PENGUIN BOOKS
CLICHÉS AND CURSES

Deidre Isaac is a Malaysian author who was born and raised in Sandakan, Sabah. She started her reading journey on Wattpad, and her love for books has only bloomed since then. A hopeless romantic at heart, her favourite genre to read is romance, with a promise of a happy ending. When she's not spending her time reading, you can find her watching Formula 1 during race weekends. Clichés and Curses is her debut novel.

You can connect with her on Instagram and Wattpad at @inabookdaze.

ADVANCE PRAISE FOR CLICHES AND CURSES

'*Clichés and Curses* plays with classic romance tropes in such a fun way! A swoony, adorable story that feels like a warm hug for readers.'

—Amelie Rhys,
author of *Alive at Night*

'*Clichés and Curses* is a love letter to college romance. It is everything you could want in a cute, fun, and heartfelt story about what it means to be young and falling in love. This definitely needs to be on your TBR!'

—Bobbi Maclaren,
author of *The Edge of Summer*

Clichés and Curses

Deidre Isaac

PENGUIN BOOKS

An imprint of Penguin Random House

PENGUIN BOOKS

Penguin Books is an imprint of the Penguin Random House group of companies
whose addresses can be found at global.penguinrandomhouse.com

Published by Penguin Random House SEA Pte Ltd
40 Penjuru Lane, #03-12, Block 2
Singapore 609216

First published in Penguin Books by Penguin Random House SEA 2025

ISBN 9789815295399

Typeset in Garamond by MAP Systems, Bengaluru, India

To my past teen self,
who thought she could never write a complete book.
(SPOILER ALERT: YOU DID IT)

PLAYLIST

'The Only Exception' - Paramore

'Maybe Don't' - Maisie Peters (feat. JP Saxe)

'Waterloo' - ABBA

'Safety Net' - Ariana Grande (feat. Ty Dolla $ign)

'Valentine' - Laufey

'Treacherous (Taylor's Version)' - Taylor Swift

'Andante, Andante' - Lily James

'In Agreement' - Lizzy McAlpine

Prologue

I've always been a hopeless romantic.

Growing up on fairytales and the promise of a 'Happy Ever After' tends to do that to a three-year-old girl. While I have those to thank, my hopeless romantic self was shaped by the one story I got to witness every day.

The love my parents shared and how it began.

My parents' love story is one that you have probably heard a million times before. He was the bad boy, she was the good girl, and both were pretty much on two different sides of the world—at least in high school terms.

But of course, no matter how far off each other's radar they were, one could never escape the power of 'being partnered up'.

You guessed it, they got partnered up for a class assignment in high school. And just like every single time you have seen this story played out, they got together and lived happily ever after.

But does one ever question, what happens post the happily-ever-after?

In the case of my parents, they did live the life expected of a couple formed from a high school cliché.

Each morning, as far back as I can remember, my parents, my sister, and I would gather around at the dining table for breakfast, and no matter how rushed or how late to work my dad was, he never left without kissing my mom goodbye. Every Friday after work, he would always bring a bouquet of flowers for her to put in a vase for the dining table—celebrating the end of a work week and the beginning of spending quality time with the family for the weekend.

But as time went by, these little occasions were getting rarer. The time between one kiss to the next was getting longer and the flowers were starting to wilt, because there weren't new ones to replace them with.

And, ultimately, my parents' love story ended on a day I remember vividly.

The day my parents sat me and my sister down at the dining table, sitting across from us with gloomy expressions on both of their faces.

The same dining table that was used to display their love for each other was now tainted and overshadowed by the memory of that one day. It mocked me of everything the table had once meant, when that one word was uttered.

A word that was spoken only once and yet it kept repeating in my eight-year-old mind.

Divorce.

My parents were getting a divorce.

'Do you not love us any more?' my then fourteen-year-old sister, Eliza, had asked as her eyes started to fill with tears.

'Of course we do,' my mom answered as she reached out her hands, clasping them with Eliza's. 'And we will always be there for the two of you, no matter what.'

'Then why can't you be there for us together? Do you not love each other any more?' I voiced out, grabbing both my parents' attention as I said my first words since they delivered the news to us.

They both looked at each other for a moment, not knowing how to answer my question.

'We just think it's best for us to go our separate ways,' my dad then said, looking into my eyes, as if he was willing me to understand he would've spared us this pain had there been a better way.

But the damage was already done.

That was strike one.

While my parents' divorce had ruined my views of love and wants for a 'Happy Ever After' with my own cliché love interest, the bruise slowly started to fade when my sister introduced Nathan to the family. It eventually disappeared on the day Eliza called me on Facetime, telling me that Nathan got down on one knee and popped the question, asking her to spend the rest of their lives together.

With tears streaming down her face as Eliza tried her best to recount the story of how he proposed—a customized crossword puzzle was involved—through her sobs of happiness, I started to believe that maybe 'Happy Ever After' did exist for love stories with cliché love interests.

Being the ambitious woman she was—and still is—
Eliza steered clear of any romantic entanglements until
she graduated college. At her first job of being a journalist
as a fresh graduate, Eliza was hired alongside Nathan—
another graduate who was equally motivated to prove his
worth to extend their stay at the company, making them
natural work rivals.

And just like déjà vu, they were partnered up to work
on an article together. Long story short, spending more
time together led them to discover that they had more
similarities than they thought, both in their way of thinking
and big career goals.

They ended up submitting one of the best stories the
organization had ever received.

Nathan proposed just over a year after they officially
got together. Their families and friends surrounded them
at their engagement party, joining them in celebration on
their road to happily-ever-after.

But of course, real life had other plans. It came as a
phone call I received from my sister.

'Hey, little sis. Are Mom and Dad there with you?'
my sister had asked, her voice shaky as if she had been
crying. It was a Friday night, and I was catching my
parents up on my week. Dad usually came over to have
dinner with us whenever he could, but Fridays were
a constant.

'Yeah, they're here,' I told her. 'Is everything okay?'

The line was silent for a moment, and I was starting to
get worried. 'Eliza?' I called out.

'Can you put me on speaker please?' Eliza answered
instead.

I placed the phone in the middle of the kitchen island as Eliza started explaining why she was calling.

Eliza and Nathan were planning to move to New York City once they got married, living out their lives as journalists in 'The Big Apple' together. But while that was Eliza's ultimate goal, Nathan didn't share it so much. The downfall came when he got another job offer, the one he had been dreaming of.

The setback?

It was all the way in San Francisco.

The other side of the country.

It left Eliza and Nathan with a very difficult decision to make.

They tried compromising on things—making plans to visit each other, prolonging their engagement. But ultimately, they didn't want to hold the other person back, not when they both perfectly understood the price they had each paid—the time and effort they'd put in, the sacrifices they had made—in hopes of having their dream offer to finally be within their reach.

In the end, they decided to break off the engagement, just three months later.

It was sad to think how their biggest similarity with one another—the one that had brought them together—would also be the one to rip them apart.

And that was strike two.

For a long time, I wondered if there truly was such a thing as 'happily ever after', or if that was just a concept created to give hope. Maybe love stories with cliché love interests weren't meant to last after all; maybe they were just meant for stories, a thing of fiction.

Or at the very least, they weren't meant to last for my family. I had enough proof to believe in that.

'Happy Ever After' is a part of fairytales, but we tend to forget that curses exist in the same stories too. What if my family was cursed to have doomed relationships because of who they choose to be with? Seeing it happen once had already convinced me of the curse, but watching it repeat made it harder to ignore. And what if the only way to prevent this from happening to me was to avoid these cliché love interests from entering my life?

If that's the case, then I'll just have to make sure I won't be struck out.

Chapter One

Avoiding the curse is easy when you know what to look out for.

The key is to always be one step ahead. With my vast knowledge of all things clichés from all the romance movies I've watched and the endless Wattpad books I've read, I was confident I wouldn't fall under the curse.

In all the romance stories, the cliché love interest has always been the same type of guy. The one that the main character will always brush off ever having a romantic relationship with, because it's such an unrealistic scenario—a 'never gonna happen' situation. Whether it be the mysterious bad boy who doesn't engage with anyone, or the rival they've been competing against, the two leads have either never crossed each other's path or stayed away from one another.

And here's where the catalyst comes in.

The catalyst is the one responsible for bringing the main character and the cliché love interest to spend more time with each other. In the case of how it began for my parents—with it happening again to Eliza—it was the 'being partnered up' scenario.

And so, the game plan was simple: identify the cliché love interest in every situation and ensure that the scenario doesn't fall upon me, and whoever the curse decides to lay on my path.

While the years of middle school were spent rigidly following this plan, I had started doing it subconsciously once I entered my high school years.

At the start of any school year, I made sure to befriend, or at the very least make an acquaintance, with someone in each class. So if any partnered assignment came up, I wouldn't be accidentally stuck with anyone that I had categorized as a cliché love interest. There were instances where the curse could've made its appearance, when the teacher decided to pair up the students themselves, but thankfully it didn't.

And so, I had lived those years of my life unscathed from the curse.

When college came around, I was confident the curse would be avoidable, given the large size of the campus and the number of students that surrounded it. Attending a university where its highest pride was the baseball team, it's no surprise that the cliché love interest would be the star athlete himself, Colton Reed.

You could tell God really took his time when he made Colton. On top of his great talent at the sport itself, the Big Man had also decided to give him romance hero swoon-worthy features—with his tall frame and messy hair that I never saw tamed. Though, the latter might have to do with the fact that I had only got to see his hair during those split seconds of him not wearing a cap or a helmet when he was on the field.

And though my life might've been focused on avoiding the curse, I was still the same girl who grew up with cliché love stories. So, you couldn't be too surprised to learn that I harboured a crush on Colton, especially with the fond memories I have attached to baseball.

When my family was still in our bubble of being picture-perfect, my Saturday afternoons were spent playing catch in our backyard with my dad. Considering my parents never had a son, my dad rarely shared his love for baseball. That was until I found a baseball glove lying in the garage one day and asked him about it.

'What's this?' questioned my six-year-old self, my hand holding it as I inspected the hand-shaped leather.

'Ah, that's a baseball glove. You wear it so it'll protect your hand when you're catching a ball,' my dad explained to me, his eyes looking at the glove fondly with a tender look on his face.

'Can we play?' I asked my dad, interrupting him from his reminiscing.

My dad's head jolted back a bit at my unexpected request. 'You want to play catch?'

'Yeah!' I had exclaimed. 'It sounds like fun.'

He laughed at my excitement, ruffling my hair. 'Sure. Go wait out back, I'll try to find us a baseball.'

That one random afternoon snowballed into a love for the sport and the creation of a special bond between my dad and me: from playing catch in the backyard to attending little league baseball games held around town, and spending time together watching the Major League Baseball, or MLB, games on TV.

Even after my parents got divorced, I always went over to my dad's place every Sunday and we would watch a live game together with a box of pizza sitting between us. It didn't matter what team was playing, it had just become our tradition.

Even though I never religiously followed the sport, baseball held and still holds a special place in my heart.

When it had come to choosing where I would be spending the next four years of my life, a college that has one of the best collegiate baseball teams in the nation wasn't one of my requirements, but a very welcome bonus nonetheless.

I still remember the day I saw the college team play for the first time in our own baseball stadium. It was my freshman year of college, and I was so excited to see a live baseball match, even if it was just one of those exhibition games they did during the off-season. It also happened to be the day the college was introduced to the star-athlete-to-be.

The game held my attention fairly well, but when it was Colton's turn to bat, he became my sole focus. He had a certain aura to him as he walked up to home plate. It wasn't necessarily arrogant, but more of a confident one, as if he knew just how good he was and he was ready to prove it.

When Colton took his place and prepared his stance to swing the bat, I felt time stand still. My mind was alerted with the knowledge that I was going to witness something remarkable that would forever be marked in my memory.

Once the players were ready, the pitcher threw the ball.

Colton missed.

Strike one.

The ball went back to the pitcher's glove and Colton readjusted his grip on the bat.

Colton got into his batting stance again and the ball was tossed the second time.

He missed again.

Strike two.

While the ball was tossed back to the pitcher, Colton set down the barrel end of the bat as he took a deep breath, his back rising and falling along with the number '23' on his back.

When he was ready, Colton picked up the bat once again, all eyes of the crowd on him.

The pitcher threw the ball the third time and Colton swung.

The sound of the ball hitting the bat echoed throughout the stadium as the ball flew across the field and continued to fly past the fence.

Just like that, the silence from the crowd was replaced by a thunderous roar of cheers for Colton as he started to run the length of the infield.

First base.

Second base.

Third base.

Home plate.

He hit a home run.

The crowd continued to erupt in excited shouts as the commentator's voice blared through the speakers, 'And that was a home run hit by a new freshman on the team! A beautiful swing, if I do say so myself. I have a feeling we're going to be seeing more of him on the field pretty soon.'

And so, Colton's star athlete reputation was born, as well as my silly little crush.

I've always been careful not to crush on any guy that would fall under the 'cliché love interests' category—another precaution I had decided to take to prevent myself from falling under the curse, and for the most part, it had been easy.

The whole 'bad boy' persona never really appealed to me, at least not in real life. It was fun to read about them in books. My phase of exclusively reading Wattpad books with the 'bad boy' trope pretty much explained how addicting they were. But if that fiction ever became reality, I already knew I'd be asking where the exit was.

And in terms of having a rival, whether academically or in other situations, I never did have one. I'd never been competitive enough to earn myself one.

That had left me with one last option, the star athlete, which in my humble opinion was the best one.

I might be biased, but I sincerely believe anyone who grew up with the *High School Musical* movies has a default setting of automatically having a crush on the school's star athlete—courtesy of the one and only, Troy Bolton.

I mean, who could forget the scene, where Troy got knocked down and Gabriella stood up in the bleachers mid-game singing his name to encourage him?

Was it over the top? Yes. Was it just as iconic? Most definitely.

While crushing on the star athlete definitely went against my precautionary rule, Colton seemed like a justified exception. We ran in two completely different circles, pursuing a degree in two very different majors. The chances of us ever crossing each other's path were slim to none. Almost non-existent.

But of course, it was never zero.

Our furthest—and only—interaction with each other dated back to a brief encounter last semester, when I was still a sophomore.

A run-in that I liked to refer to as *the incident.*

It was a late afternoon on a Wednesday. The sun had already started its descent, and the track team was hard at work on the field.

I sat on the bleachers with my close friends, Lily and Claudia, while we waited for Nina—the other part of our quartet, who was also my roommate and my best friend—to finish her training session. That day was one of those rare occasions that semester when I got to witness Nina in action. Her training usually ended hours after my final class, so we would just see each other back in our apartment. But one of my lecturers had decided to hold a replacement class, indirectly extending my stay on campus for the day.

On the other hand, Lily and Claudia had a club meeting that ended at the same time as my class did, and so all four of us agreed to have dinner together, taking the opportunity to hang out, since we were still on campus after all our day's responsibilities had been settled.

As the track team was wrapping up their training for the day, I decided to make a stop before leaving. 'I'm going to the bathroom,' I said to Lily and Claudia, getting up from the bleachers.

'Okay,' noted Lily. 'We'll just meet up at the entrance then?'

I gave her a nod. 'Sure. And can you bring my bag for me?'

Once they agreed, I made my way to the bathroom.

There were a few bathrooms scattered around the stadium—including the newly added single-stall ones located on the other end of the building—so I just went to whichever was the closest. Thinking Nina wouldn't be out for another twenty minutes, I decided to take my time, occasionally stopping to read some of the newspaper headlines of the college's track team achievements on the bulletin boards.

The bathrooms finally came into view, two doorframes standing right next to each other. I was a few steps away from entering the women's bathroom when I momentarily paused mid-walk as someone stepped out of the men's bathroom.

And. He. Was. Shirtless.

But not for long, *unfortunately*.

He was putting on a shirt as he stepped out of the door, briefly stopping at the doorframe to wear it perfectly. Only when his head popped out of the neck hole did I register who it was.

It was Colton.

And then, it fully hit me.

I had just seen Colton shirtless.

I might have only caught a glimpse of his abs for about five seconds, but they had been tattooed to my brain forever.

Putting his arms through the other two arm holes, Colton smoothed down the T-shirt on his torso. As if he could sense my attention on him, Colton swerved his head in my direction, his eyes meeting mine. He fully caught me in the act of shamelessly gawking at him shirtless and watching him put a T-shirt on.

Fuck.

A playful smile made its way to his lips. 'Like what you see?' he teased me.

Without giving it a second thought, I just verbalized the first thing that came to my mind.

'Very much,' I blurted out and willed myself to walk at a normal pace as I stepped into the women's bathroom.

Once I was inside and the coast was clear, I finally let myself freak out.

'What just happened?' I muttered to myself. Bringing my hands to my cheeks as they start to heat up. 'What did I just do?'

Was I flirting? Was that flirting? Did that even *qualify* as flirting?

Normally, I wouldn't have been so bold to say something like that. Maybe it was just the spur-of-the-moment kind of thing, my mind temporarily malfunctioning after being caught like that.

As I paced back and forth in the bathroom—my brain going a mile a minute on how to deal with the consequences of what had just happened—it occurred to me that freaking out wasn't necessary. While I never thought I would run into Colton, I knew there was a slight chance I would.

At least it didn't happen at a place I frequently went to; that day was just a rare occurrence. In the grand scheme of things, we probably wouldn't ever see each other again, logically. Colton and I didn't have mutual friends—at least, none that I was aware of—and we were studying different things on different sides of campus.

And even if we were to bump into each other again, he probably would've already forgotten about the whole thing by then. I was freaking out over nothing.

Reassuring myself of this fact, I splashed my face with some water from the sink before *finally* going into one of the stalls.

By the time I reached the entrance to meet up with Lily and Claudia, Nina was already there with them. My backpack was slung over one of her shoulders.

'Finally,' Nina exclaimed once she saw me coming. Her eyes narrowed in question when she noticed the flush on my face. 'Are you okay?'

'What? Yeah, I'm fine. Are we leaving?' I answered, reclaiming my bag from her. 'Thanks.'

'You're welcome,' Nina replied. 'And yes, we're leaving. What are your thoughts on Thai for dinner?'

'Thai sounds perfect to me,' I said and that was the end of it.

There are moments in life that you just want to keep to yourself and as we sat in the Thai restaurant catching up with one another, I realized *the incident* was one of them. I didn't particularly understand why. All three of them were well aware of my silly crush on Colton, so I knew they would've loved to hear this little story.

But for some reason, even with the numerous opportunities to bring it up during dinner, I just didn't. I had decided to keep this small interaction with Colton to myself.

As I tucked the memory into my mind, I reminded myself that was all it could be. A memory. Anything further would mean tempting the curse, and I wouldn't allow that to happen.

Time went by, with *the incident* being my only interaction with Colton, and real life proving that it was just a coincidental encounter rather than what fiction would claim a fated one.

But of course, just when I thought the curse's claws were starting to loosen their hold on me, it had only just begun working its magic.

Chapter Two

My legs were folded as I sat in my favourite spot at the campus coffee shop with a book in my hands. The weather was taking a turn from the sunny morning. The rain had only started getting heavier after the tiny drops that fell half an hour ago. A tiny flash of lightning appeared, quickly followed by the soft sound of thunder.

It was perfect.

In certain circumstances.

Not when you realize you got carried away by the book you're reading to the point where you were going to be late for class.

'Shit,' I cursed out. Quickly but gently, I shoved the book into my backpack and rummaged through it to find my umbrella.

But as my hands continued to search through my pile of things over and over again, I tried to remember the last time I used it. Then it hit me: I used it yesterday and left it to hang near the front door of my apartment. I was in such a rush in the morning; I must've not noticed it when I left.

'Are you kidding me?' I whisper shouted at myself. The one day I didn't bring my umbrella also happened to be when I absolutely needed it.

Groaning out my frustration, I zipped up my bag, checking once again to make sure I didn't leave anything behind before heading to my next class of the day. My mind already dreaded taking the longer route to shield myself from the rain.

Tardiness wasn't uncommon for me. But considering it was the first class of the semester, I wanted to make a good impression or, at least, not draw attention to myself and get called out by the lecturer in the upcoming weeks. My class was to start in five minutes and if I quickened my pace, I might be able to reach there just a few minutes later.

Fortunately, the coffee shop—my favourite one on campus—wasn't too far from the building where my elective was going to be. After having spent two years here, I was pretty familiar with all my classrooms. However, my next class, Introduction to American Sign Language or ASL, was held at a different part of campus—the one that I rarely visited.

Once I safely arrived inside the building, I took out my phone on my way up the stairs to the second floor. I was thankful for my foresight in finding the classroom; otherwise, I would have been even later than I already was.

I was panting by the time I reached the door. I made sure that I was at the right one before twisting the door handle and heading inside.

My mouth was already preparing to apologize for being late when I noticed that the front desk was empty.

The instructor wasn't there yet. I let out a sigh of relief.

Awkward apology avoided.

I quickly turned my attention to the rest of the classroom, searching for an empty seat. The space wasn't anything extraordinary, same white walls and floor tiles—both things that had definitely seen better days. However, the tables and chairs were different.

Instead of the usual task chairs, the classroom was fully packed with rectangular tables from the front to the back, each one capable of comfortably fitting two people. Most of the tables were filled, except for the one at the back of the room, which was perfectly fine by me.

I made my way to the table and took my seat in time, just as the front door opened and a man, who looked to be in his fifties, stepped in.

'Good morning, everyone,' the man, whom I presumed was our instructor for the class, greeted us. He had a briefcase with him which he softly placed on the desk. 'Sorry for the slight delay. Just give me a few minutes and then we can start the class.'

Taking out my notebook and pencil case from my backpack, I turned to a blank page and wrote the day's date, along with the class name.

Once he settled himself, he opened the briefcase, taking out a piece of paper from a pile that was already covering the desk. 'It seems that everyone is already here,' he said. 'So, let's get started. Hi, every . . .'

He was interrupted mid-sentence by the squeak of the door, signalling the arrival of someone new.

'Hey. I'm sorry for running late, the rain caught me off guard,' I heard a masculine voice say as I was going through my bag to find the class syllabus that I had printed out yesterday.

'No worries, Colton. We were just about to get started,' our instructor replied. 'I think there's a seat available at the back.'

My hand stopped mid-task when I heard the name. Colton.

There's no way it was *that* Colton, right? I mean, it was a pretty common name.

The universe wouldn't be that cruel.

But boy was I mistaken.

Because lo and behold, the Colton that was standing at the front door was none other than Colton Reed, the beloved star athlete of the college.

And he was heading straight to my table.

I was so focused on getting myself ready for the class that I didn't even realize the seat our instructor was referring to was the one at my table. I gave a quick scan to the rest of the classroom to see if there were any other empty seats.

But nope, the only seat available was the one next to me.

My pulse started to speed up. My mind was freaking out.

I tried steadying my erratic heartbeat as Colton pulled out the chair next to me and took his seat.

'Hi,' he greeted me, a small smile on his face.

'Hi,' I croaked back, giving him a tiny wave, internally groaning at its awkwardness.

I tried to think of something else to say to shake off my embarrassment, but luckily, I was saved when the instructor decided to start his introduction once again.

'All right, I think everyone is finally here, so best to get started.' He cleared his throat before he began talking again, and this time he was also conversing in the sign language we were supposed to study. 'Hello, everyone. I'm Mr Albert. I'm a CODA, which is Child of Deaf Adults, and I'll be your instructor for this class. Welcome to *Introduction to American Sign Language (ASL)*.'

He continued with what would be covered on the course syllabus throughout the semester, as well as all the assessments.

I was looking through my own printed paper, my eyes searching for any assignments that required a partner. I let out a breath of relief when I couldn't find any.

As long as we're not partnered up together, I'll be fine, I thought to myself.

But it seemed I may have celebrated too soon.

'And, to those of you who have already printed out the syllabus, I do recommend you print a new one due to some new changes,' Mr Albert announced.

Changes?

He can't possibly mean . . .

'As you are all aware, ASL is different from other languages because it doesn't use any verbal words. Although most of your assessments will be individual, I decided to add one that requires you to be in pairs,' he explained, confirming my worst fear.

'There might only be one paired-work assignment, but I advise that you frequently meet up with your partner to practice. It'll be a lot easier for you to grasp the language that way.' His phone rang at that very moment. Looking at the screen, he picked it up and excused himself from the class while he took the call. 'I'll be back in just a minute. You can take this time to find your partner.'

Once he stepped outside, the room instantly came to life with everyone's chatter, conversation upon conversation, breaking through the silence.

I tried to find someone whom I could partner up with, but it seemed everyone was already acquainted with the person next to them, which meant . . .

'So,' Colton said, snapping me out of my inner turmoil. 'Do you want to partner up?'

'Umm, I don't think that's a good idea,' I answered him.

'Why not? Are you thinking of dropping out of the class?'

'No, but . . .' I paused trying to come up with a reasonable excuse. 'I'm just not sure if you'll be able to free up some time to practice ASL with me. I mean, doesn't the baseball team train almost every day?' My eyes widened in horror at my words. I had basically just revealed I knew who he was—so much for wanting to be nonchalant about it.

While I may not have known anyone else on the baseball team, I knew Nina, who was also a college athlete. After being roommates with her for years, I knew just how much dedication it took to commit to being one. Other than training with the team, Nina also set aside time to train on her own. I can't begin to imagine just how much more the baseball team trained, especially with their goal of defending their place as the nation's collegiate baseball team champion.

Understanding dawned on Colton. 'You know I'm on the baseball team then. I mean, we do. But I can make time to practice ASL with you, I'll be helping you just as much as I'll be helping myself. I want to get a good grade too, you know?' he added teasingly.

A blush rose to my cheeks. 'I didn't mean to assume that you didn't care about your classes.' At least I didn't mean it entirely, but you can't blame me for thinking that the baseball team might get a free pass after winning the Men's College World Series, especially in a small elective class such as this one.

'I know,' he answered with a tilt in the corner of his mouth. 'And I understand where you're coming from— but trust me, the first thing our coach told us before we started each of our training was to not slack off our classes. It's either meeting the average grade requirement or he wouldn't let us on the field. Anyway, what I'm trying to say is, if I were to be your partner, I promise to set out time each week for us to practice together.'

I took a moment to think over his words. While his engagement was not my biggest concern, it was nice to be reassured of his seriousness towards this class. But of course, I would still have the curse to think about.

'How can I trust you to stay true to your word?' I asked, instead.

Colton looked taken aback by my question, but he quickly recovered. 'I guess that means you'll just have to trust me,' he answered, his tone firm and void of any teasing.

Should I?

God, Clara—it's just for a class. Stop making it so complicated.

'Can you give me some time to think about it?' I told him.

'Seems fair,' he nodded. 'I'm Colton Reed, by the way; I'm a junior.' He held his hand out as he introduced himself, even though I had already indirectly admitted to knowing who he was. But I appreciated him for trying to help me feel less embarrassed about it.

'I'm Clara Healy, also a junior,' I replied, shaking his offered hand.

'Nice to meet you, Clara.'

The sound of the door opening snapped our attention back to the front of the class as Mr Albert stepped back in. 'Okay, so where were we?'

'I think that's everything for today. Class dismissed,' Mr Albert announced.

I took out my phone from my backpack to check the time and noticed that he had ended the class ten minutes early. Not surprising, since it was only the first class of the semester, but still any class that ended early was always much welcomed.

'I'll see you next week, then. And will you let me know if we can be partners?' Colton asked as we were packing up our things.

'Yeah, I'll let you know by then.'

'All right. See you around, Clara.' He stood up from our table, backpack strapped to his shoulder and went his way. He gave me one final wave as he opened the front door and stepped into the hallway.

I gave him a head start of a few minutes before exiting the classroom myself. I don't think I could have handled the awkwardness of us walking in the same direction after saying goodbye.

Realizing it was my last class for the day, and that I didn't have anything left to do on campus, I decided to just head back to my apartment.

The pouring rain from earlier had come to an abrupt stop while we were still in class. The lingering mist greeted me as I walked out of the building, instantly putting a grin on my face.

My daily commute from the apartment to campus and back was usually by bus, occasionally hitching a ride from Nina if we happened to leave at around the same time. But as I was walking to the nearest bus stop, it seemed like a missed opportunity to not stay in the cool breeze for a little while longer.

I ended up walking past the bus stop and continued.

This wasn't the first time I walked back to the apartment ever since Nina and I had started living off-campus for our sophomore year. However, this was my first time walking back to the new one we leased for our junior year. I wasn't sure how long of a walk this was going to be, but my estimation was around half an hour.

This gave me the perfect amount of time to determine what it was exactly that had incidentally led me to being *almost* partnered up with Colton.

As my mind ran through everything that had transpired, I realized I couldn't just trace it back to one thing. It was a combination of all the little things.

Me rushing out the door in the morning, making me forget to bring my umbrella with me. The book I was reading in the coffee shop earlier and how invested I was until I lost track of time. Having to take a longer route to class because of the unexpected rain, and again, the absence of my umbrella.

If you were to remove all these minor details, I would have made it to class earlier. I could have had the chance to choose a different seat next to someone else and get acquainted with them in case there were any paired assignments coming up. That way, I could have avoided sitting next to Colton and the whole 'being partnered up' scenario, even though we were in the same class together.

I halted my steps when it finally hit me.

How did I not see it?

It was the curse.

Every single thing could be seen as a common mistake. If each of them had occurred separately, I wouldn't have thought too much of it. But it had taken place consecutively, as if domino pieces falling in line—with the last one being me having to partner up with Colton.

'No. No, no, no,' I muttered to myself, shaking my head.

I was always careful about these things. I had a system to make sure this didn't happen. But I must have lost focus, since there was almost zero possibility of us ever being in the same class together, with us majoring in two different things. It never occurred to me that we would share a class in an elective course.

The one time I slipped up, and here was the curse, already working its charm on me.

It might have made it this far, but I could still put a stop to this. I hadn't said yes to being partners with Colton yet. Moreover, this was still only the first week of classes—there was a chance that other people might drop the class which would allow me to find someone new to be my partner instead.

All I had to do, once I saw him the next week, was to tell him that pairing up together can't workout. I had already given him a reason, even though it wasn't real. *He'll understand*, I thought.

I had managed to avoid the curse this far, there was no way I was going to let it get to me because of a minor mishap on my part. Not when I could still stop it.

Chapter Three

I was reheating previous night's leftover lasagna, when I heard the front door open.

'Honey, I'm home!' Nina announced, entering our apartment.

College had had its fair share of ups and downs in the past couple of years, but it had also given me one of the greatest blessings of my life: on the day that I had stepped foot into my dorm room for the first time, I was introduced to my roommate, and now best friend, Nina Alvarez.

When it came to choosing a roommate, I had decided to request one and let the university do the searching, instead of doing it myself. Keeping my fingers crossed, I'd hoped to get along with whoever I ended up being roommates with.

Thankfully, we did, even catapulting into one of the greatest friendships I've ever made.

When it had come to discussing our living plans for our sophomore year, it was a no-brainer that we wanted to live together again.

And here we were, rooming together again for the third year running.

'Welcome home, babe!' I replied, matching her enthusiastic tone.

'I smell something delicious. Is it food? Are you making food?' she rushed out her words as she stepped into the kitchen, the mouthwatering smell of the lasagna slowly filling the air.

'I'm just reheating our leftovers from last night,' I told her. 'You came home just in time.'

'Oh, thank god. I'm starving,' she said dramatically as she set down her bag by the kitchen island. Then, she headed over to the sink to wash her hands before plopping herself on one of our kitchen stools in our newly leased apartment.

Nina and I had decided to switch to a new apartment for the new term. The old apartment was fine, but we had realized that we wanted to have our own bathrooms instead of sharing one.

Our new apartment wasn't anything special: just one open space with a kitchen a few steps away from the doorway, a countertop thrown in the middle of it to separate the kitchen from the living room, and windows that showed off a view of the streets below. Not to forget, there were three doors on the right wall: two of which led to bedrooms with their own attached bathrooms; the middle door covering a washer and a dryer.

When Nina and I had toured the building and this particular apartment last semester, we had instantly fallen in love and knew this was the one. The apartment was still slightly messy, since I had only moved in a week ago, but even so, I knew we had made the right choice moving here.

Just as I was taking out the plates and utensils, the alarm of the oven went off. Wearing mittens, I took out the heated lasagna, making sure to position it perfectly with the coaster. Nina wasted no time scooping it up and putting it on her plate. By the time I took off the mittens and went to sit next to her, she was already savouring her food.

I let out a small laugh and scooped out a proportion of my own, filling my plate.

Silence enveloped us as we enjoyed our reheated leftovers, the sounds from the streets below being our only companion.

'I'm so glad we decided to make lasagna last night,' Nina eventually said, moaning out her satisfaction in between bites. 'This was exactly what I needed after today.'

'I guess training was harder than usual today?' I asked her, taking a bite of my own. Nina had arrived back on campus a week earlier than me, as was required by the track team. But the coach had decided to allow them an extra two days off the previous weekend to let them prepare for the semester.

'It was brutal,' she groaned out. 'Coach had us running drills like a maniac. It was as if he was punishing us for taking the time off he gave us. I can already feel how sore I'm going to be this week.'

'It'll get better,' I said, trying to cheer her up.

'Yeah. Hopefully, I'll get used to it by this time next week,' she said, letting out a wistful sigh. 'Anyway, enough of my whining. How was your day?'

For a moment, I considered telling her about what had happened today in ASL class and how I could possibly end up partnering with Colton Reed for a class assignment.

Nina had known all about my crush on Colton, just as I did about her crush on Miles, his teammate. But I had never told anyone about the curse before, and I didn't want to get her hopes up over something that wasn't worth mentioning— not when this thing with Colton couldn't go any further than us just being mere classmates.

'It was okay.' I shrugged. 'I decided to walk back to the apartment today, instead of taking the bus—but that was pretty much the highlight of my day, along with this lasagna,' I answered, my spoon pointing at whatever was left on my plate.

She let out a laugh. 'The lasagna also happens to be the highlight of my day.' She scooped up another bite, before adding, 'Wait, wasn't your first ASL class today? How did it go?'

Being roommates for two whole years together, Nina had been a witness to my disappointment each semester, when I couldn't fit the ASL class into my schedule, as it had always clashed with my other mandatory classes.

When the stars had finally aligned for me to be able to take it this semester, she was just as ecstatic as I was to learn that ASL was going to be on my list of classes I would be attending.

'It was,' I nodded. 'Nothing much happened since it was just the first class, so it was mostly just an introduction to what we can expect in the course.'

But I did sit next to Colton for almost a whole hour and got to talk to him, I added in my head.

Just as she was about to reply, her phone, placed next to her on the kitchen island, started buzzing with tons of notifications. She picked it up to see what the fuss was about. A look of excitement crossed her features at whatever it was.

'Good news?' I asked.

'The best,' she replied, turning her attention back to me. 'Do you have any plans this Saturday night?'

I mentally went through my agenda and to-do list. 'I don't think so, I might just spend the morning unpacking and organizing my things.' I had to stop procrastinating and get it done while I still had some free time on my hands.

'Great! The track team is throwing a party at the team house on Saturday night to celebrate the end of the first week—or so they say,' she explained, rolling her eyes.

The sports teams in our college were notorious for throwing parties on a weekly basis. It was almost as if they had a social calendar to ensure there was always a party happening on weekends. And it seemed like we were kicking the semester off with the track team.

'I'm down for that. It'd be nice to catch up with everyone,' I agreed. It had been a chaotic week: with moving out of the state, settling into a new apartment, attending classes, and deciding which ones I wanted to take for the semester. I hadn't had the chance to talk to anyone other than Nina.

'That settles it. The party starts at 8 p.m., so that gives us some time to grab dinner before we head out.'

'Sounds like a plan,' I confirmed.

As I continued to devour our homemade lasagna, it occurred to me that Colton might be attending the party too, since he was on the baseball team. Anyone and everyone who was a college athlete, tended to show up to these parties—regardless of which sports team was throwing it. Even so, this wouldn't have been the first party I attended which bore the possibility of Colton's presence.

Last semester, when it had been the baseball team's turn to throw the week's party, Nina was adamant about going and begged me to come along. While I was hesitant at first, I had eventually given in, figuring it would be a good way to celebrate after submitting a heavy assignment. I had stuck close to Nina the whole night, cheering on Claudia and Lily as they played beer pong against college athletes.

At that point in time, *the incident* had happened more than a month ago, but I was still slightly nervous about unexpectedly running into Colton, and the small chance of him remembering our little encounter. My worries ended up being for nothing, when the night flew by without Colton and I crossing paths with one another.

My fingers were crossed: I wanted it to repeat this upcoming Saturday.

The rest of the week was uneventfully filled with attending more classes, organizing my calendar with test dates, and assignment deadlines. I also had finally managed to unpack everything out of my luggage. Before I knew it, Saturday rolled around, and it was time to get ready for the party.

As I was curling my hair in my room, I heard knocks coming from the front door.

'I'll get it!' shouted Nina.

It wasn't a minute later, when the sounds of excited shrieking met my ears. I quickly curled the last patch of my hair and went out to the living room to greet our guests. Nina, meanwhile, went back to her room to add some finishing touches to her makeup.

'Hey!' I exclaimed, once my eyes landed on Claudia and Lily.

'Clara!' I barely managed to hear my name being called out, as I was pulled into Claudia's arms. She squeezed me with her tight hug before I could even blink.

'That's enough. You're suffocating the poor girl.' I heard Lily say.

'Let me be. I haven't seen her in months.' Claudia waved Lily off, continuing to hold me in her embrace.

'I missed you too, Claudia,' I said, softly patting her arms until she eventually pulled away.

'All right, my turn.' Lily playfully pushed Claudia to the side, before taking me in for a hug.

Not wanting to be left out, Claudia put her arms around both of us, making it a group hug instead.

'Attachment issues,' I heard Lily whisper into my ear.

'I heard that!' Claudia admitted.

I let out a light chuckle.

In our freshman year, when Nina and I were roommates staying at the dorms, Claudia and Lily had also been rooming together across the hall from us. One day, during the orientation week, I had left the door open, and they both came over to introduce themselves. All four of us were glued to each other for the rest of the week, always waiting for each other before heading out for the next activity. By the end of the orientation, we had already formed a group chat.

The proximity, ever since, had only increased our friendship with one another. Even as our sophomore year came, and all of us had been living off campus in different apartment buildings, we still made time for each other whenever we could—especially if any two of us were free, while being on campus.

'We're pregaming with Fireball, by the way,' Claudia said, once our group hug finally came to an end.

'And we also brought pizza!' Lily gestured to the bottle of whiskey and the two boxes of pizza sitting on the kitchen island.

Once Nina was ready and joined us in the living room, we finally indulged in the pizza, catching up on the happenings of the past week. We hadn't seen each other all summer, but that didn't slow down the messages from flooding our group chat, updating each other in real-time about anything that had happened in the last three months. But nothing beat seeing each other in person, and I took a moment to soak it all in.

Finishing off the last slice of pizza, I cleared away the boxes and pushed them to the side. I placed it in full view, to make sure we'd bring it with us on our way out later to throw it down the garbage chute. Nina took out four shot glasses as Claudia opened our pregame drink of choice.

Pouring out the whiskey into shot glasses, we each took one and raised it as Lily proposed a toast.

'To a new semester!' We clicked our glasses and drank—all of us wincing from the taste.

We took one more shot before leaving the apartment and made our way to the party.

Even though the invitation might have said the party was starting at 8 p.m., it had already been in full swing by the time we arrived—just thirty minutes after the said time.

We asked the Uber driver to drop us off a few houses away, as cars had already been filling up the driveway of the venue. The sound of music got louder as we got close, the ground thumping along the beat of the song that was playing. Upon reaching the front door and stepping inside the house, the smell of alcohol and sweat welcomed us.

We slowly squeezed our way through as we headed to the kitchen to get some drinks. There, we were met by the sight of the track team casually hanging out.

Lucy, another junior on the team, was the first to see us.

'You guys made it!' she said, giving each of us a hug when we were within an arm's length. Once the others realized who Lucy was hugging, they all greeted us too.

'It's nice seeing you all again,' I told them.

During the first semester of my sophomore year, when Nina and I had just started rooming together off-campus, one of my classes ended late—almost at the same time as Nina finished her training. So, I always hung back around campus, waiting for her before we headed back to the apartment together. Usually, I would stay at the library or the coffee shop while waiting for Nina's training to be over, then meet up with her at the entrance of the track field later.

Some members of the track team would occasionally hang out to grab dinner together after their training. Seeing that I had been waiting for Nina, they asked if I wanted to join them. Initially, I thought of bluntly rejecting, for fear that it might get awkward, since I was neither on the track team, nor a college athlete myself. But with much persuasion from Nina, I had decided to take the offer.

And I'm glad that I did, because they had ended up being some of the coolest people I know, accepting me into their friend group with open arms.

Since all my classes ended early last semester, I usually went home by myself, instead of waiting for Nina. Even then, they would still invite me whenever they wanted to have dinner together, and I just ended up meeting them wherever they decided.

The party was only getting louder with more people coming in through the front door every few minutes. I was leaning against the kitchen counter, with a beer-filled red solo cup in my hand, when someone decided to take the empty spot next to me.

I looked to see who it was and was met by an unfamiliar face.

'Hey,' he greeted me, smiling.

'Hey,' I greeted back, my mind trying to recall if we'd ever met before.

'I'm Aiden,' he introduced himself, holding out his hand to me. 'The new roommate of the house.' The house he was referring to was where the party was happening in full blast. This place had been the go-to spot for the track team to throw their parties, considering almost everyone who lived here was on the team—unofficially making it the track team's house.

'Nice to meet you.' I shook his hand. 'Are you on the track team as well?'

'Nope. Just your average college student.'

'Same here,' I said, raising my cup. 'What made you decide it'll be a good idea to live with the track team and their wild streak of throwing parties?' I asked, gesturing to the chaos that had increased tenfold since we got here.

'The rent was good,' he shrugged. 'And I have my own bathroom. Plus, I get the whole house to myself while they're at practice. If that means I'll have to put up with their wild parties every now and then, I'll take the offer.'

I chuckled lightly at that, because that's definitely a perk of living together with a college athlete. Don't get me wrong; I love Nina to bits and pieces, but I also love having some alone time while I chill in the living room and cozy up on the couch with a good book in my hands. So, the solitary time Nina gave me when she was off to training has very much been appreciated.

'So, the pros outweigh the cons?' I teased him.

'Pretty much,' he replied, his tone matching mine. 'And they did warn me they were going to throw some parties throughout the semester. But as long as it didn't happen on weekdays, I'm okay with it.'

Our conversation came to a stop when Nina suddenly appeared in front of me. She snatched my cup from my hands and placed it on the countertop.

'You can continue talking later, it's time to dance!' She grabbed my hand, taking me with her in the direction of the music.

'I'll see you around,' I told Aiden before letting her drag me to the dance floor.

It was a little over 10 p.m. when I started reaching my tipping point for the night. It had been nice seeing and catching up with people after the summer break, but I could already feel the last of my social battery being drained out. There were days when I could continuously talk to everyone and hang around until hours passed midnight, but there were also days when I just wanted to go home early and be in my bed.

That night was one of the latter.

I was standing in the corner of the living room, my place of solace for the last fifteen minutes, when Nina came up to me after finishing her round of beer pong.

'Hey, you okay?' she asked, with concern in her voice seeing the tired expression on my face.

'Yeah, I'm fine,' I gave her a small smile. 'But I'm reaching my limit for the night, so I think I'm just gonna head back to the apartment.'

'Oh, sure,' she said, her eyes looking around the room. 'Let me go find Claudia and—'

I cut her off. 'You should stay. You deserve it after this week's training.'

'Are you sure?' she asked, hesitantly.

'Hundred percent,' I reassured her. 'Go and have fun; I'll probably head straight to bed once I reach the apartment.'

'Okay,' she replied, her tone still contemplative. 'But promise you'll text me the second you step foot inside our apartment.'

'I promise,' I told her, holding out my pinkie finger.

She laughed when she saw what I was doing, but sealed the pinkie promise anyway.

I went to search for Claudia and Lily, along with the members of the track team I was familiar with, to tell them I was leaving. I hugged each of them goodbye before heading to the front door of the house.

Blurting out numerous excuse me-s as I squeezed my way through the crowd of people blocking the way to the entrance, I finally emerged victorious on the front porch of the house, taking a deep breath to recompose myself.

Even though the girls and I had taken an Uber to the party, the new apartment that I shared with Nina wasn't too far. Our last apartment building was merely a few streets from our new place. It was barely a thirty-minute walk, twenty if I walked at a faster pace. I was pretty sure I had already sweated out all the alcohol from the dancing, but my skin still felt a bit warm. The cool night air only made it more inviting to walk my way back to the apartment.

As I was walking down the front yard, willing my mind to recall the route back to my place, I didn't realize I had barely been focusing on my path until I accidentally bumped into something.

Or, rather, someone.

A hand immediately reached out and grasped my arm, steadying me from a fall.

'Oh sorry. Didn't see you there,' I apologized to whoever it was, my mind still reeling from the collision.

'Clara?' the person asked, in a voice that sounded oddly familiar to me.

But that might have just been my mind playing tricks with me.

I finally looked up to see who it was.

And turns out, my mind was, in fact, *not* playing tricks.

The person standing before me, was none other than the star athlete himself, and my potential partner for ASL class.

Colton Reed.

Chapter Four

'Clara?' Colton asked once again, confusion written on his face.

I didn't realize I was plainly staring at him, while my mind went off in a turmoil over what could have possibly led me to end up in this situation.

How did I manage to run into Colton twice this week?

'Colton. Hey,' I greeted him.

Once I finally got over the shock of running into him, only then did my mind register the warm sensation that was on my arm. Looking to see where it came from, my eyes met with Colton's right hand gripping it.

I must have been looking at his hand for a bit too long, when he finally let go of his hold.

'Oh, sorry,' Colton apologized, pulling his arm back. 'Are you okay? I'm sorry for bumping into you like that. I was reading some texts on my phone,' he explained, gesturing to his phone in his other hand.

'It's okay,' I reassured him. 'My mind was occupied elsewhere too, so I wasn't really focusing on where I was going either.'

My words hung in the air between us and the silence that followed got a bit too long. So, I thought I would save us from the awkwardness and go about my way.

Just as I was about to say goodbye, Colton asked, 'Were you leaving?'

So, I guess we're making conversation now.

'Yup. I think I had enough partying for the night,' I answered. And that's when I noticed our collision had happened because we were walking towards each other. 'Did you just arrive?'

'Yeah,' he said sheepishly. 'To be honest, I wasn't thinking of coming, but the baseball team was here. So, I thought I'd drop by and hang out for a bit.'

To think . . . that if I had left a bit earlier . . . I could've avoided running into him here . . .

'Plus, someone has to be the designated driver,' he added.

'You don't drink?' I blurted out before I could stop myself, my curiosity getting the better of me.

'Not when I'm driving.'

My head jolted back slightly at his words. I did not expect that from him.

'You seem surprised,' he read the expression on my face.

'I am, a bit,' I was truthful. 'That's very responsible of you. So do you always drive your teammates home?'

'Most of the time,' he shrugged. 'But I don't mind, driving them home is a small price to pay than having them drive themselves home.'

'That's really sweet of you to do that.'

It was. It's nice to have someone looking out for you that way.

A small but genuine smile made its way to his face. 'Thanks.'

God, he looks even cuter when he smiles.

'Well, go and have fun,' I told him, pushing that thought away. 'It was nice talking to you. I'll see you on Wednesday.' I waved at him and moved past, ready to start my night walk back to the apartment.

But as I made my way down the sidewalk to the end of the street, I heard my name being shouted.

'Clara, wait!'

Stunned, I halted my steps to a stop. Turning around to see who was calling me, I was met by the sight of Colton walking towards me in quick strides.

'Where did you park your car?'

I narrowed my eyes at his sudden question. 'I didn't. I don't have a car.'

A questioning look appeared on his face. 'Did you order an Uber?'

'No.'

'Is someone picking you up? Your boyfriend maybe?'

For the life of me, I couldn't tell why he specifically mentioned boyfriend. But I decided not to dwell on it. 'Nope. Don't have one of those either.'

'Then how are you going home?'

'By foot,' I gestured to my feet.

'You mean, you're walking back?' he asked somewhat outrageously, alarmed by my plans.

'Yeah,' I confirmed. 'My apartment isn't too far from here—a thirty-minute walk. Tops,' I pointed in the direction of my apartment building.

Colton seemed to be lost in his thoughts mulling over something. When he finally made up his mind, he said, 'Let me drive you home.'

What.

'What?' I verbalized my thought out loud, a bit bewildered by what he had said.

I must have misheard him; there's no way he just offered to drive me back to my apartment.

'Let me drive you home,' he repeated.

Turns out I *had* heard him correctly.

'That's not necessary,' I told him. Sharing a class was still safe territory curse-wise, since we didn't really have to talk to one another unless absolutely necessary. But being in a car together seemed to be pushing it a bit too far for my liking. 'And you should already be inside, hanging out with your teammates.'

'They can wait,' he answered without missing a beat. 'Come on. My car is parked over there.' He started heading towards the fleet of cars chaotically parked on the driveway. His steps slowed down to make sure I could catch up with him.

Think of an excuse. Any excuse.

'Are you sure about this? Won't your girlfriend be mad?' I argued with him. I wasn't one to mingle in college gossip, but that didn't mean I was too far out of the loop. And, according to the gossip floating around, rumour had it that Colton didn't date, nor did he have a girlfriend.

But that was *just* a rumour, and it didn't hurt to at least confirm the suspicion. The last thing I wanted was to be caught up in some couple drama because of a simple friendly gesture.

'Don't have one,' he confirmed, his steps never faltering.

'Colton, you really don't have to do this,' I tried negotiating with him once again, throwing out one last ditch effort for him to change his mind. 'I'm really okay with walking back.'

'Then do it for my peace of mind,' he answered me, his voice firm. Then, he added in a softer tone. 'Please?'

It was the soft *please* that melted the rest of my resolve. Here was Colton, kindly offering to drive me back to my apartment. And here I was, trying to come up with excuses to reject his offer, simply because of a stupid curse.

I re-evaluated my options once again, and honestly, the idea of walking back started to sound less appealing by the second. Curse or not, I was pretty sure I could handle a short car ride with Colton.

'Okay,' I finally agreed. 'Where did you park?'

Colton's car was parked a bit further from the party venue, since he had arrived late. Whatever space that was available near the house had already been filled.

While walking to his car, I told him the name of my apartment building and the street it was located on. The building was situated on a familiar street, so I wasn't surprised he knew where it was, without me having to navigate.

We finally reached his car, and just as I was about to open the door to the passenger seat, Colton beat me to it and opened the door for me instead.

'Milady,' he said with a teasing smile, a slight bow in his stance.

I wasn't sure what he was doing, but decided there was no harm in playing along. 'Milord,' I answered back. His eyes lit up at my reply and my heart squeezed just a tiny bit at his reaction.

Once I got myself into the passenger seat, Colton shut the door and went over to the driver's side. As he turned on the engine, music started playing from the car's speakers.

And it was playing 'Mamma Mia'.

By ABBA.

My eyes widened a bit upon recognizing the song. But then, I thought it might have come from a radio station. I tried to see what channel he was tuning into, when I saw that the song was playing from a CD. My eyes widened a bit more.

Before I could stop myself, the words were already out of my mouth. 'You have an ABBA CD?' I didn't even try to conceal the surprise in my voice.

'No.'

'Oh, is it someone else's—'

'I have five of them,' he clarified.

I'm pretty sure my eyes couldn't have gotten any wider than they did then, as I whipped my gaze over to him.

'You have five ABBA CDs?' I was bewildered by this new information about Colton.

'Yup.' He paused while he was reversing the car. 'It would've been all of their albums, but I'm still missing a few of them to complete my collection.'

I've always believed that one's music taste says a lot about a person. Sometimes, it even takes a lot for people to be comfortable enough to share that part of themselves. I could tell that Colton might have been slightly embarrassed by me stumbling upon this part of him, seeing how quiet he got. A shade of red was starting to appear on the tips of his ears.

Trying to think of something to say to save him from the unwarranted embarrassment, I told him, 'I love ABBA.'

'Yeah?' he replied softly, the feeling of unease slowly melting away.

'Yeah,' I affirmed. 'I only know their popular songs though. But from what I have heard, I love them.'

I realized that it was the exact thing to say, when I saw his tense shoulders started to relax, and a smile lit up his face. 'Let me guess. Are all the songs you know from the *Mamma Mia* movies?' he asked, his voice teasing.

'Busted,' I admitted. It was true, and I refused to be ashamed because those movies were my comfort watches.

He let out a laugh at my reply, and Lord, if it wasn't the sexiest laugh I had ever heard.

Get it together, Clara.

'Okay fine, yes that's as far as my knowledge of ABBA music goes. You definitely know more of their music than me, if you have five of their albums. Is there any story behind it?' I asked. 'If you're willing to share, I don't want to pry,' I then added.

'Not at all,' he started, both eyes on the road. 'My parents are huge record collectors, that's one of the things they had in common before they even knew each other. Of course, when they got married, their collections only grew. My mom usually played whatever record she was feeling for the day. Since she works from home, every day when I came home from school, music had always been playing.'

He paused his story when we reached a junction, making sure we were heading the right way before he continued.

'Anyway, the summer before I started high school, my mom randomly decided it was the summer of ABBA, so she exclusively played all the ABBA albums until the summer ended. And it was a good summer, so any time I hear an ABBA song, it always brings me back to that time in my life. You know, before life got complicated with high school,' he said with playful sarcasm. 'I always blasted ABBA in my room afterwards. When my parents got me this car as a graduation gift, I went ahead and bought the actual albums. So now, I choose to blast them in my car instead. Just me, ABBA, and the road ahead.'

'How very poetic of you,' I told him once he finished recounting his story. A corner of his mouth lifted, giving way to a small smile at my reply. 'But why buy their albums instead of just playing it from your phone and connecting it to the car?'

'That might have been my parents' record-collecting influence. I don't know,' he trailed off. 'There's just something about having them physically, I guess. Does that make sense?' he then added, struggling to put his thoughts into words.

'No, I get it,' I told him because I did. I might not be an album or a record collector, but I am a reader. And every reader knows there's something magical about collecting books and creating your own mini library as your collection grows bigger.

'I feel the same way about books. Don't get me wrong, I like the convenience of eBooks, but there's just something special about having them in your physical hold. It's like you're willingly letting them take up space in your life, for nothing more than just your own happiness,' I explained. 'And I think that alone is a good enough of a reason as any.'

Other than the ABBA song that was playing from the speakers—one that I didn't recognize—and the muffled hum of the car's engine, the car was filled with silence. I looked over at Colton, silently hoping he wasn't weirded out by what I had just said.

But I found him risking a glance my way, a genuine smile on his face when he broke the silence, and said, 'You're right. That's exactly it.'

My pulse skyrocketed and I'm pretty sure I was blushing, for my face felt warmer than it did a few seconds ago.

I quickly looked away from him, trying my best to calm myself down, and willing the blush to go away. The radio continued playing ABBA songs as Colton drove ahead, and my lips titled up recognizing the melody of 'SOS' as I recalled the scene of Meryl Streep and Pierce Brosnan singing it in the movie.

'So, what's your favourite ABBA song?' I asked Colton.

'That's a fully loaded question.'

'Why? You can't seem to pick just one?'

'Can *you* pick just one favourite book?'

'Touché,' I replied. 'Okay then, what's your favourite ABBA song at the moment?'

'Hmm. I'm gonna go with "One Last Summer",' Colton answered after a moment.

'Seriously?' I exclaimed. 'Don't tell me it's because summer just ended.'

'In that case, I won't tell you.' A smile tugged on his lips.

I blew out a dramatic sigh, shaking my head in mocking disappointment. 'Okay. Then what about your favourite ABBA song to sing? Like, if you were asked to sing one of their songs, what would it be?'

'"Waterloo", hands down,' he answered with no hesitation. 'But what about you? I know you said your ABBA song knowledge is limited, but I doubt you don't have a favourite to sing to.'

I took a moment to pick one out of the few that I loved singing to, and then, I decided to just name them all.

'I think it depends on what I'm feeling,' I told him. '"Andante, Andante" is a good one if I'm feeling a bit sentimental. "The Winner Takes It All" is for when I want to belt. But honestly, I'd probably pick "Waterloo" as well if I just want to have fun.'

'Glad to know we're on the same page.' He nodded, that small smile still ever-present on his face. 'We're here by the way.'

I looked out the window and saw he was right. I wouldn't even have noticed that we were already on my street if it weren't for him pointing it out and asking me where he could drop me off.

'There's a drop-off spot, just in front of the building. In front of that red car,' I told him, pointing at the said vehicle. Our street was filled with a variety of shops and restaurants. Most of them were already closed for the night, except for a few restaurants that offered to serve alcoholic drinks until 2 a.m. All of them were packed with people wanting to make the best of their Saturday night and it seemed like the night was only getting started for them.

Colton stopped his car in front of my apartment building before unbuckling his seat belt and getting off. Confused, I watched him from the windshield, when he finally stopped at my side of the car and opened the door for me.

'You didn't have to do that, but thank you,' I told him, climbing down from the car.

'You're welcome,' Colton replied. 'So, I'll see you next Wednesday then?'

And that's when I remembered.

Right.

I was supposed to tell him I couldn't be his partner for ASL class the next time I saw him. Me running into him unexpectedly at the party and his offering to drive me home totally threw me off and made me forget all about it. But just as I was about to tell him my decision, I stopped myself.

This isn't fair of me to do this to him.

I might've already given him a reasonable excuse on why we could't be partners, and he seemed to have understood where I was coming from, but he did offer a solution on how we could make this work. While I didn't know him well enough to know if I could fully trust him to stay true to his words, the vulnerability he had shown me during the conversation we had in the car seemed a good enough indication that I could trust him to be a good partner.

And darn it, I *liked* talking to him, and I wanted more chances to talk to him again. Not that I would admit it out loud.

It was easy to get over my crush on him, when I had nothing to back up the infatuation with, other than the fact that he was cute, and a star athlete. But now that I knew he liked listening to ABBA to the point that he voluntarily collected their albums, drove his drunk teammates home, and extended the same gesture towards *me*, brushing off this crush had gotten a tiny bit harder.

And the more time I spent with him, the higher the chances I had of tempting the curse.

But none of those reasons were his fault, and he shouldn't have to bear the consequences because of me. Plus, the curse would have worked only if he *actually reciprocated* my crush, so I might have been a bit over my head to think that could happen.

'Clara?' Colton called out, snapping me out of my train of thought.

'Oh, sorry,' I said, getting out of my head. 'Yeah, I'll see you next Wednesday.' Then, placing the puzzle that would change my entire semester, I added, 'partner.'

I don't know if Colton caught what I meant by that last word. But it seemed he did when a beaming smile lit up his entire face, his eyes crinkling with happiness.

'I'll see you in class then,' he said. Momentarily pausing for dramatic effect, I assume, before he added 'partner.'

We exchanged phone numbers, and I waved him goodbye on my way inside the building. I went straight to the window of my apartment to catch a last glimpse of his car, just in time, to see him driving off. I decided to stay there for a moment as I recalled what I had just done, and how I should move forward with my impulsive decision.

Crushes are a weird thing. I feel like most of the time, you tend to build up that person in your head with daydreams, only to have it crushed once you actually got to know them. God knew I had my fair share of those, which is why it was fairly easy to brush off my crushes before. But something told me this crush on Colton might be different, but maybe that was just the spark of hope burning in my heart.

Even so, I had to be careful in pursuing whatever it was, because crushes or not, Colton was a cliché love interest, and I had to make sure to protect myself from succumbing to the curse.

I made sure I texted Nina before starting my nightly routine. As I took off my makeup for the night, something else occurred to me. It usually took around five minutes from the track team's house to get to our old apartment, ten in case of some traffic. Considering how close that building was to our new one, my guess was it would've taken the same amount of time.

But the car ride with Colton seemed to be longer than usual, even though there wasn't much traffic on the road.

That spark of hope—the rebel that she is—and my inner romantic self, unanimously decided that Colton had unintentionally driven slower to prolong our conversation.

I immediately pushed away those feelings. *I must be more tired than I thought.*

I tried reading a chapter of *It Happened One Summer*, the new romance book I had just started, but ultimately decided I couldn't process any words, when a yawn escaped my mouth.

As my head hit the pillow, my mind started reliving the later events of the night on repeat when I finally drifted off to sleep, a smile present on my face.

Chapter Five

A feeling of excited anticipation had slowly been building up since the night of the party. I couldn't fully understand what it was until Wednesday came around, and I was on my way to this week's ASL class.

I made it to class earlier this time. For a moment, I thought about switching to a different seat than where I had sat previously. However, since the class was held in a classroom instead of a lecture hall, I felt that there was an unspoken rule: where you sat during the first week would be your unofficial assigned seat for the rest of the semester. Plus, the class did rely on students being in pairs, the wise decision would be to just sit where I had sat last week.

Not wanting to disrupt the peace and avoid any kind of confrontation that might erupt, I went to the back of the class and took my seat.

The class wouldn't begin for another ten minutes, so I took out my book from my bag and tried to read whatever I could before Mr Albert got there.

I didn't even manage to read a page when the seat next to me was pulled out and snapped me out of focus.

'Hey,' Colton greeted me, a smile on his face.

My heart started to flutter as he took the seat beside me. It seemed the excited anticipation was my heart waiting to get the chance to talk to Colton again.

Traitor.

'Hey, partner,' I greeted him back, closing my book. 'How has your week been so far?'

'Good. Practice is starting to get rough, but nothing out of the ordinary, with a match coming next weekend.'

Right, I remembered receiving an email about it a few days earlier. They only had three exhibition matches in total, two of them were away games, and the last one was to happen in our own college baseball stadium.

'But don't worry,' he continued. 'I'll make time to practice ASL with you. When are you free?'

'I should be asking you that, since you're the one fully booked up,' I pointed out, arching a brow at him.

Compared to his life packed with baseball practices, my schedule for the week had consisted of me either finishing my book and starting a new one, or finishing the show I had been watching, and starting a new one. I would find some time to do *actual* work in between. 'But I'm free after this, if you have time to spare.'

He thought about my offer for a while, perhaps going through his schedule for the week. 'I think I can do that. I don't have a class after this, and practice doesn't start in a few hours.'

'So that settles it then.'

Before we could continue our conversation, we were interrupted by Mr Albert opening the front door and entering the classroom.

'Good day, everyone,' he greeted, setting down his briefcase on the desk and taking out a piece of paper out of it. 'I hope you already found your partners for the class. I was supposed to do this last week: so, before I forget again, please write down your name and your partner's here, for my own record,' he said, gesturing to the paper he was holding in his hand.

He passed the paper down to the first row of tables in the classroom. 'All right, now let's get started.'

Halfway through the class, the piece of paper finally made its way to us, after the person sitting next to our table passed it to me.

As I looked at the list of names, I couldn't help but think of it as a contract of me willingly going through with this decision, risking myself to the possibility of being struck by the curse.

Was I actually going to do this?

I was so caught up in my head, rethinking my decision, that I didn't notice Colton talking to me.

'Hmm?' I hummed non-committally, turning to him.

'Having second thoughts?' Colton asked teasingly, snapping me out of my inner dilemma.

Caught off guard by him voicing out the exact thing I was contemplating in my head, a shadow of doubt appeared on my face, but I quickly masked it away.

Colton must've caught it, because the look on his face slowly started to lose its glint.

Last chance to back out, Clara.

'Nope, no second thoughts. I guess you're stuck with me for the whole semester,' I told him and wrote down both our names on the paper, him spelling out his name for me so I didn't misspell it.

It's official then.

There was no going back now.

'I think that will be all for today. I'll see you all next week,' Mr Albert announced, dismissing the class.

I started packing up my things, Colton did the same beside me. 'Should we go to one of the coffee shops on campus to practice?' I suggested, zipping up my backpack.

'Anywhere is fine.' He shrugged. 'We don't have to stay on campus, you know? I have my car and I'd be happy to drive you anywhere.'

'But you have practice later, wouldn't you prefer to stay on campus?' I didn't want to make this any more of a nuisance for him.

'I'll make it; practice doesn't start in a few hours,' he reassured me.

I considered his offer. I had been wanting to try out that new bubble tea shop that had just opened a few streets away from my apartment, but I hadn't had the opportunity to visit it just yet.

'Since you're offering, do you mind if we go to a bubble tea shop instead? There's one near my apartment building and I can just walk home afterward,' I told him.

'Sure,' he nodded, before adding, 'on one condition though.'

I looked at him suspiciously. 'What's that?'

'I'm driving you home,' he said with a teasing look in his eyes, then quickly got up from his seat and rushed his way to the door.

I sat there stunned, my mind slowly registering what had just happened.

Did he say he was driving me home?

I snapped out of my daze and rushed after him, only to see him lean on the wall next to the door frame in the hallway, waiting for me, with a crooked grin on his face.

'Come on,' he said to me, nudging his head as he made his way to the stairs. I noticed that he was walking at a faster pace than normal as if trying to outrun me before I could argue with him about his so-called 'condition'.

When I finally caught up to his pace and was walking side-by-side with him, he slowed down his strides. We made it out of the building, and I could just about make out where his car was, amid all the others in the parking lot.

'You don't really have to drive me home, you know?' I tried reasoning with him as we walked together toward his parked car. 'I'm perfectly capable of walking.'

'And I'm perfectly capable of driving you home.'

'Then, let's just go to the coffee shop on campus,' I told him.

'No problem,' he said, 'But I'm still driving you home afterward.'

'Colton,' I called out, my tone exasperated. 'You don't have to do that. I can just—'

I hadn't even finished my sentence, when he abruptly stopped walking. I paused in my steps as well, just as he turned to face me. 'Look, I am not letting you walk back home when I am fully capable of driving you. The way I see it, you have two options. One, we practice at the coffee shop, and I'll drive you home when we're done. Or two, we practice at the bubble tea shop, and I'll drive you home when we're done. So, what is it going to be?'

I blinked at him. 'I didn't say I was going to walk back home from campus. I was going to take the bus.'

'Not happening.' He shook his head. 'Your only options are the two that I gave you. So where are we practicing ASL today?'

His firm tone had me so momentarily stunned, that I unknowingly stayed quiet as it passed. I felt like I should have been put off by it, but I was not. Moreover, I was drawn to it.

Colton must've mistaken my silence as a reaction to him being stern with me. He then added, this time in a much softer tone, 'It's your choice, Clara.'

I took both the options into consideration, and it doesn't seem like either was fair to him, since he had been offering to drive me home no matter where we went. So, I guess he meant it when he said it was up to me.

A slightly better choice would be the coffee shop, since he only needed to drive me back home and back to campus for practice. However, I couldn't deny that craving in my heart for a bubble tea fix, ever since I had heard about the new shop.

'Fine, the bubble tea shop it is,' I said, giving in. Then, deciding to play him at his own game, I briskly added, 'But

I'm paying for the drinks,' before fastening my steps to his car and leaving him standing there.

That was one point for Colton and one point for me.

That day's ASL lesson focused on learning the alphabet and perfecting the placing of the fingers for each letter. Since ASL is a visual language and more about hand movements, as well as facial expressions, it's hard to convey them on paper. But Mr Albert had still provided us each with a printed sheet of paper with the hand placements for each alphabet as reference. He had also encouraged us to practice using them daily, so eventually—hopefully—it would become a muscle memory.

'Try spelling out words of whatever object you see or names of the people you meet every day. Before you know it, you'll be spelling in ASL effortlessly,' he had suggested during class.

'Okay,' I said, putting down my bubble tea. 'My turn.'

Colton and I were sitting across from one another at a table placed in the corner of the bubble tea shop. Aside from us, the shop had been quite vacant, with only one other table occupied, providing us with a pleasant environment to practice ASL. While the tables might be mostly empty, that hadn't stopped the inflow of customers preferring to have their bubble tea to go, if the sounds of the door opening and closing were anything to go by.

Following Mr Albert's advice, Colton and I took turns spelling out random things or names that came to mind, with the other person having to say what word was spelled.

After I finished spelling my word, I waited for Colton to say it.

'Bobs?' he guessed, a look of confusion written on his face.

I shook my head. 'Nope. But you're close.' I spelled it again and he finally caught on.

'Oh, boba.' He nodded. 'I keep messing up the A and the S.'

'I think that calls for a break,' I said, taking a sip of my bubble tea. I looked around the shop and admired how well-designed it was. I took in the ambience it was putting out—with its bohemian theme decorations and potted plants occupying one of the other corners.

'So why did you decide to learn ASL?' Colton asked, taking my attention away from the shop and to him.

'I don't think there was a concrete reason, to be honest,' I told him. 'I've always found sign language fascinating and when I was registering for my classes during my freshman year, I saw they had offered ASL as an elective. I just had a feeling in my gut that wanted me to take it. I know the class wouldn't be anything advanced, but I figured it was a great place to start.'

'Freshman year?' Colton arched an eyebrow.

'Yeah. I wanted to take the elective since my freshman year, but my other classes always clashed with the ASL class time. So, when I could finally take it this semester,

I jumped at the chance and here I am now.' Then I added in a playful tone, 'stuck with you as my partner.'

He chuckled lightly. 'What do you mean when you said you find ASL fascinating?'

I took a moment to mull over his question. 'I think there's something beautiful in communicating without words. I mean, I know learning ASL is a necessity for some people. But I don't know,' I shrugged. 'People always go on and on about the beauty of different languages, but ASL is a language too. And I just don't think it's appreciated as much as it should be. To me, communicating in ASL feels like you're talking to another person in secret, where you don't have to utter a single word.'

The silence that followed was a bit unnerving, so I kept my eyes down to my bubble tea, worried I might have scared off Colton with my random ramblings. But when I finally dared to glance at him, he had a genuine smile on his face.

I could feel my cheeks start to heat up with the way he was looking at me. 'Anyway, enough about me. What's your ASL story?'

He took a long gulp of his bubble tea—that he was already close to finishing—before he started narrating. 'I'm not sure how much you know what entails if you're on the college baseball team, but as long as you're a part of it, you're required to attend a few charity events here and there. You know, to keep up a good public appearance?'

I nodded for him to continue.

'We attended an event last semester for kids. Just teaching them how to throw, catch a baseball, and how to swing a bat,' he said to me. 'And I noticed this one boy sitting in the corner all alone. So, I went over to him to say hi and started talking, but he just waved back at me and stayed silent. I thought he was just shy, but then one of the volunteers at the event told me that the kid was Deaf.'

His voice started getting softer as he continued telling the story.

'And since no one there knew ASL, the kid pretty much glued himself to the corner. I asked one of the volunteers for a notebook with some pens and we just used the notebook to write down whatever we wanted to say and pass it to each other to communicate,' he continued, his face wearing a tender look, matching his soft tone. 'Eventually, he wanted to try swinging a bat, and I ended up just spending the entirety of the event with him. When I got home that day, it got me thinking that ASL might be something I want to try and learn. So, when I saw it was being offered by the university, I thought it'd be a great opportunity to start. I know I won't be fluent but I'm hoping I'll at least learn a few sentences to use for future events.

'And here I am now, stuck with you as my partner,' he finished off with a smile, throwing my words back at me.

I gave him a smile of my own, while internally trying to calm down the chaos that had been going through my mind at that very moment.

I knew there was a chance I'd be tempting the curse, when I agreed to us being partners for this class. But I had also relied on the fact that my crush on Colton would be gone once I learned he's nothing like the Colton my infatuation had built him up to be. Nothing like the fantasy hero version of him I thought about.

Turns out the real Colton was much better.

A small part of me had been hoping for him to say he took the ASL class for the sake of fulfilling the requirements, and that it was the only one available. This would have tremendously helped me dissolve this silly little crush that I had on him to overcome the curse.

But, instead, he was telling me he had decided to take ASL so he could talk to Deaf kids?

I think my crush on him had just grown.

The curse really is cruel.

'That's very thoughtful of you.' I finally said, after a beat of silence.

'It's the least I can do,' he shrugged.

'What was his name?'

A fond smile tugged on his lips. 'Phillip.'

'Well, I think he deserves a toast from us. What do you say? To Phillip?' I raised my bubble tea, which he laughed at before tapping his bubble tea with mine.

'To Phillip,' he replied as both of us took a sip of our drink.

As I was chewing down the boba, I couldn't help but think whether I wanted to hug Phillip or strangle him for unintentionally being the one to bring Colton into my life.

I internally sighed at the thought.

Guess we would have to wait and see.

This area of town had always been the hub of anything and everything for the people living here—whether temporarily or permanently. Rows and rows of restaurants, small shops, boutiques, and bars filled up entire streets, with the occasional apartment buildings smacked in between. I might have lived there for the past two terms, but new shops had always been opening every time I returned after the summer break.

Once we had decided we were done with our ASL practice for the day, we finished up our drinks and left the shop. The girl working behind the cashier waved us goodbye.

Colton's car had been parked a few shops away from the bubble tea shop, so it was quite a walk, and I took the time to admire the slow bustle of the street. It might have been a college town, but there was a certain air to it, which made you want to live in the present moment, rather than hustle at every second.

As we were walking in the direction of his car— Colton standing in the middle between the road and me—I noticed there was a grocery store across the street from where he had parked. Buckets of flowers carefully wrapped and neatly stacked covered its front.

'Hey,' I stopped him from opening my car door. 'Do you mind if I go take a look at the flowers over there?' I pointed to the grocery store.

He looked at where I was pointing. 'I don't mind.'

I assumed he would have waited for me in the car, while I headed over there and looked around. But he surprised me by locking his car instead, and said, 'Let's go.'

We made sure to look on both sides of the road before crossing. Once the roads were clear, I felt a gentle push coming from my back. I turned my head slightly to see what it was, finding Colton standing by my side, his hand at my back and guiding me while we crossed the road. I couldn't fully feel his touch with my backpack in the way, but I could imagine how warm it would be.

I quickly shook that thought out of my head. 'You don't have to come with me, you know? And again, I can just walk back to my apartment. It's not that far,' I reminded him once again as we reached the opposite street.

'It's fine,' he told me, pulling his arm back to his side once we reached the sidewalk.

'Are you sure? I don't want to make you late for practice or anything.'

Colton turned to me, putting both of his hands on my shoulders, and stared straight into my eyes. 'Yes, I am sure.'

I wasn't fully convinced, and he must've seen it from the look on my face. With a small smile on his face, he said gently, 'Practice doesn't start in another hour, and campus isn't even a ten-minute drive away from here. I already have everything I need in the car. So yes, I am sure of this, and I am driving you back home. Stop doubting me.'

'Okay,' I replied, giving him a small smile of my own. I appreciated Colton for using logic to back up his reasons, and it did help settle a part of my guilt. Since we were already on this side of the street, I might as well take a look.

A sweet scent filled the air the closer I got to the store. The beautiful flowers took up almost half of the sidewalk, while the radiant colours of the petals welcomed me in their embrace once I was close enough to fully admire their beauty.

Colton stood patiently by my side as I took my time looking at them. My hands gently caressed each of the flower petals that I had passed by.

I was admiring the red tulips when I heard Colton ask, 'Do you have a favourite flower?'

I tilted my head at him and caught him looking at the gardenias, his hands reaching out and touching the petals softly with his fingertips.

And I couldn't take my eyes away from him.

My crush on Colton had been superficial, I would freely admit to that. It was shaped by seeing him from afar in the stands, as he scored points for the baseball team, fully living up to his reputation of being a star athlete. But at that moment, he had just seemed like nothing more than another guy, admiring flowers with a fond look on his face.

Colton's eyes met mine and I instantly looked back at the tulips, a rush of heat filling up my cheeks. 'I don't really have a favourite flower. I just like whatever looks pretty,' I answered him. 'Bonus if it's in pink.'

'So pink flowers then?'

'You could say that.'

I finally got to the section of flowers that had first caught my attention from across the street. The pink roses.

Looking at the flowers, I thought about whether I should bring some home. Nina and I had never really put flowers in our apartment before. But I was pretty sure we had a vase somewhere that I could put on the coffee table in the living room to brighten up the space.

'What are you thinking hard about?'

My head snapped up, seeing Colton standing closer to me than he did moments before. Close enough that our arms had almost been touching.

'I'm thinking about whether or not I should get some flowers for my apartment,' I told him, my mind stuck in a dilemma.

'Go for it,' he urged me.

I raised a brow at him. 'You think so?'

'Why not?' He shrugged. 'I mean, if having flowers in your apartment makes you happy, then why not get them? Isn't that a good enough reason as any?'

I couldn't fight back a smile even if I tried. 'You're right, that reason alone is enough.'

And before I knew it, I was walking back to the car with pink roses in one arm.

Colton opened the passenger door for me and offered to hold my flowers while I climbed into the car. I thanked him as he passed them back to me, closed the door, and made his way over to the driver's seat.

When we arrived in front of my apartment building, Colton parked his car at the drop-off spot and once again stepped out of the car to open my door for me.

'Thank you.' I smiled at him. 'I'll see you next week then, partner?'

He gave me a nod. 'Next week it is, partner.'

Chapter Six

In the next few weeks that followed, my Wednesdays had started to fall into a bit of a routine.

My mornings consisted of having breakfast at the apartment and heading down to campus for my classes. Then, I would meet up with Claudia and Lily for lunch. Although we were taking different classes, our schedules seemed to align with one another, and we took it as an opportunity to meet up and hang out until our next class.

After lunch came the afternoon portion of my Wednesday, which was slowly becoming my favourite part of the week. It started with ASL class, then going to the bubble tea shop to practice ASL with Colton.

The Wednesday after our first practice, Colton had asked me if I wanted to go to the same bubble tea shop again, to which I had enthusiastically agreed. The week after that, it just became the normal spot for our weekly sessions.

Once we were done with our practice, we would head over to the grocery store across the street, where I would get new flowers for the week. Nina had given an excited stamp of approval to me bringing home flowers that first time.

'I can't believe we never had these in the apartment before,' she had said, while admiring the pink roses. It was then I decided to continue bringing them home, choosing a different kind every time based on whatever I felt like getting that day, though they were always pink.

And of course, the routine always ended with Colton driving me home.

As the weeks passed by, I started to learn more and more about Colton Reed: how he started loving baseball ever since his family brought him to a batting cage for one of his birthdays, how his comfort food was his mom's homemade spaghetti that she cooked every Sunday morning—a tradition he had carried on by himself once he left for college—and how he has a younger sister who he was extremely protective about.

Naturally, my questions about his family meant he would bring up a few about mine as well. I contemplated telling him about my family situation, as talking about my parents' divorce wasn't necessarily a fun fact about myself. But ultimately, I decided I could confide in Colton about it.

'My parents got divorced when I was eight. They're still good friends though and my dad still comes over to my mom's place so we could all have dinner together. And they always make sure that we're always together to celebrate the holidays, so I'm grateful for that,' I told him. 'And I have an older sister named Elizabeth, but she usually just goes by Eliza. She's six years older than me, but pretty much my best friend in the whole world. She's a journalist who currently lives in New York City.'

I avoided looking up to see Colton's reaction to what I had just told him and kept twirling the straw in my bubble tea. My eyes focused on the boba going in circles.

Finally, I stopped spinning when I felt something warm placed on top of my other hand on the table.

It was Colton's hand.

I chanced a glance at it and finally turned my attention to his face. He gave me a small smile and gently squeezed my hand.

And that was it.

He acknowledged my story and said we didn't have to talk about it any more, communicating with only an expression, and my hand in his.

Communicating without words.

I gave him a smile of my own in return.

My streak of a similar Wednesday routine eventually came to an end.

After our ASL class for the week ended, I suggested to Colton that we just stay on campus.

'Stay on campus? Are you sick of bubble tea already?' he teased.

'Definitely not,' I shook my head. Can one even get sick of bubble tea? Probably, but not me. Yes, I admit I had started to develop an obsession with the drink, but I was consuming it in moderation, only once a week during our ASL practice session.

'My friends invited me out for dinner,' I started explaining. 'They're on the track team and heading out right away after their training. So, I'm just gonna stay on campus until they finish.'

Nina had informed me the night before that the team was planning to grab dinner once they were done with their training and invited me along to join them. Because I hadn't got a chance to hang out with them again since the party, I told Nina I would wait for them on campus. In the meantime, I wanted to be able to get some work done at the library.

'Okay,' he nodded. 'But the real question is, do you still want to get bubble tea?'

I furrowed my eyebrows at him, failing to see what bubble tea had to do with this. 'How is that relevant?'

'Well. We could still go practice at the bubble tea shop and come back. I mean, I'm coming back to campus for my practice either way. Or, we can go get some bubble tea to go, and come back to practice on campus,' he suggested. 'So, what is it gonna be?'

If there's one thing I had learned after spending all that time with Colton, it was that you have to pick your battles with him. I could point out how unfair both options were for him, but from my previous attempts at doing so, it wouldn't get very far.

At the same time, I couldn't help the butterflies in my stomach every time Colton offered me choices that gave me some kind of benefit, even if he was just doing it for nothing more than being a good friend.

I took a moment to consider the two options he had given me. As much as I liked spending time in the bubble tea shop, a change of scenery sounded like a good idea.

'Do you have a place in mind where we can practice ASL?' I asked him instead.

I could see the exact moment his eyes lit up. 'I know just the perfect spot.'

'Then bubble tea to go it is.'

I tried getting the answer out of Colton as to where the 'perfect spot' was, while we were getting our bubble tea, only to have him answer me with, 'You're just gonna have to be patient.' This was accompanied by a glint of mischief in his eyes.

When we arrived back on campus with our drinks, my suspicions only grew when he took up a parking spot in front of the baseball stadium.

'Come on,' he said, after opening my door. I grabbed the drinks and got out of the car.

Noticing that I was carrying the drinks, he grabbed them from me. 'Let me get those. It's a bit of a walk though, is that all right with you?'

I gave a slow nod, still confused about where exactly he was bringing me.

The walk lasted for a while, and I noticed that we ended up passing the baseball stadium and were walking up a hill in the clearing behind it, towards a clump of trees.

Colton finally came to a stop at one of the trees at the edge of the grove, and I reached a few seconds later.

'We're here,' he announced, setting down the drinks and his bag at the foot of a tree as he sat down on the grass.

Leaning against the trunk with his legs extended in front of him, he closed his eyes and took a deep breath, exhaling it slowly with a peaceful look on his face.

There was a sense of calmness in him at this very moment. From all the time we had spent together so far, Colton had never shied away from openly expressing himself, but this was the first time I had ever seen him truly relaxed.

I couldn't stop staring at him. I wanted to capture this version of Colton in my head to hold on to when the semester was over, and there was no ASL class to practice for any more.

He must've felt my gaze on him, when he peeked one eye open to see me still standing in the same spot as before.

'Come sit,' he said, patting the spot next to him.

I hesitated for a moment. But since the afternoon weather gave way to a pleasant atmosphere, and the sun had been shining brightly for the past few days, I figured the grass was dry.

Without further second-guessing my decision, I put down my bag and sat next to Colton, following his lead by stretching my legs out in front as I leaned against the tree.

We spent the next few minutes in silence: listening to the rustle of trees, and the sounds of birds singing.

I started closing my eyes as well and inhaled a deep breath, gently exhaling it.

Colton was the one to break the silence.

'I discovered this spot during my freshman year,' his voice was soft.

I opened my eyes and turned my face to him, and he turned his to mine.

'How did you find it?' I asked, urging him to continue.

'It was the week before the first baseball team practice, and I thought I would stop by to get a feel of this place. I was pretty nervous about it, so I thought I would just take a jog. I didn't know what came over me to jog this far, but I did, and stopped right here to catch my breath,' he said pointing at the spot we were sitting on.

'The next thing I know, I just sat here for the next twenty minutes, taking deep breaths and looking out at the baseball field, ' his face turned to face the front, and there it was, the baseball field in all its glory.

'And I just felt a lot calmer than I did, I was still nervous but less than before. So, if I ever feel like I need a moment to step back from anything, or when the idea of playing baseball seems a bit more daunting than usual, I always find myself coming back here. Just looking at the field. It helps me to remember why I love the sport so much and why I started it in the first place,' he said.

I took a moment before saying anything, letting the story sink in. 'And does it work?'

'Most of the time.' He shrugged, his voice slightly lowered as if he was embarrassed by what he had just told me.

I gave him a small smile. 'Thank you for sharing this with me.'

My words hung in the air as the breeze passed through the tree. As his soft gaze met mine, I hoped he could sense how honoured I had felt for him to have brought me there.

A small smile found its way to his lips. 'You're welcome.' We just looked at each other for a minute before his eyes narrowed in confusion.

'What?' I asked, sensing something wrong.

'I just realized. You didn't get flowers this week.'

I jolted my head back slightly in surprise. I didn't even think he would notice, but he might have caught on to that, since he had been the one who saw me getting them every week.

'Yeah, I didn't think it was worth the trip today, since I won't be home until later tonight, so I didn't feel like carrying them around. It might also be a bit weird bringing flowers into the library,' I added the last part jokingly. 'I might get them this Friday though; I love having them in my apartment and so does my roommate Nina. Just not getting them today.'

Colton just nodded.

'As much as I would love to just sit here and admire the view, I think we have some ASL to practice,' I said, turning my whole body to face him and crossing my legs.

'Yes, we do.' He turned to me doing the same, and thus began our practice session under the tree.

I tapped my phone to check the time and saw that the track team would be finishing up their training in half an hour, plus some additional time or so for them to shower and get ready before we went out for the night. I still had one question left to finish for my class tomorrow, and I mentally calculated what time I should leave the library so I could be there before they got out of the locker rooms.

Thinking I had enough time to finish up that one final question, and knowing that I wouldn't have to worry about it during dinner later, I opted to continue with my work.

After twenty minutes of searching for answers, paraphrasing, and adding thoughts of my own, I could finally turn off my laptop with a peaceful mind and call it quits for the night.

I checked the time once again and saw I still had some time left to spare. The walk from the library to the track field was short, so I took my time to gather up my things, rechecking that I hadn't left anything before leaving the building.

I took the steps down from the library to the pavement and was greeted by the golden hour. A smile made its way to my face as I took in the beautiful skies and the multitude of colours filling it. I took out my phone to capture the moment into a forever memory.

As the sky started to get dark, I fastened my steps toward the direction of the track field.

Our college's athletic centre took up a huge area of campus ground. All the fields and stadiums were built close to one another: the track field was located right next to the baseball stadium, and the two shared a huge parking lot which stretched from one end of the track field to the other end of the baseball stadium. In the middle, there stood a covered walkway that connected to the intersection between the two buildings.

Usually, I waited for Nina at the entrance of the track field. However, she had texted me earlier, saying that she parked on the baseball stadium side of the parking lot. So, I decided to just wait for her at the intersection instead.

I looked around the parking lot to see if I knew any of the cars that were still left. I recognized quite a few of them, including Lucy's car, which meant the track team was yet to come out of the locker room.

My eyes then traitorously drifted off to where Colton's car was parked. Since we were already on campus, our ASL practice session had run a bit later than usual, with Colton not having to drive me home and back here. When the time was cutting close to him arriving late to practice, we finally headed our separate ways. I couldn't stop that disappointed feeling in my chest when we had to say goodbye.

And that's when I noticed his car was still there, which meant . . .

'Clara!' a familiar voice called out to me.

I turned to where I heard the sound coming from, and was met with Colton walking up to me.

'Colton, hey,' I greeted him. 'Did you guys just finish practice?'

'Yup,' he said, popping the 'p'. 'Were you waiting for your friends?'

'Yeah, they should be out by now. And then we're heading out for dinner.'

'Cool,' Colton replied, running his hand through his hair. That's when I noticed, he looked *nervous*. 'I wanted to ask you something. I thought I would text you about it, but since you're here, are you—' But before he could finish, I heard footsteps coming towards us.

'Clara!' It was Nina, walking hurriedly to me in her excitement.

I could see the exact moment she registered who I was talking to as she started to slow down her steps. Her face was in disbelief as she stared at Colton.

'Nina,' I said in a slightly louder voice, bringing her eyes back to me.

She finally snapped out of her daze and turned to me. 'Clara, hey.'

This was getting awkward real fast.

But I barely had the time to come up with something when I heard someone call out Colton's name.

It was Miles.

I could hear the sharp intake of breath Nina took as he made his way to us.

With Colton covering us from Miles's point of view, he hadn't noticed me and Nina standing next to Colton until he reached us.

'Oh, I didn't know you had company,' he said as a way of greeting.

'Yeah,' Colton replied sheepishly. 'Miles, I'd like you to meet Clara. She's my partner for ASL class,' he gestured to me, then gesturing to Miles, and said, 'this is Miles, my roommate.'

'And his best friend,' Miles pointed out, a grin on his face.

'Right, my best friend when he's not embarrassing me.' Colton gently shoved him.

Miles just laughed him off. 'I'm not embarrassing you,' he remarked. '*Yet.*'

'Nice to meet you, Miles,' I said, smiling at him. 'This is Nina, *my* roommate, and best friend,' emphasizing 'my' as I introduced her, earning a laugh from the two baseball players.

I softly nudged Nina, silently asking her to say something.

'Yeah, I'm Nina,' she murmured.

'Well, it's nice to meet you both.' He nodded at us, though I couldn't help but notice how his eyes were focused on Nina, who was trying her best to avoid his gaze.

Turning to me, he prompted, 'You're Colton's partner for ASL class?' Though it sounded more like a statement than a question.

'Yeah?' I replied hesitantly, unsure of why he was asking for a confirmation.

He quickly darted his eyes to Colton before a smug grin appeared on his face. 'So, *you're* the one he's been seeing every Wednesday before baseball practice.'

I didn't even have the time to react to that when I heard Colton call out. 'Miles.'

'What?'

'Shut up.'

But that only made his grin grow bigger, followed by a burst of laughter when he saw the unamused expression on Colton's face.

'Okay, okay. Point taken.' He conceded once he calmed down, putting his hands up in mock surrender. Turning his attention back to me and Nina, he added, 'So I'm guessing I'll be seeing you two on Saturday?'

'Saturday?' I raised my eyebrows in question.

Instead of answering me, Miles whispered to Colton, 'You didn't invite them?'

'I was about to,' Colton whispered back to him, exasperated. Facing me once again, he said, 'The baseball team is throwing a party this Saturday at the team's house. You're both invited if you want to come, and you can bring your friends too.'

A party hosted by the baseball team.

'Oh, umm,' I stammered, not knowing how to respond to the invitation. 'Thanks for the invite. We'll think about—'

'We'll be there.' Nina cut me off.

'Great,' he said with a grin on his face. 'Do you guys know where the house is?'

'Yup, I got it covered,' Nina confirmed to him.

He gave her a nod. 'I'll see you two on Saturday then.' And directing his gaze at me, he added, 'Partner.'

'See you on Saturday,' I replied. 'Partner.'

Turning to Miles, he asked, 'You ready to go?'

Miles nodded and waved us goodbye with a 'See you on Saturday!' before running to Colton's car.

Colton just shook his head at his roommate's antics, turning around to give us one more smile before he went his way.

I had already been dreading the moment that was to come, once I saw the guys go into Colton's car and leave the parking lot. Once we couldn't see his car in our line of vision any more, Nina finally let out a loud screech.

'How? What? When?' Nina struggled to grapple with her thoughts and what to ask first.

'Later,' I told her instead, seeing more members of the track team slowly come out.

'Why were you talking to Colton? How does Colton know who you are? How long has this been happening?'

'Later,' I repeated. 'Once we're home.'

'You promise?' she said, holding out her pinkie.

I smiled and sealed my pinkie with hers. 'I promise.'

Dinner with the track team was always a fun time and tonight was no different, except I wasn't the only non-athlete at the table. They had also invited Aiden to join, and it was nice to get to know him a bit better.

We finally arrived back at the apartment at a quarter to ten, but I knew the night was far from over.

Just as Nina was about to say something, I interrupted her. 'Let me shower first, please. I've been out for almost the whole day.'

'Fine,' she huffed. 'But I'm kicking down your door if you're not out here in thirty minutes.'

I started laughing at her, but the look on her face assured me she wasn't kidding. 'Thirty minutes,' I nodded.

After I finished my shower, I went out to the living room to see Nina already sitting on the couch with a mug in her hand.

'Chocolate milk?' She picked up the other mug that was on the coffee table.

'Thank you,' I said, taking it from her.

We sat down in silence as we each took sips of the milk before she finally put down her drink and crossed her legs, facing me.

'Spill.'

I let out a sigh and put down my drink.

Where do I even start?

'As you already know, I'm taking the ASL class this semester, and turns out Colton was too. We ended up sitting next to each other on the first day and partnered up. Mr Albert, our ASL class instructor, recommended everyone to practice ASL with their partners, so we decided to meet up every Wednesday to practice,' I said, letting her take in this piece of information.

'Since when have you started practicing?' she asked.

'Second week of classes?' I said sheepishly, preparing myself for her reaction.

Nina's eyes widened, 'You're telling me you have been talking to your crush, Colton Reed for weeks now?' I could tell she was struggling to keep her voice at a normal volume.

'Yeah,' I confirmed.

And here came her big reaction.

Putting her hands on both my shoulders, she started shaking me. She let out a squeal before pulling me into a hug and started rocking us.

'I take it you're not mad?' I asked, slightly confused by her reaction.

'Mad?' she said, taking me out of the hug and back to putting her hands on my shoulders. 'Why would I be mad?'

'I don't know.' I shrugged. 'Maybe for not telling you earlier. I feel like if this were happening to you, you would have told me right away.'

'Because that's who I am. God knows I can't keep anything like that to myself. Of course, I'm not mad. You don't owe me anything,' she said and then let out a wince. 'But I am sorry for forcing this out of you. I should've just let it slide until you were ready to tell me.'

I knew Nina meant no harm. I would have told her a lot sooner about it, if it weren't for my fear of being struck down by the curse with this arrangement with Colton. While I would have loved to take my time and figure out how to tell Nina without getting her hopes up, I was glad it was finally out in the open.

'It's okay. To be honest, I'm glad you know now.' I smiled instead.

She gave me a smile in return. 'So, where have you two been practicing?'

'At the bubble tea shop a few streets from here.'

Nina nodded before a look of suspicion covered her face. 'Wait. Didn't you start getting flowers since the second week of classes as well? Does that have anything to do with Colton?' She raised her brow at me.

Damn her deductive skills. I blamed it on all the true crime podcasts she was always listening to.

'There was a grocery store that also sold flowers near the bubble tea shop. So, I usually just buy them after we practice. Then, he drives me home.'

'He drives you home?' Nina screeched out.

'Yes, he does. But it's not a big deal. He was just being a good friend.' I shrugged it off.

Nina just gave me a teasing smile and said, 'Whatever you say, Clara.' Picking up her mug, she took another sip of the chocolate milk.

'I'm serious, we're just friends,' I told her.

'Mmhmm,' she hummed knowingly, taking another sip. 'I'm just saying, you still have the rest of the semester to go. Anything could happen.'

I just took a sip of my own chocolate milk from my mug.

She was right, anything could happen. I just had to make sure whatever it was, didn't give room for the curse to linger around.

Chapter Seven

A thought occurred to me as I was walking up the steps to the baseball team's house.

I had never caught a single glance of Colton the first time I went to a party hosted by the baseball team. But the second time around, it was Colton who had invited me to the party.

It just went to show that life, truly, is full of surprises.

Taking slow and steady breaths, I tried to calm down my nerves, feeling grateful that we had decided to pregame before coming there. The music got exponentially louder once Nina opened the front door to the house, me tagging along behind her with Claudia and Lily.

On our way to the kitchen to get some drinks, we were intercepted by Miles.

'You made it!' he exclaimed when he saw us.

'Hey,' I greeted him. Remembering he hadn't met the other two yet, I said 'This is Claudia and Lily. They lived across the hall from us in the dorms during freshman year.'

'Nice meeting you two.' He nodded in greeting. 'Now, let's get you girls some drinks.' Leading us into the kitchen, he poured us drinks in red solo cups.

He passed one to each one of us. 'Here you go.'

I thanked him, taking it from his hand.

'So, here's the rundown. Drinks are in the fridge and the ice cooler, the dance floor is in the living room, and beer pong is happening in the dining room if you're up for it,' he explained. 'I'm still looking for a partner for my round, by the way.' This, he directed at Nina with a flirtatious glint in his eyes.

'That depends on how good your aim is,' Nina retorted, before taking a sip of her drink. Miles might have caught her off guard the other day, but it wouldn't be the case that night. With the added liquid courage from the two Fireball shots we had each gulped before coming there, Nina was fully prepared to face her crush head-on.

Miles' head jolted back slightly at her response, surprised but intrigued at her newfound confidence which wasn't there the last time they had seen each other. 'Are you questioning my skills?' he asked.

Nina arched a brow at him. 'I'll believe it when I see it.'

Keeping her gaze on Miles, she took another sip from her cup—her eyes daring him to take up her challenge.

Shooting Nina a smirk, Miles took up her bait. 'Challenge accepted. Come on.' He ushered us to the beer pong table.

A round had been in session between two baseball players against two basketball players. Looking around, I noticed that most of the baseball team was there, and I slowly started to scan the faces to see if I could find the one who had invited me, trying my best to be subtle.

'He's not here,' I heard someone whisper to me. Turning my head to see where it came from, I saw Miles looking at me.

So much for being subtle.

'Oh,' I trailed off, struggling to think of what to reply to that.

'Something urgent came up, but he said he'll be back in an hour or so,' he continued.

I just nodded my head at him, bringing my attention back to the round of beer pong that was on.

I couldn't help the feeling of disappointment emerge at Colton's absence. I hadn't even realized, until that very moment, how much I was looking forward to seeing him outside of our Wednesday ASL practice sessions.

What was so urgent? And why didn't he tell me anything?

I quickly brushed the thoughts out of my head.

Colton did not owe me anything just because he had invited me to the party. I was pretty sure he invited most of the people there, which didn't make me anything special. I rationalized myself.

Did I put a bit more effort into my looks tonight in hopes of seeing him?

Maybe. Okay, fine. Yes, I did.

But I refused to let this affect me further.

I was at a party at the baseball team's house with my best friends.

Looking around at all the people having a great time, I told myself to forget about Colton.

Let the fun commence.

After participating in a few rounds of beer pong myself and doing very poorly, Lily took me out to the dance floor to sweat the alcohol away. I even caught up with some of the people I had known from my other classes, along with those on the track team who had made it that night. I have to admit, I was having a lot of fun. But, as the clock got closer to eleven, my energy was starting to drop.

Excusing myself from the group I was with, I went to search for a bathroom to get some alone time and clear my head for a few minutes.

As I passed through the kitchen, I noticed that the back door was open, with people coming in and out of the house. I decided to change where I was heading, after seeing there weren't many people outside.

Exactly what I needed.

I went back to look for the girls to inform them where I was going, so they wouldn't panic when they couldn't find me inside.

Heading over to the dining room, I saw Claudia and Lily play against two baseball players at a round of beer pong, while Nina was in conversation with someone.

I squinted my eyes to get a better look at who she had been talking to.

It was Miles.

Observing her body language, she was definitely flirting with him, and from the looks of it, he was flirting right back at her. I internally squealed and chanted '*Go best friend*' in my head, happy that they were hitting it off.

I decided to not distract them and went straight to the backdoor, stepping outside to the backyard, thinking I'd be gone just for a short while.

There were groups of people scattered all around, but everyone seemed to be in their own little bubble. I wasn't planning on being out there for long, just enough to get my bearings straight before heading back in.

However, as I glanced around, I saw an unoccupied seating area.

I could stay out here for a bit.

Sitting down in one of the chairs, I took off my sandals and lifted both my legs, bringing them to my chest. I placed my crossed arms on my knees and rested my head on top of them. Closing my eyes, I let the night breeze cool off the warmth on my skin.

Moments later, I heard movement come right next to me, seeming like someone had just taken a seat in the chair beside mine.

I lifted my head, and an unfamiliar warm feeling settled inside me when my eyes landed on a face I didn't think I would be seeing that night.

An unfamiliar warm feeling?

It's probably the alcohol.

Colton smiled at me when our gazes locked.

I smiled at him in return. The almost silence enclosing us in its embrace.

Choosing to not break the silence, Colton signed to me instead.

'*Hey, partner,*' he signed.

I smiled at him, signing back, '*hey, partner.*'

Although we had been learning ASL for weeks, we were mostly still learning new words as there was a lot left to cover. We were only recently introduced to how sentences in ASL were structured, and asking questions in ASL was in our syllabus for a future class. So, instead of signing it perfectly, Colton just signed each word to me and added a question mark at the end.

'*You okay?*' he asked.

I arched a brow at him, slightly amused by the way he was signing, and gave a nod. '*Just tired,*' I signed back to him.

Colton nodded, then signed. '*You want me to go?*'

I shook my head at him. '*Stay.*'

Seconds passed by as I waited for Colton to say something, but he didn't. His head was turned upwards, looking at the night sky. I followed suit, admiring the full moon along with the stars.

We just sat like that, enjoying each other's presence in comfortable silence, stuck in our own little world.

The only thing that would have made that moment better was if Colton had his arm around me and my head was on his shoulder.

I immediately stopped my train of thought—shaking my head as if I was trying to physically remove the visual of it from my mind.

That can't happen, you know it can't.

I let out a wistful sigh.

The needle to burst our little bubble came in the sound of my phone buzzing against my pocket. I took it out and saw that it was an incoming call from Nina.

I answered it right away.

'Where are you?' Nina asked, worry in her voice.

I let out a wince, I must have been out there longer than I had thought. 'I'm outside, in the backyard.'

'Oh, thank god,' she breathed out. 'We couldn't find you anywhere, so we thought you left.'

'Nope, just getting some fresh air,' I reassured her. 'I'll meet you inside.'

'We were actually about to leave.'

'Is everything okay?'

'Beer pong got a bit out of hand,' she trailed off. 'They added vodka into the drinks to level up the game, and I think Claudia overestimated her alcohol tolerance again.'

'Is she okay?'

'She's all right, about to crash, but still fine.'

I let out a sigh of relief, glad to hear nothing bad had happened. 'That's good, so should I meet you on the front porch instead?' I suggested.

'Yeah, see you in a bit,' Nina said before she hung up.

'Is everything okay?' Colton asked me, a worried look on his face.

'Yeah. I think we're done for tonight, we're just about to head back.'

'How are you getting home?'

'Probably an Uber,' I answered.

'I'll drive you home.'

Normally I would have politely rejected his offer and insisted that we could get ourselves home just fine. But this time, I just said, 'Thank you,' gave him a smile of appreciation, and left it at that.

Colton must have been expecting my usual antics, and when the two words finally registered to him, his eyes widened in amusement. 'No arguments today?'

'No arguments today,' I confirmed.

With that, we both stood up and made our way to the front porch, taking an alternate route along the side of the house, rather than facing the party crowd.

'There they are,' I pointed out once I saw them.

Claudia stood in the middle of Nina and Lily, her arms wrapped around each one of them. I could tell they had been struggling to hold her up, considering Claudia was a foot taller than both of them.

'Did you order an Uber yet?' I asked once I approached them.

'Not yet,' Nina said. 'Can you do it?'

'You don't have to,' Colton chimed in. 'I'll drive you home.'

Both Nina and Lily immediately turned their head to look at Colton, finally noticing I had company.

Deciding to quickly introduce them, I gestured to Colton. 'Colton. This is Lily and Claudia, Nina and I used to live across the hall from them during my freshmen year.' Turning to Lily, I said, 'This is Colton. We share a class this semester.'

'Nice meeting you,' Colton said. But it seemed like Lily was still a bit too surprised to speak.

Trying his best to ignore Lily and Nina's stares, Colton turned to me instead. 'I had to park my car a couple houses away from here, you guys just wait while I go get it,' he instructed before heading off.

'Okay.' I nodded, watching him as he went to fetch his car.

I kept staring after him, trying my best to prolong the moment as much as I could, before I had to face the shocked looks on my friends' faces.

'Did I drink way too much tonight or did Colton Reed just offer to drive us home?' Lily asked.

'Both?' I shrugged.

Lily just arched a brow at me, while Nina had an amused look on her face.

'He's just being a good friend,' I tried explaining.

'Mmhmm,' Nina hummed, clearly not believing me.

'I'm serious.'

'I didn't say you weren't.'

I didn't get a chance to continue defending myself, when I heard a car door slam shut, and saw Colton opening the door to the back seat.

'He's here,' I pointed out.

Nina and Lily hauled Claudia across the yard while I helped carry their purses.

Colton rushed towards us. 'Do you need any help?'

'No, we got it,' Lily insisted. And she was right, it wasn't the first time one of us had got a bit too drunk. By that point, we pretty much knew what we needed to do.

Upon reaching his car, we tried our best to situate Claudia inside the back seat. Lily entered the car from the other side to gently pull her in, while Nina slowly pushed her. Once all three of them were in the car, Colton shut the door and opened the car to the passenger seat for me.

'Thank you.' I smiled at him, getting in before he closed it.

I told him the street Lily and Claudia's apartment was located on, before he started driving. He nodded and said he was familiar with the location.

The car ride continued in silence, with only the hum of the car and Claudia's soft snores filling the void.

I was about to suggest turning on the radio to diffuse the awkward tension in the car, but stopped when I remembered that there might be an ABBA CD in there. A sudden feeling of possessiveness came over me at the prospect of Colton having to share with them the story of him and his collection of ABBA albums.

I quickly swept the thought away.

Where did that come from?

'Thank you for inviting us by the way,' I said instead, figuring that was safe territory.

'No problem. Glad you all had fun.' He smiled.

Nina just snorted. 'I think this one had too much fun.' Softly nudging the shoulder where Claudia's head was rested on.

Colton just let out a small chuckle.

'Did I, somehow, not see you, or were you not at the party?' Lily blurted out.

'Good observation,' Colton nodded. 'I had something urgent outside, I just arrived about twenty minutes ago. I was in the house for a bit, then I headed out to the backyard.'

I tensed up slightly at that, knowing without a doubt that Nina would figure out we had been outside together, expecting her to say something.

But I was saved from the interrogation, when I noticed that the car was turning into Lily and Claudia's apartment street.

'Thank God,' I muttered to myself.

I pointed out to Colton where their building was, and he parked at the drop-off spot right in front of it.

Colton got down, opening Nina's door first, and then, mine.

We both thanked him as we got out of the car.

Nina slowly started to drag Claudia from her seat, with Lily softly pushing her from the inside.

Putting one of her arms around my shoulders, Nina took the other arm. Colton helped shut the door, while Lily went ahead to unlock the apartment building.

'I'll wait for you two down here,' Colton said.

I nodded in acknowledgment before facing Nina. 'Let's go.'

Lily waited until we crossed the door before closing it and heading straight to the elevators. Fortunately, we didn't have to wait long, when the doors immediately opened. Once we reached the floor, Lily held the elevator door open, making sure we were all out of it before rushing to their apartment to unlock the door.

We tried our best to haul Claudia as quickly as we could, and made it into the apartment finally. Then, we went straight into Claudia's bedroom, gently putting her down on the bed, and plopping her so she was lying sideways.

A bucket had already been there, beside the bed. I assumed Lily put it there when we were still dragging Claudia across the corridor.

Once she was comfortably situated, we left her room, gently closing the door behind us.

'Mission accomplished,' Nina huffed out, her breathing at a much normal pace than mine. 'You ready to go?'

I just nodded my head, still slightly out of breath.

We hugged Lily and waved her goodbye before heading back down to Colton's car.

I was anticipating some questions from Nina as we waited for the elevator and during the ride back down, but she just said nothing. When we stepped out of the elevator, Nina grabbed my arm, taking me by surprise.

'You don't need to tell me anything if you don't want to, but I'm here if you ever want to talk about it,' she reminded me. After rooming all these years together, and her being as observant as she is, Nina pretty much could tell when something was affecting me. But this time, I wasn't prepared to talk about it just yet.

While her words were different each time, they held the same meaning: She'll be there for me when I am ready to voice out the things I've been keeping to myself.

'Thank you.' I smiled at her.

Colton was on his phone, leaning against the car, when we stepped outside of the apartment building. Upon hearing us, he looked up.

'Everything good?' He pocketed his phone away.

'Yeah.' I gave him a nod. A yawn escaped my mouth as I tried to cover it with my hand.

Colton smiled. 'Time to get you two home.'

He opened the door for Nina first, closing it when she got inside before opening mine.

There was a bit of traffic on the way back to our apartment. The night seemed to have caught up to Nina, when I heard soft snores coming from the back. Colton and I were back to sharing the silence, just like we did in the backyard.

Just when I was about to ask him where he had been before he arriving at the party, Colton stunned me with his words.

'You look beautiful tonight, by the way,' he said.

My eyes widened in surprise. 'What?' I blurted out, thinking I heard him wrong.

'I said you look beautiful tonight,' he repeated.

'Oh, thanks,' I replied sheepishly, caught off guard by his compliment. 'Although, I definitely looked a lot better earlier in the night before we had to drag Claudia home,' I added playfully, trying to brush it off as a joke.

But Colton wasn't having it.

Briefly turning his eyes in my direction, he deadpanned, 'You still look beautiful to me.' His gaze was soft as he looked at me before facing the road once again.

'Thank you,' I breathed out, looking down at my hands, trying to cover up the blush on my cheeks. I tried to think of what else to say, but Colton—once again—beat me to it.

'I'm sorry for not talking much just now. Back at the house,' Colton continued. I looked back at him. His eyes had been facing the road, but they looked apologetic. 'I saw you were sitting alone in the backyard and thought you could use some company. You looked like you were enjoying the silence, so I didn't want to intrude on it and bother you with my talking.'

My heart squeezed listening to him.

This boy.

'Thank you,' I said again, speechless over his thoughtfulness. 'I appreciate it.'

Colton continued to drive, with me in the passenger seat next to him, and Nina with her soft snores at the back. We settled back into the silence while he drove us home.

As I lay in my bed that night, I couldn't help but go over everything that had happened with Colton that night: right from when he sat beside me in the backyard of the baseball team's house signing at me, to him dropping us home, and me signing *thank you* to him when he opened the car door for me.

My mind kept going back to what he had said in the car.

You looked like you were enjoying the silence, so I didn't want to intrude on it and bother you with my talking.

How did he know?

As much as I loved spending time with my friends, my social energy was nearing zero by the end of the night. I knew Colton would've respected my decision if I had said yes when he asked me if I wanted him to leave.

But I had also meant it when I said I didn't want him to leave, knowing I could still come up with enough energy to talk to Colton if he wanted to.

But he only spoke to me in ASL to ask if I was okay, just letting the silence envelop us, because he thought that was what I would've wanted.

I didn't think my heart could take it.

And to make matters worse, the silence we shared wasn't awkward at all.

I hadn't felt the urge to talk to him just so he wouldn't feel out of place or uncomfortable by my lack of energy to make conversation. Instead, I had learned that Colton was not only someone I liked spending time talking to, but someone I could spend time in comfortable silence with.

Ever since that conversation in his car the first time he drove me home, I had realized that agreeing to be partners in the ASL class could have made me like Colton even more as I got to know him better. I knew my crush on Colton alone wasn't enough for the curse to work, but how far was I willing to let myself fall deeper into this crush, without risking myself from getting hurt?

Because anything, beyond this friendship that Colton and I share now, cannot happen.

Not that I thought Colton liked me in that way, but just the idea of him being with someone else had already broken my heart a little.

But what if he does like me that way? The traitorous thought popped out of nowhere, entertaining that small possibility.

I quickly dismissed it.

Even if he does, I won't risk it.

While unexpected, the ASL class had brought me Colton, who was now a friend I could confide in.

And I wouldn't let my stupid crush and this stupid curse ruin it for me.

Chapter Eight

The soft chatter of people conversing, and the aroma of coffee surrounded me as I immersed myself in my current read.

It was a Thursday afternoon, and my next class was to start in a little over thirty minutes. I hit up the group chat to see if anyone was free to hang out. Both Nina and Lily had been on their way to their next class, while Claudia had just reached home after finishing her last class of the day.

For one brief second, I thought about texting Colton. Even though I might have fully considered him to be a friend, instead of just a partner whom I was only acquainted with for that one class, I still hesitated. Other than the first time he had driven me home, and the previous Saturday's party, all the times Colton and I hung out outside of class were only for our ASL practice sessions, which seemed to be more of a necessity than choice.

Texting him to ask if he wanted to casually hang out would mean we are friends who willingly chose to spend time with each other. And after my revelation, it wouldn't be a wise move on my part when my crush on him was only growing bigger with the more time we spent together.

The smart move would be to distance myself from Colton, other than our necessary ASL practice sessions—at least, until I could get over my infatuation with him.

Choosing not to dwell on it any further and overcomplicate simple matters, I opted to go and wait at the coffee shop alone. I thought I might as well use this time to read my book.

The semester was starting to get hectic with midterms and deadlines piling up, and I hadn't been in the mood to read, but I nonetheless wanted something to get lost in as a small reward for submitting the assignments and finishing midterms. This led me to pick up my all-time favourite book for the third time, *You Deserve Each Other* by Sarah Hogle.

When I had been reading the book for the very first time, I knew I stumbled upon something special. After finishing it, the book had undoubtedly become my standard for romance books. Growing up with Wattpad meant I was exposed to tons of love stories and, as I grew older, those virtual stories transitioned into romance books instead. While I love reading stories about people falling in love throughout the book, *You Deserve Each Other* struck something different in me. Reading about how drifted apart Naomi and Nicholas were, and falling in love with each other all over again, had me thinking that happily-ever-after was not something that happened once; but instead, it could happen again and again, when you choose for it to be.

But then again, it was fiction.

And things like that were just easier to believe when it was fiction and not real life.

I sat in the corner of the coffee shop with both my legs in the chair, making myself comfortable. I was at one of my favourite parts of the book—where Nicholas brings Naomi to a house that he bought for them to live together and save their relationship—when I was interrupted.

'Hey, Clara.'

I looked up to see who it was, and was momentarily surprised to see Aiden, the only non-athlete living with the track team.

'Aiden, hey,' I greeted back, closing my book. 'How've you been?'

He just shrugged. 'Surviving. Midterms have been kicking my ass.'

I groaned in agreement. 'Tell me about it. I still have one more tomorrow and then I'm sleeping through the weekend.' My sleeping schedule had been all over the place that week, and I couldn't wait to sleep in on Saturday without the sound of an alarm waking me up.

Aiden just chuckled.

'Do you want to sit?' I asked him, standing up to offer him the chair across from me on which my bag sat.

'It's okay. I was just about to head to class anyway. Just thought I would say hello,' he explained.

'Well, it's nice seeing you. Hopefully, we'll get to catch up when the track team decides to go out for dinner again.'

Aiden paused for a beat, seeming like he was contemplating something when he said, 'Or we could see each other before then.'

I raised a brow at him, puzzled at what he meant by that. 'What do you mean?'

'I mean, other than sleeping in, do you have any other plans for Saturday?' he asked me.

I shook my head. 'None so far.'

'Well then, how about going on a date with me.' Before adding, 'If you want to.'

I widened my eyes in surprise, slightly taken aback by what he just said. *Aiden is asking me out on a date?*

We had never really hung out alone, and this was only the third time we ever saw each other. But apart from those two occasions, Aiden seemed like a fun guy to be around, and isn't the point of going on a date with someone to get to know them?

But what about Colton? My traitorous heart couldn't help but point out, catching me completely off guard.

What about Colton? He has nothing to do with this. My brain replied harshly, stamping on whatever brought on that thought in the first place.

Besides, Colton was just a friend that I, unfortunately, had a crush on. And I wouldn't be betraying him by agreeing to go on a date with someone else. Plus, it might have just been what I needed to help myself get over my crush on him: to go out there and see what else the world had to offer that wasn't Colton Reed.

My inner turmoil must have been longer than expected, when I heard Aiden call my name again as I went over my decision in silence.

'Um, Clara?' Aiden waved his hand in front of me.

'Oh, sorry. Um, sure. I would love to go on a date with you,' I finally answered him.

A look of glee appeared on Aiden's face. 'Great!' he exclaimed. 'I'll see you on Saturday then.'

We exchanged numbers before he headed towards the door and went his way.

After he left, I went back to reading my book.

But no matter how hard I tried, I couldn't help getting distracted by what I had just agreed to.

Was it wrong of me to say yes to a date with Aiden, when I clearly liked someone else? I didn't think so. And while a part of me did feel guilty for agreeing only in hopes it would help me overcome my infatuation with Colton, it didn't mean I wouldn't treat that as an actual date. No, Aiden doesn't deserve that. But it did mean that I needed some help from Nina to figure out what to wear for the date.

Glancing up at the clock in the coffee shop, I saw that I had around ten minutes before my next class. Knowing that I wouldn't be able to get any reading done, I packed my stuff and started heading to class, hoping that the walk would help me clear the mess in my head.

I knew that going on a date with Aiden was the right decision if I wanted to salvage my friendship with Colton, by allowing myself to like someone else.

But even with all these rationalizations, I couldn't fully shake off the feeling of sadness and betrayal my heart had been feeling, no matter how hard I tried.

Out of courtesy for Nina and her midterms, I decided not to tell her about the date until Friday night, when she was finally done with her training for the day. To celebrate both of us surviving that week, we decided to have dinner at our favourite Chinese restaurant a few streets away from our apartment.

Even though we lived together, we had been missing each other the whole week. With Nina's dual athletic and academic obligations, I had decided to cook dinner for us throughout the week, but ate alone and left Nina her portion before locking myself in my room as I prepared myself for whatever test was coming up the next day. Whenever Nina returned to the apartment, she would come knocking on my door to let me know she was home, before having her dinner and locking herself in her room as well.

The best thing about living with someone after a while is how you get into a routine of things subconsciously. When we had started living together off-campus last year, and midterms week was coming up, I had simply decided to cook dinner for the both of us throughout the week, as I had more free time in my hands than Nina. But the grateful look she gave me every day that week had made me realize how that small act of kindness might have meant more to her than it did to me. When midterms results were released, the first thing she did was hug me, thanking me countless times as the results from each new class came out one by one. She never really said what she was thanking me for, but I'm pretty sure I got the message. Since then, it became a norm for me, with us celebrating the end of midterms week by eating at the same place we were sitting in that moment then.

The Chinese restaurant had opened just a week after we started our freshman year, and we had been frequent customers ever since. Once the waitress put our food down on the table, we instantly dug in. I let out a moan once the taste hit my tongue—the mix of spices perfectly blended in the fried rice.

'I have been looking forward to this since Monday,' I told Nina, once I swallowed down that first spoonful.

She nodded her head. 'Me too. This is honestly what kept me going this week.' Using her spoon, she pointed at her plate of rice and her sweet and sour chicken. 'The promise of good food.'

'Nothing beats good food.' It was true, nothing does. We actually wrote down 'close to good food' as one of the requirements when we were choosing an apartment building—even with our last one. We had really lucked out with the place we chose, considering how the area was surrounded by numerous restaurants.

We continued eating in silence, enjoying our celebratory meal of the week, with me trying to figure out how to break the news of my date with Aiden.

'Anyway,' I started. 'I need your help for tomorrow.'

'Sure. What's happening tomorrow?'

'I'm going on a date.'

Nina instantly stopped chewing her food, her eyes widened in shock.

'What?' I narrowed my eyes at her, alarmed by her unexpected reaction.

Once she swallowed down her food and took a sip of her drink, she asked, 'With Colton?'

'What?' I repeated, even more confused. 'No, with Aiden. Why would it be with Colton?'

'Aiden?' she questioned, raising an eyebrow. 'You mean, the one living with the track team Aiden?'

I nodded. 'Yes, that Aiden.'

'I didn't know you liked Aiden.'

'I mean I don't *not* like Aiden,' I replied. 'But he seems like a nice guy.'

There was a slight pause before she said, 'Then, what about Colton?'

'What about Colton?' I questioned it back to her, failing to see how Colton fit into this.

'I mean, you like Colton. I just don't understand why you're going out with Aiden,' she explained.

Still failing to see the relevancy. I tried explaining in bullet points, ticking off each item with a finger. 'First off, Aiden actually asked me out. It's hard to go out with someone *aka Colton* who didn't ask me out. Second, yes, I do like Colton but we're just friends. And third, why are you so surprised that I'm going on a date with Aiden? I've been on dates before when my crush on Colton was still ongoing.'

'That was different. Back then it was a passive crush, based on his looks and his star athlete reputation,' Nina started explaining. 'But I don't think it's a passive crush any more with how much time you're spending together.'

'What do you mean exactly?'

'What I mean is, your crush on Colton, a few semesters ago, was based on a fantasy—like mine used to be on

Miles. It was all in our heads, because we didn't know them. We made up the romantic scenarios ourselves and just put their faces on it. So, of course, I didn't question you going on dates before. But now, you actually know Colton, and I'm damn sure you're liking the real person a lot more.'

I scoffed. 'How can you possibly know that?'

'You're happier on Wednesdays,' Nina pointed out. 'At first, I thought maybe something good happened on that one random Wednesday but then I noticed it every week. There was a certain happiness in you. Once you told me about the practice sessions you had with Colton, that's when I realized it's because of him.'

My breath hitched. I didn't know if this was one of those moments where having an observant roommate was a blessing or a curse.

'Okay fine. Yes. I like Colton, more now than I did before,' I admitted. There was no point in denying it, when it was true. 'But we're just friends and it's not like he likes me back.'

Nina just raised an eyebrow. 'Really, Clara? You cannot be that oblivious.'

I just stared at her confused.

'He likes you too.'

I quickly shook my head, dismissing her words. 'Don't do that, don't give me that hope.'

'The night of the party at the baseball team's house when he finally arrived,' Nina continued, ignoring what I said. 'The first thing he did was he went up to Miles and asked him where *you* were. When Miles said he didn't know, he went to look for you.'

'And how did you know that was what happened?' I asked, even though I could already guess how.

'I was with Miles when he asked. It was like nothing else mattered to him than getting to see you.'

The butterflies in my stomach were pretty much out of control at that point, no matter how hard I tried to calm them. Normally I wouldn't trust anyone's accusations of these things, but that came from Nina, who had only ever looked out for me and said things as they were, even if they were hard pills to swallow. This just made her accusations a lot harder to brush off, and really making the spark of hope in my chest grow bigger.

'Even *if* you are right,' I finally said, 'These are still merely your observations. I'll only believe Colton actually likes me back if he ever says the words, "I like you" to me.'

'That's fair.' Nina nodded, ending that conversation.

As we continued eating our meal, and my mind finally calmed down over everything that we discussed, something struck me over what Nina said just then.

'Hold on a minute. What do you mean, used to be on Miles? Is there something going on between you two that I should know about?'

And lo and behold, my best friend and roommate flushed on the spot.

'There is,' I exclaimed.

'We've just been texting. That's all. I mean, midterms and training have pretty much filled my time this week, but it was nice to text him once in a while,' Nina said, sheepishly.

'And?' I urged her to continue.

'And nothing. That's the extent of it.' She shrugged.

'Well, I'm happy for you,' I said.

'And I'm happy for you for going on a date tomorrow. But what exactly do you need my help with?'

I couldn't help but laugh at her question, her joining me seconds later.

'Gosh, how did we stray so far away from the main thing I wanted to talk to you about,' I said, after calming myself down. 'I need help picking out an outfit and I need your brutal opinions and fashion sense, please.'

'Consider it a done deal. My training is until mid-noon, so I'll be home to help you out. The date is at night, right?'

I nodded. 'He's asked me to be ready at six.'

'Yup, I will definitely be home by then,' Nina confirmed.

We spent the rest of the dinner catching up with whatever had happened that week, no matter how small or big. As I sat there listening to Nina recount what had happened during her training the day before, I couldn't help but be grateful to have stumbled upon her in my life.

'I'm glad you're my best friend,' I said once she finished her story.

She gave me a giant grin. 'I'm glad you're my best friend too.'

Chapter Nine

I was lounging around on the couch with Nina, rewatching an episode of *F.R.I.E.N.D.S.*, when I got a text message from Aiden.

Aiden: I'm here.

It was finally Saturday, which also meant it was the day of my date with Aiden.

He had texted me the other night, informing me that for our date, we would be catching a movie at the theatre and have dinner afterwards. I chose a more comfortable outfit, since we would mostly be sitting all night. After Nina annihilated my closet, she finally decided on what I would wear, which consisted of a casual dress paired with a cropped cardigan in case the theatre was cold.

Clara: Okay. I'll be down in a bit.

I quickly texted him back before heading back to my room to grab my purse. Taking one final look in the mirror, I slowly inhaled a deep breath, and then exhaled it just as slowly. Once my nerves calmed down—though only slightly—I picked out my favourite sandals that had a bit of a height to them, completing the look before I headed to the front door.

'Okay,' I called out once I finished putting on the other shoe, 'I'm leaving.'

Nina got up from her spot on the couch and met me at the doorway. 'Have fun, okay? And call me if you need anything,' she said, hugging me.

'Will do.' I waved her goodbye and went out the door.

Once I arrived at the lobby of the apartment building, I could see Aiden waiting on the sidewalk through the glass door. While he had offered to come up to my apartment to pick me up, I told him to just wait for me in his car, since it was a Saturday night and parking would be filled.

'Hey,' I said when I reached him, smiling at him.

'Hey,' he greeted me and gave me a hug.

Catching me off guard, I tried to conceal my surprise as quickly as possible and hugged him in return, awkwardly giving him a pat on his back.

'My car is just right here,' he said after pulling away, pointing to a black sedan. 'Come on.'

Aiden opened the passenger door for me. 'Thank you.' I smiled at him and got in.

'So, we have two movie options. I wasn't sure what you would be down for, so I haven't bought the tickets yet,' he told me once he got into his car and started the engine. 'Options are either a horror movie or a rom-com. Both movies start at around seven, so which one do you want to watch?'

I took both options into consideration. But ultimately, I decided I wanted a good night's sleep tonight. 'A rom-com sounds good.'

'Then, the rom-com it is,' he nodded as he took out his phone. 'Let me just buy the tickets now.'

Looking at the time, I saw that it was only ten minutes past six and the cinema was only a quick drive away, so finding a parking spot also wouldn't take long. 'I think we can get the tickets once we get there,' I suggested instead.

'Sure, let's get going then.' He put down his phone and started driving, making our way to the movie theatre.

The parking lot at the movie theatre was a lot fuller than usual, courtesy of it being a Saturday, and also the end of midterms week. There were still a few more parking spots available a bit further, but we lucked out when we managed to find a spot that wasn't too far from the entrance.

Parking the car, Aiden then killed the engine before getting out and coming over to my side to open my door.

'Thank you,' I said once I got down. The night air was a bit chilly, so I could only guess how cold it would be inside. I was grateful that I decided to bring my cardigan with me.

'Let's go,' Aiden said, offering his arm.

I gave him a smile and hooked my arm around his.

When we got inside, it was packed. Checking the time, we still had around twenty minutes before our movie started.

'I'll get the tickets, and you'll get the popcorn?' I suggested.

'Sure. Do you want your own popcorn or?' he asked, leaving his question hanging. I smiled at his thoughtfulness in ensuring that I was comfortable with everything.

'We can share the popcorn. I don't think I'll be able to finish one on my own. Though, I do want my own drink.' I pointed at him, with a playful seriousness on my face.

He let out a light laugh. 'Got it. I'll be right back. Let's meet up over there.' He pointed to the Minions cardboard cut-out.

I nodded and we both went our separate ways.

The line to buy the tickets wasn't too long, but it seemed like everyone wanted to watch the same movie at this showtime. Looking at the screen, it was visible that the hall was more than halfway filled. I would have preferred to sit somewhere in the middle, but all the available choices were too close to the screen for my liking. I went ahead and chose the seats at the side, which were slightly further from the screen.

Having bought the tickets, I was about to wait for Aiden at the spot where he had pointed out, but I thought I would see how far in line he was.

I went to the food and beverages area and spotted him already at the counter, making his order. I just waited for him at the end of the row of counters.

'Let me get that,' I said, taking my drink from his hands, when I saw him struggle with the two drinks and a large popcorn in his hold.

'Thanks.' He looked up at the line of numbers that indicated which halls were already open for seating. 'What hall are we in?'

I looked at the tickets in my hand. 'Hall 7.' Glancing up, I saw that number seven was lit up. 'Our hall is open. Is there anything else you want to get, or should we head inside?'

Aiden shook his head. 'I think I got everything, let's head in.'

The movie turned out to be a lot of fun. A rom-com was exactly what I needed after this week.

'What did you think of the movie?' Aiden asked once we left the movie hall and headed back to his car.

'Honestly, it was really good. I haven't been to the cinema in a while, so thank you for bringing me here,' I replied, smiling at him.

He opened my car door for me and closed it once I got inside.

'What did you think of it?' I asked him once he got in the car.

He didn't say anything for a while until after he reversed the car, and we were on our way to our next stop for the night. 'I liked it. Nothing beats a feel-good movie after midterms week. Anyway, I'm guessing you're hungry. We can head back to your street to get dinner or go somewhere close by. I think there's a diner around here.'

As much as I would have loved to go and eat somewhere familiar, I did want to check out the diner he was talking about. 'The diner is fine with me,' I told him. 'Nina and I need more food options, so if the food is good, I can bring her with me next time.'

Turns out the diner was barely a five-minute drive from the movie theatre. Before I knew it, Aiden was already turning on his blinker and driving the car into the diner's parking lot. It was about nine, but the parking lot was still quite full. So, we had to wait around for a bit.

Aiden parked his car, once again opening my door, and we finally made our way inside.

We chose a booth that was at the end of the diner, and I looked around to take in the surroundings of the eating establishment. From my observation, I could sense the theme they had been going for was the typical diner that you would go to when you're on a road trip. It honestly reminded me of Radiator Springs from the movie *Cars*.

It also occurred to me that the diner was only half-full when we got in, which I found a bit odd, since the parking lot was full.

Aiden must've noticed the confusion on my face when he said, 'Most of the people park here while they go to the bar over there.' He was pointing towards a lit-up bar across the street from us.

I nodded at him. 'Have you ever checked it out?'

'I haven't actually. But from what people have told me, it's more catered towards people in their thirties, and I heard they do karaoke on the weekends,' he said with a slightly sour look on his face.

'I take it karaoke isn't your thing?'

'Not really,' he answered.

I just gave him a forced smile in return. Guess I had found a thing we were incompatible about. I mean, it wasn't really a big deal, but I love going to karaoke, so it did suck he didn't feel the same way.

Does Colton like karaoke? The thought unexpectedly popped into my head.

I quickly pushed it away.

Aiden was about to say something else when the waitress reached our table with two menus in her hand.

'Hello there! My name's Tracy and I'll be serving you two tonight,' the waitress greeted us. She looked to be in her mid-fifties, but her sweet smile and cheerfulness gave off a youthful aura that made her seem younger. 'Here's our menu. Can I get you something to drink while you look?'

'Root beer for me,' Aiden answered.

'Just water, please,' I told her.

'Coming right up,' she said as she went off.

I looked at the menu to see what was available and saw that they had a small Italian cuisine section, which included spaghetti and meatballs.

Perfect, just what I was in the mood for.

Tracy came back just in time with our drinks.

'Here you go. Water and a root beer,' she said, setting down our drinks. 'Are you two ready to order?'

I nodded at her. 'I'll have the spaghetti and meatballs, please. What about you, Aiden?'

'I'll have the chicken tenders, with French fries and mashed potatoes on the sides,' Aiden told Tracy.

She quickly jotted down our orders and left.

Time for the awkward talking of the first date part of the night.

'The diner looks cute,' I said, looking around the place. 'It reminds me of Radiator Springs.'

'Radiator Springs?' Aiden asked, his eyebrows scrunching slightly.

'You know. From *Cars*,' I clarified.

He just shook his head. 'Doesn't ring any bells.'

'It's okay,' I reassured him. How does someone not know the movie *Cars*? Or maybe, I just have a bigger obsession with Disney than your average person. Though I couldn't help, but add it to the list of things we were incompatible about.

'How did you get close to the track team by the way?' Aiden asked finally, breaking our awkward silence.

'I was roommates with Nina during our freshman year when we were living in the dorms. When we lived off-campus during my first semester of sophomore year, my classes on Wednesday ended almost at the same time as her training, so I just stayed back and waited for her instead of going home first. Then, they decided to invite me to dinner with them whenever they went out, and the rest is history.'

'So, you're like the honorary member of the track team?' Aiden said, taking a sip of his root beer.

'I guess you could say that,' I shrugged. 'What about you? How did you end up living with the track team?'

'My brother attended the same college as us. We were living in an apartment together until he graduated last year. I was just going to stay in our apartment and find a new roommate, but then Lucy said they had a room available at the house. So I thought, why not.'

'How did you know Lucy?'

'We had a class together and we ended up being in the same group for one of the assignments. She had invited me to one of the house parties and that was how I got to know the rest of the team,' he continued. 'And when I told them I was looking for a new roommate, Lucy offered me a room in the house, since a senior was moving out.'

'Oh right, Josh was living with them,' I said, remembering the senior he was talking about. 'And how has living with them been so far?'

'Pretty good. Apart from the occasional parties that they throw, they're pretty good roommates.'

'Well, I'm glad to hear that.'

Tracy finally arrived with our food. Two plates filled up both of her hands before she set them down on the table. 'Here you go, darlings. Enjoy your meal! Let me know if you need anything else.'

We thanked her and started on our food.

The spaghetti was pretty good. Of course, I still preferred the one at the Italian restaurant on my street, but this was enough to satisfy my cravings.

'Do you want to try?' I asked Aiden, offering my plate to him.

'It's okay. I don't really like spaghetti.'

I instantly stopped chewing my food.

Each to their own food preference, but how am I supposed to be with someone who doesn't like spaghetti?

I decided to try again. 'Are you sure? It's pretty good.'

'I'm sure. You can try my chicken tenders if you want,' he said instead.

And that was strike three.

I couldn't help but internally let out a sigh.

I like to think of myself as being open to the idea of love by going on dates, but sadly my luck with them had always been poor. It wasn't that the date was bad or anything, I would even go on to say that I never really had a bad date before. The bad luck stemmed from me not hitting it off with the person I was on the date with.

I knew that going on dates—specifically the first date—was to get to know someone, but I always had this list of strikes going off in the back of my mind, whenever I found something we were incompatible about. My personal rule was this: I wouldn't go on a second date if there had been three strikes on the first date, which meant I had only gone on first dates all my life.

Unfortunately, Aiden would also be added to my list of guys I went out with, who only made it as far as the first date.

We continued eating our meal, occasionally bringing up random questions to ask the other person.

'Sooo,' Aiden trailed off, once he finished his mashed potatoes.

'Soo,' I repeated.

'This was fun.'

'It was.' I nodded.

'Though I'm sensing a *but* in there somewhere.'

I gave him a forced smile. 'I had a great time *but*—'

Aiden let out a slight wince once he heard that forsaken word.

'I did have a great time and you're a nice guy, but I don't think things are going to work out between us,' I finally said.

He just gave me a forced nod, his lips sealed tight.

'But thank you for taking me out tonight. I appreciate it after the week that we had.'

'You're welcome,' Aiden said, a small smile on his face. 'We're still friends though, right?'

'Definitely.' I gave him a smile in return.

'I guess that's pretty much the end of our date for tonight. Let me just get the check and then I'll drive you home.' He got out of his seat and went to the cashier to pay for the meal.

While he was gone, I couldn't help but glance at the bar across the street. There was an urge in me that seemed like it wanted me to go and check it out, and I was just not ready for the night to be over. I wasn't twenty-one yet, so I wasn't sure if I would be allowed inside if they decided to ask for my ID at the entrance.

Aiden came back minutes later. 'Let's go.'

'I think I'll just stay here for a bit,' I blurted out, unsure of why I said it.

His eyebrows narrowed in confusion. 'Are you sure?'

'I'm sure,' I confirmed, finally making up my mind. I thought about telling him the truth about wanting to check out the bar across the street, but I didn't want him to feel like he had to agree because of me, especially since he said karaoke bars weren't really his thing.

'I think Nina might want to come and check this place out.' I mean I was *technically* telling the truth. I was pretty sure Nina would have loved to see this diner, but it just won't be tonight.

From the look on his face, Aiden still looked unsure about leaving me behind.

'I'll be fine,' I reassured him. 'I'll see you when I see you.'

Seeming satisfied with my reply, he gave me a hug and waved me goodbye before he went his way.

I let out a sigh as I watched him head for his car.

'Date didn't go so well?' I heard someone say. I looked to see who it was and found it was Tracy, the waitress.

Not seeing the harm in venting to her, I said, 'It was okay. He's a nice guy but I just didn't think he was for me.'

Tracy just nodded. 'Hang in there, honey. The right one will come along eventually.' She started picking up our empty plates. 'And who knows? Maybe the right guy will be the next person entering the diner.'

I let out a small laugh. 'I wish I had your optimism, Tracy.'

She joined me with a laugh of her own. 'Well, there's no harm in seeing the brighter side of things, is there?'

I shook my head. 'I guess not.'

She just smiled at me in return, as she picked up the plates. 'Anyway, can I get you anything—'

The ringing of the bell at the door cut her off, signalling a new customer entering the diner.

Out of curiosity, I glanced over to see who it was.

I couldn't really see his face, since he was looking the other way, though something about the jacket he was wearing seemed very familiar to me. I squinted my eyes to get a better look, but before I could, the person turned his head, and I could clearly see his face.

My eyes widened in surprise as my mind registered who it was.

It was Colton.

Chapter Ten

Colton was looking around the diner, his eyes searching for something—or maybe someone—when he finally settled in my direction.

I momentarily tensed up. My pulse was racing, nervous that he caught me here on a date with someone else. But I dismissed the thought as quickly as it appeared, confused as to why I should be worried when I'm not doing anything wrong.

As my brain tried to rationalize the situation, that's when I heard Colton call out a name.

But instead of calling my name, he called out someone else's.

'Tracy!' he exclaimed.

I slowly calmed myself down and let go of whatever tension that I had been feeling just then. But the moment didn't last long enough, when I noticed Colton was walking towards Tracy—who was standing right next to my table.

'Hello, Colton,' Tracy greeted him with a kiss on his cheek. 'Is it break time already?'

'Yeah,' he nodded. 'The bar wasn't as crowded, so they thought I could appreciate an earlier and a slightly longer break,' Colton answered.

Noticing that Tracy was carrying the empty plates, his eyes turned to the table.

Then, they landed on me.

'Clara?' Colton asked, his eyes widening.

'Clara?' I heard Tracy say, with a hint of surprise in her tone.

'Hey, Colton.' I gave him an awkward wave.

'Fancy seeing you here on a Saturday night,' Colton teased.

For a moment I thought about telling Colton that I was on a date with someone. There wasn't any harm in telling him, but something was holding me back, so I stopped myself before the words could come out.

'I was out with a friend just now; they just left,' I said instead. Technically, it wasn't a lie. It just wasn't the full truth, so I didn't have to feel too bad about it.

I chanced a glance at Tracy, expecting to see a look of disappointment on her face about my partial honesty with Colton. But to my surprise, I saw a look of amusement instead—as if she was approving of my little white lie. Using that as encouragement, I continued explaining, 'We went to watch a movie and thought we would check this place out since it was close by.'

'Well, I'm glad you did,' he said before he furrowed his eyebrows when he saw what I was holding in my hand. 'What are you drinking? Is that water?'

'Yup, just water.' I shook the half-empty cup, the water inside sloshing around.

'You're telling me you didn't drink anything else from the menu?' he said, his tone slightly serious.

Raising a brow at him, I said, 'Why do I feel like I just committed a crime?'

'Because you were. But not to worry, we can still fix this. You're not leaving until you try the best drink in this place.' Then, turning to Tracy he said, 'Tracy, I need two chocolate milkshakes.'

Tracy let out a small laugh. 'Two chocolate milkshakes coming right up,' and left us, carrying the dirty plates with her.

'Two chocolate milkshakes?' I pointed out.

'You didn't think I was going to let you drink one alone, did you?'

I let out a light laugh. 'Definitely not.'

'Do you mind if I sit?' Colton said, gesturing to the empty seat across from me.

'If you must,' I playfully sighed.

Colton gave me a playful grin before taking his seat.

'So, to what do I owe the pleasure of running into you here on a Saturday night?' I asked him.

'Do you see the bar over there?' he said, pointing to the bar I had been thinking of going to.

I nodded my head. 'Yeah?'

'My aunt and uncle are the owners. They told me one of the workers couldn't make it tonight, and needed some help, so here I am,' he explained.

My eyes widened in surprise. 'Wait, you have an uncle and an aunt who own a bar? That's so cool.'

He just shrugged, his way of shyly accepting my compliment.

'Do your friends know?'

'Some of them do, but not a lot of people,' he said sheepishly. 'It's not something I like to parade about, since people think it means I can get free alcohol for a party.'

'That makes sense.' I nodded in understanding.

'Plus, the bar is more geared towards older people than college students. So, I rarely run into anyone there when I do go and help out.'

'Do you go help them out often?' I asked.

'Every once in a while. They only started asking me recently since I just turned twenty-one before the semester started,' he told me. 'I was actually there last—'

But before he could finish his sentence, Tracy was back at our table. This time holding a chocolate milkshake in each hand.

'One chocolate milkshake for the lady and one chocolate milkshake for the gentleman,' Tracy said, putting down the drink on the table one by one.

We both thanked her as she left our table, heading off to take the order of a new customer that just walked in.

'Prepare to have your mind blown,' Colton said.

I raised a brow at him. 'You seem pretty confident I'm going to love this.'

'Trust me, you will.'

'Well, here goes nothing,' I said before taking a sip.

Wanting to keep Colton on the edge of his seat, I took my precious time tasting it, holding up a finger to him as I took another sip.

Thinking I prolonged this long enough, I finally said, 'Okay, you're right. My mind is officially blown.'

'I told you so,' Colton said before taking a huge sip of his own. 'Now that is a chocolate milkshake.'

I took another sip and just enjoyed the burst of flavour the drink had to offer. 'God, this is so good. Where have you been all my life?' I said dramatically.

Colton just laughed at me.

'You know, it's really your fault for not bringing me here sooner,' I teased him.

I was expecting Colton to tease me right back. But when I looked up at him, instead of a playful grin, he had a solemn look on his face.

'I'll just have to make it up to you by bringing you here any time you want,' he deadpanned, his voice devoid of anything playful.

The butterflies in my stomach started to erupt, as my brain went haywire with all different types of questions.

What did he actually mean by that?

But as much as I wanted to ask the question out loud, I refrained myself.

Nothing good would come out of me dwelling on the questions of what-ifs, when all we could ever be was friends.

Wanting to shift the tension, I asked him, 'So I'm guessing you come here often?'

It seemed like Colton understood what I was doing, and we were back to our usual selves. 'Every time I go help out at the bar. But I do come here occasionally whenever my sweet tooth is craving something. Most of the time, I'm specifically craving their chocolate milkshake.'

'So, like, once every two days?' I teased. I had learnt a number of things about Colton over the last few weeks, but his sweet tooth might have been one of my favourite fun facts about him.

'More like once every three days.' He smiled. 'Nah, it's just once a week at most, considering I've been getting addicted to bubble tea for the past few weeks.'

'I wonder how that could have happened,' I said to him, my voice teasing. 'It's a cute diner though, I can see why someone would like to come here, even if it's just for the chocolate milkshake.'

'There's a sense of comfort to it, I think,' he nodded while I took another sip. 'Or maybe it's just that it reminds me of Radiator Springs.'

I was pretty sure I had been gaping at him when I registered his words in my mind.

It was just a coincidence that we both had the same thought, right?

Right?

I must've been stunned into silence, because Colton started waving his hand in front of me. 'Clara?'

'Oh sorry. I just remembered something I had to do before class on Monday,' I lied. 'But you're right. My first thought when I came into this place was how it reminded me of Radiator Springs as well.'

His eyes widened a bit in surprise, seeming as if he was just as shocked as me by having the same thought when a small smile appeared on his face.

I quickly changed the subject. 'Anyway, going back to the topic of your aunt and uncle's bar. My friend told me it's somewhat of a karaoke bar. Is that true?'

He nodded his head, gulping down his drink before answering me. 'They only do karaoke on the weekends though.'

'You mean like today?'

'Yes, like today. You want to check it out?' His head gesturing to the bar.

I hesitated for a moment. My brain was telling me it was a bad idea, when the goal was to stay away from Colton. But my heart couldn't help it, wanting to say yes to his offer.

Maybe my brain had been drained from all the midterms I had to take that week, because my heart was winning the argument by the second. Plus, we were only checking out a karaoke bar, which didn't really constitute a romantic spot for me.

And a part of me was just not ready to say goodnight to Colton just yet.

It was only for a few hours, what harm could it possibly bring me?

Sealing my fate, I said, 'I would love to.'

We finally finished up our drinks, with Colton offering to pay for us both, even though I insisted I could pay for my own.

'You can pay for mine next time,' he said to me with a wink.

The wink caught me completely off guard—so much so, that I didn't even try to stop him from paying. Colton must have taken my silence as an act of defeat, even though I was trying to calm my racing heart down.

We waved goodbye to Tracy before walking out of the diner. Passing the parking lot, we stood side-by-side on the sidewalk, waiting for the perfect time to cross the road.

'Come on,' Colton said, taking my hand in his as we made our way to the bar.

The sound of the music from the bar got louder as we got nearer. I saw a sign hanging beside the entrance that said '70s Groove'. There wasn't a line at the door, but from what I could see on the outside, the bar looked full.

'I think it's full,' I told Colton, expecting him to let go of my hand since I thought we might have to wait outside for a bit.

But instead, he held my hand tighter and said, 'There's an empty table,' before pulling me inside.

As we were walking inside, I tried my best to conceal my disappointment when Colton let go of my hand. But the feeling was only temporary, when he put his hand on my back instead, as he led me to our table.

The table that Colton brought me to was located at the back of the bar, in a slightly elevated area, than the seats in the front that were closer to the stage. As we got closer to our seats, I noticed there was a 'reserved' sign placed on the table.

'Thank you.' I gave Colton a grateful smile when he pulled out my chair for me.

'Reserved?' I asked him once he settled himself on the seat beside me.

A blush appeared on Colton's face, but that might have just been a trick of my imagination due to the dim lighting of the bar. 'I texted my aunt when we were at the diner to reserve a table for us before we got here,' he explained.

'That's sweet of you. Thank you,' I smiled. 'I saw a sign outside that says "70s Groove". What does that mean?'

'Oh, that's the karaoke theme for the night. Usually, they'll just let everyone sing any song they like. But on Saturdays, they have a theme,' he explained.

'So that means you can only sing songs from the seventies tonight?'

'Exactly,' he confirmed.

At that moment, a lady, who looked to be in her forties, stopped by our table.

'Colton!' she greeted him, before turning to me and asking, 'And who do we have here?'

'Aunt Edna, this is Clara. My partner for a class this semester,' he introduced me.

'Clara, you say?' she asked suspiciously, raising an eyebrow at Colton. 'Well, it's nice to meet you.'

'It's nice to meet you too. I love what you've done with the place,' I told her. The insides of the bar were truly an aesthetic of their own. One of the walls was just pure red bricks, and there was another one filled with album covers, ranging from the classics to new ones.

'Why thank you, this bar is my heart and soul, so I appreciate the love,' she replied, her tone filled with pride as she looked around the place. 'Anyway, can I get you anything to drink? It's on the house.'

I was about to insist on paying, when Colton shot me a look, as if he already knew what I was about to say.

Rescinding back on what I was about to offer, I told his aunt, 'I'll have a margarita please.'

'Just a Sprite for me,' Colton added.

Giving us a nod, Aunt Edna went her way to get our drinks.

'Just a Sprite?' I arched a brow at him.

'Well, you're going to need someone sober to drive you home later.'

'I don't think I agreed to let you drive me home,' I said to him, my voice teasing.

Colton was quick to reply. 'You'll just have to get used to me driving you home.'

My stomach flipped at his words, his tone firm and *possessive*. But the last part was probably just my imagination running a bit wild.

Colton had driven me home numerous times before, but something felt different about this one. My automatic response was to reject his offer, reassuring him I could go home on my own, if he wanted to drink tonight. But, instead, I just accepted his kind gesture with a grateful smile. 'I appreciate that. Thank you.'

Aunt Edna was back at our table moments later, holding our drinks in her hands. 'Here you go,' she placed down the drinks as she turned to Colton and said, 'and you're off for the night by the way.'

'Shit. Did I take you away from work?' I forgot he only went to the diner for his break.

'Don't worry about it, honey. We can manage the bar from here, you two just have fun,' Aunt Edna reassured me. 'And call for me if you need more drinks.'

'Thanks, Aunt Edna,' Colton said before she left us.

I took a sip of my margarita, my eyes turned to watch the people singing on stage. They looked like they were having a great time, not caring whether they were off-beat or singing the wrong tune.

'You look like you want to go up there,' I heard Colton say next to me.

I turned my attention back to him and shrugged. 'It looks like a lot of fun. But I definitely do not want to be up there alone.'

'Then, I'll go up there with you.'

My eyes widened, and then I let out a small laugh at his suggestion. But I stopped when I realized he wasn't joining me and instead had an amused expression on his face.

'You're not serious?'

'I never kid around about karaoke.'

'You don't have to go up there just because I want to.'

'I know, but I do want to,' he said, before adding, 'On one condition though.' Holding up a finger.

I tilted my head. 'Which is?'

'I get to pick the song, and you won't know what song I picked out until we get on stage.'

I gave him a suspicious look. 'And how are you so sure I will actually *know* the song that you chose?'

'You'll just have to trust me on this one.'

I took a moment to think about it, but I already knew my mind was made once he said he would go up there with me. 'Deal.' I held my hand out to him, and we shook on it.

'I'll be right back,' Colton said as he left our table to submit our names for our turn on stage.

I let out a sigh. While I do like karaoke, it's mostly in a privately rented room with my closest friends—a pastime the girls and I grew fond of ever since we discovered a karaoke box in town our freshman year—not in a public space like this.

What did I just agree to?

Colton came back moments later, retaking his seat. 'There's two more songs including this one, and then it's going to be us.'

I just gave him a silent nod and took another sip of my margarita. We settled into silence—well, as silent as you can get at a karaoke bar—as the next person got up on stage and sang the song they had selected, belting out the lyrics slightly off-pitch when they reached a high note.

Noticing how quiet I got, Colton asked, 'Are you okay?' His voice filled with concern.

'I'm all right.' I tried to wave off my nervousness but the squeak in my voice might have given it away.

'We don't have to do this, you know?' Colton reassured me, sensing my uneasiness. 'I can still go there and cancel.'

The thing is, I did want to. As much as I would have loved to just sit there for the rest of the night and be content with listening to other people singing on stage, I knew that a part of me would regret backing out of this, once I got home later that night.

'I want to do this. I'm just a bit nervous, that's all.' I started rubbing my hands together, trying to warm them up once I felt them starting to get cold.

Noticing what I was doing, Colton took my hands and put them between his. His thumbs slowly rubbing the back of my hands.

'Does this help?' he asked.

'It does,' I replied, giving him an appreciative smile.

I didn't know how long we stayed like that, both of us looking down at my hands that were clasped between his.

'Next up, give it up for Clara and Colton!'

Upon hearing our names, we raised our heads and looked at one another.

'You ready?' Colton asked, a small smile tugging on his lips.

I gave him a nod, and Colton finally let go of my hands. Just for a split second before grasping one of them as he got off his seat and waited for me to get off mine. I eyed my drink and decided to just finish it up. I was going to need that extra liquid courage for when I'm up there.

Leading us to the stage, Colton let go of my hand to take two mics from the DJ and passed one to me.

At that moment, I was grateful for my cardigan for giving me the sense of being less exposed. I braved myself to look at the crowd, but my courage only lasted for one fleeting second before I let my eyes fall to my feet.

But as I felt a warm sensation covering my left hand, I turned my gaze to look where it was coming from: finding Colton's hand wrapping mine.

I peered up to look at his face and was met by his encouraging smile.

I gave him a smile of my own and the song finally came on.

It took me a moment to register what song it was. But once I recognized the melody, my eyes instantly widened. Seeing the expression on my face, Colton's smile turned into a massive grin.

It was 'Waterloo'.

By ABBA.

I was still too stunned by the song choice to start singing, so Colton started instead, his head banging to the beat of the verse. And as he went to the chorus, Colton started stepping sideways—one step to the right and to the left repeatedly—bringing me along with him since our hands were still connected. The movements slowly calmed down my nerves and I was starting to enjoy following the rush of the music.

As if sensing my ease, Colton raised his hand that was holding mine, indicating I take the next part.

I started singing, my voice slightly awkward, and my tone quiet. But Colton kept nodding his head, encouraging me, and I started singing a bit louder.

Letting go of my hand when the next verse came, Colton started dramatically walking backwards to the side of the stage. That was when I realized that he had been acting out the lines. I continued with the next line, repeating his head banging from earlier, when the beat came, following his dramatic antics.

We continued the rest of the song, just singing to each other—some lines on our own, some lines together. And before I knew it, we were nearing the end of the song. As we sang out the last line, Colton took my hand, twirling me around again and again as the outro played, until the song finally came to an end.

He stopped spinning me and wrapped his arm around my waist on the final beat of the song, my hands instinctively going to his chest. We just stared at each other for a few seconds and for that brief space in time, only Colton and I existed.

And it wasn't until I heard the sounds of clapping and cheers that I remembered where we were and what we were doing: singing karaoke on stage in a bar full of strangers.

Snapping out of our little moment, Colton finally freed his hold of my waist and grabbed my hand. Facing the crowd, we took a bow before leaving the stage, passing the mics back to the DJ.

As we were walking back towards our table, people kept cheering, their eyes following us. I just smiled at them, while Colton waved at them as if he was royalty.

I was laughing at how ridiculous he was being, when he turned his head at me—an amused look on his face as if daring me to do the same. Taking up on his challenge, I copied his wave. That was how we ended up, walking back to our seats, waving one hand in the air, the other one interlocked with each other.

'Now that's what I call a duet!' I heard the DJ say, once we finally got ourselves back into our seats. 'Everyone, give it up for my nephew and his date for their performance of ABBA's "Waterloo"!'

The crowd erupted in cheers and thunderous claps once again.

'Nephew? The DJ is your uncle?' I asked Colton once the crowd settled down and the next person was walking to the stage.

'Yup,' he nodded. 'It was his idea to have the themed karaoke.'

I thought about pointing out how his uncle might have mistaken this little hang-out with Colton for a date. But it seemed like an honest mistake, considering it was a Saturday night, and we were the only two people at our table, so I just let it slide.

And okay, maybe there was a tiny part of me that liked the fact that it looked like a date to someone else.

'Are you okay? You look a bit flushed.' I heard Colton ask, a slightly worried look on his face.

I put my hands up to my cheek, and he was right: it did feel warm.

'I'm okay. It might have been the adrenaline rush from singing just now,' I told him. 'It might have been the margarita as well.'

'Hold on, let me get you some water.'

I was about to stop him, but he was already out of his seat.

The heat was catching up to me, so I decided to take off my cardigan. Placing it on my lap, I let the air from the AC cool down my skin.

Colton came back just a few minutes later, a glass of water in each of his hand. 'Here you go.' He set down the glasses on the table, pushing one to me.

'Thank you.' I picked up the glass and took a long gulp.

'Karaoke wore you out, huh?'

'I did just give my best performance,' I said, setting the glass—now only half full—back on the table.

Colton chuckled. 'You looked like you had fun up there.'

'I did. But it wouldn't have been as much fun if you weren't up there with me,' I told him, grateful that he had been willing to sing with me onstage. 'Thank you for being my karaoke partner, *partner.*' I emphasized the second partner with a soft nudge to his stomach.

'You're welcome, partner,' he answered, giving me a soft nudge back.

As other patrons were taking their turns going up on stage, Colton and I were stuck in our own little world: just catching up with each other, as if we hadn't seen one another in a long time, when in truth, we had just met last Wednesday for our ASL practice session. But this was the first time we had ever hung out together, not out of necessity for practicing ASL or bumping into each other at a party, but because we wanted to be with each other. There was also a certain feeling to it, a sense of assurance that we chose to spend our time with the other person.

Our conversation paused whenever someone just finished a song. We would either clap along with the rest of the crowd or just take in what the person on stage had been singing. Just like our turn, Colton's uncle didn't announce the song they had picked out. The next songs after us were also equally upbeat as ours. But it seemed the lively music of night had slowly started to simmer down, when Colton's uncle decided to get up on stage.

'Is everyone having a good time?' he announced on the mic.

The answer came in the form of a very enthusiastic 'yes,' in unison from the crowd.

'As much as I love the upbeat music, I think it's time we slow it down a bit. For my turn, I would like to invite everyone along with their partner for a little slow dance.' Colton's uncle signalled to Aunt Edna, who was now behind the DJ booth.

The first notes of the song played, and I recognized it instantly.

It was Eric Clapton's 'Wonderful Tonight'.

The tables began to empty one by one as people started taking their partners by the hand, leading them to the floor in front of the stage, slowly filling up the open space.

A smile appeared on my face, when I noticed half the bar was on the dance floor, leisurely swaying to the music, and Colton's uncle's melodious voice.

I heard a scrape of a chair moving next to me. Looking over, I saw Colton was out of his seat.

'May I have this dance, milady?' he asked, one hand offered out to me, the other behind his back. He had a slight bow to him, as if he was asking me for a dance at a ball.

I giggled at him. Putting my hand in his, I answered, 'Of course, you may, milord.'

He gave me a playful grin, and got me out of my chair once again. This time, he led me to the front of the bar where all the couples had gathered.

When we finally found a vacant spot that was slightly closed off from the crowd still in their seats, Colton let go of my hand and placed both his hands gently on my waist. He pulled me closer, while I put both my hands behind his neck.

We started swaying to the soft beat of the song, letting the music enfold us.

'Does your uncle sing every karaoke night?' I asked him, breaking the silence.

'Occasionally,' he shrugged. 'Whenever he feels like it.'

I just gave him a nod, settling back into silence as we continued slow dancing.

'I was here by the way—last Saturday night,' Colton said out of the blue.

I tried to remember what had happened last Saturday, and he must have noticed me blanking on it, when he added, 'during the party.'

'Oh, right. The party,' I answered him, stopping myself before I could say something else—things that were beyond being the just-friends territory and things that I wouldn't be able to take back once I had let them out.

Colton didn't say anything, he just continued staring at me with a contemplative look. I knew what he was trying to tell me, what he was willing me to do. He wanted me to say the words I had been holding back on.

It might have been the alcohol, it might have been our proximity, or maybe because we were swaying to one of the most romantic songs ever written. But, at that moment, I went against all logical thoughts my brain was throwing at me, and admitted what my heart wanted to say.

'I was looking for you at the party when I arrived. I was a bit sad when you weren't there, and I didn't know where you had been,' I confessed, before quickly adding, 'Not that you have to tell me where you were.'

That was definitely oversharing. I tried to cover up my embarrassment by turning my gaze down at my sandals.

But Colton stopped me when he lightly placed his fingers under my chin, bringing my eyes back to him.

'You were the first person I looked for when I arrived at the party,' he said. His tone was quiet, as if he was whispering a secret to me.

His eyes locked with mine before they darted down to my lips.

And at that moment, a sudden urge came upon me.

I wanted to kiss him.

So badly.

And I think he wanted to kiss me too.

Warning signs were going off in my brain, alerting me of how bad of an idea it was. But it seemed my cloud of judgment was fogged up by the thundering beat of my heart, which had been slowly winning the battle by the second.

And damn it, it was just one kiss. *I could just blame it on the alcohol tomorrow, right?*

Colton must have been waiting for my approval, so I gave him the tiniest bit of a nod.

I wasn't even sure if he saw it, until I could feel he had started to lean in.

Closer.

And closer.

And closer.

Until we were sharing a breath.

Until our lips were almost touching one another.

Closing my eyes, I waited for the feel of his lips on mine.

But it never came.

Instead, I felt a warmth resting against my forehead.

Opening my eyes, I saw Colton's face close to me, his forehead touching mine.

And as his uncle sang the last line of the song, Colton followed along.

His eyes stared into mine as he softly sang, '*Oh my darling, you are wonderful tonight.*'

We continued swaying to the song, foreheads pressed with one another as the outro played out. We lingered in that position, even when the song was finished, and the crowd had burst into soft cheers and claps.

Smiling at me, Colton pulled back and I could finally catch my breath. While a part of me was sad he didn't fully lean in, a part was equally relieved. It had been just a spur-of-the-moment thing. We were slow dancing, our bodies pressed closely together. I was not surprised he felt compelled to do something like that, for we had been lost in the romantic haze of it all.

Or I might have misread the moment entirely, and let my imagination conjure up what I had wanted the reality to be. Maybe Colton wasn't even trying to kiss me and just wanted to press his forehead to mine—platonically.

He proceeded to pick up my hand and raised it to his lips, gently placing a soft kiss on my knuckles. I didn't know how I was supposed to react to his gesture, but my panic was short-lived, when Colton offered his arm to me with a playful look on his face.

'Milady?' he asked. It was then I realized the kiss on the hand was part of the royal ball bit he had been doing.

When my brain finally caught up with him, I placed my arm inside his and answered, 'Milord.'

And we were back to being the Clara and Colton that I knew.

Once we got back to our table, I pulled out my phone to check the time, finding out it was almost midnight.

'Everything okay?' Colton asked me.

'Yeah.' Putting my phone back into my purse, I continued, 'I just didn't realize how late it was.'

'We can leave if you want.'

'I kinda don't want to go home just yet,' I said sheepishly.

'I didn't say anything about going home.'

I furrowed my eyebrows at him, puzzled by what he was saying. 'You have a place in mind?'

'I do,' he said, before drinking the rest of his water. 'What do you say? One last stop before I drive you home?'

At this point of the night, all my defences had already been down, and I didn't even hesitate with an answer.

Smiling at him, I said, 'Sure, why not?'

Chapter Eleven

We said a quick goodbye to his aunt, who made Colton promise to bring me back here again.

'Drive safe,' she said to him, hugging each of us before sending us off on our way.

Colton's uncle was back on his DJ duty behind the booth, so we just waved him goodbye as we made our way out of the bar.

I waited for Colton to lead the way to his car so I could follow him, but he caught me by surprise when he decided to take my hand. 'The car is this way,' he said, pulling me with him.

Considering the bar was still open for the next couple of hours, cars were still parked alongside the row of shops where Colton's drive was parked at the end. Upon reaching his car, he opened my door. Once I settled in my seat, he closed it and went over to the driver's seat.

A part of me was curious as to where he was bringing me, but a bigger part of me wanted it to be a surprise. So, I just stayed quiet as Colton continued to drive. His radio was turned on and a new ABBA song started playing.

A smile appeared on my lips upon recognizing the soft melodies of 'Andante, Andante'.

I started humming to the song and eventually sang out the lyrics in a quiet tone as I looked out the window, not wanting to disturb the silence.

But, of course, Colton caught me. Then, he started to sing in a much louder voice than mine, instantly bringing my attention to him.

He took his eyes off the road for a few seconds and looked over at me. With a smile that reached all the way to his eyes, he continued to sing, and the next thing I knew, I was singing along with him without a care in the world.

The song ended at the same time as Colton turned on his blinker and turned into a junction.

'Creamsicle Corner? Really?' I exclaimed once I realized where we were, one of the town's staples and a college students' favourite, considering it had been open even way past midnight.

'Nothing like homemade ice cream for a midnight snack.'

It seemed a good number of people had been craving some midnight snacks as well, based on the number of cars in the parking lot. There were still a few spots available, and Colton chose the one nearest to the building.

Killing the engine, he climbed out of the car, and headed over to my side.

'Thank you,' I said when he opened my car door.

We then headed inside together, as Colton held my hand like it was second nature to him.

Our midnight order consisted of two ice creams cups—one for each of us—along with some chicken nuggets and fries.

When it was time to pay, I was faster to lend the money to the cashier than Colton.

'I win!' I cheered.

Colton just chuckled at me.

When the food was ready, he picked up the tray, and we went to search for a place to sit. There were quite a few vacant tables, so we just randomly picked the one that was further away from the rest of the customers.

We settled into a comfortable silence as we ate our food. It seemed karaoke had got us both a little hungry.

The AC in Creamsicle Corner was cooler than I had expected, and the ice cream that I was happily eating did not help the situation. I hadn't put my cardigan back on after taking it off at the bar, and realized I must have accidentally left it in Colton's car.

I tried my best to not let it affect me, though I couldn't help but give a slight shiver. I tried rubbing my arm to warm myself up, but my hands were cold from holding the ice cream.

'Are you cold?' Colton asked, catching what I was doing.

'Just a little.' I shrugged as I continued rubbing my arms. I heard movement coming from his side of the seat, but I didn't notice what Colton was doing until he spoke up.

'Wear this,' he said, holding out his baseball jacket—the one he had been wearing all night—to me.

Knowing better than to reject his kind gesture when I was freezing myself, I took his jacket, and put it on immediately. 'Thank you.'

Once I put it on, I tried to take a sneaky sniff of his scent on the jacket—the one that I had slowly gotten used to over the past few weeks.

We were back to our comfortable silence, eating our food quietly, when I noticed Colton kept stealing glances my way.

'What's wrong? Did I spill the ice cream?' I asked in alarm, immediately looking down at his jacket to make sure I hadn't accidentally ruined it.

'Nothing's wrong,' he shook his head, before deciding to add, 'you look cute in my jacket.'

My eyes widened at his words. Who needed the jacket when you had Colton Reed saying these things to you? A blush instantly rose to my cheeks, and I could feel the warmth spreading throughout my body. I didn't know how to react, so I just focused my gaze on the ice cream, not daring to look his way.

He was quiet for a minute, so I decided to brave myself to peek at his face, only to see he took his phone out.

A feeling of sadness came over me; I was slightly hurt by him being on the phone.

But it was short-lived when I caught his thumb pressing the same spot repeatedly.

Realization hit me. 'Are you taking a picture of me?'

'Nope.'

'Then—'

'I'm taking multiple pictures of you.'

'Colton—'

'Smile,' he said with a massive grin on his face.

That playful grin was all he needed to dissolve the rest of my protests. 'Well, if you're taking pictures of me, it's only fair for me to take pictures of you.'

'By all means.'

Once I got my phone out, Colton started posing while my camera clicked away.

I snorted when he started flexing one of his arms.

The rest of our time at Creamsicle Corner was filled with laughter and enthusiastic voices as we recounted random stories of ourselves with one another, ranging from our most embarrassing moments to our best. As Colton recalled his story of the time he hit his first-ever home run, I couldn't help but think that it might have just been the best date I had ever had. But the sad part was that it hadn't actually been a date. Nor will there ever be one.

I tried to not let the thought affect me, but it seemed like I had failed, when a worried look appeared on Colton's face.

'Are you okay?'

'Yeah, just tired.' And right on cue, a yawn escaped from my mouth as I tried to cover it up.

'Time to get you home.'

The drive back to my apartment was filled with us singing more ABBA songs. Colton gave me full control, letting me play the songs I knew, so we could sing together. My singing eventually started to quiet down with a feeling of disappointment when I noticed he was already turning into my street.

But, instead of stopping at the drop-off spot in front of my apartment building, Colton continued to drive a bit further. He stopped only when he found an empty parking spot and parked his car.

Once the car was parked, he unbuckled his seatbelt, and went over to my side, opening my door.

'Thank you,' I said once I climbed down. 'I had a great—'

'Can I walk you up to your apartment?' Colton blurted out.

My head jolted back at his words, taken aback by his request.

Logically, it wouldn't make sense for him to walk me up, since it hadn't been a date. But that didn't mean I couldn't pretend it was one, right? Plus, it was just Colton being a good friend.

Though I won't admit it out loud, I wasn't ready to say goodbye to Colton just yet; nor was I ready for this night of make-believe to end. If I could prolong it just a little bit more before we had to part ways, then so be it—even if the walk back up to my apartment was barely five minutes.

Because no matter what had happened—or almost happened—that night, it still changed nothing. Once the night was over, we would be back to being Clara and Colton—ASL partners and friends, nothing more.

'Sure,' I said, wanting to stay in this fantasy a little longer.

Killing the engine of his car and locking it, we then started our short walk to the building. Colton opened the glass door for me once we reached the entrance. As I led him to my apartment, I found myself telling him about how Nina and I had ended up at our current place. We were waiting for the elevator when I came to a stop, realizing I was telling him about something he didn't even ask about.

'And now I'm rambling. Sorry about that. My brain tends to let loose when I'm tired,' I apologized.

'There's nothing to apologize for. I like hearing you talk,' he reassured me with a soft smile on his face. 'So how long have you and Nina been roommates?'

'This is our third year of rooming together. We were roommates during our freshman year, back when we lived in the dorms, and we just clicked instantly. It's like, we've been friends our whole life. Now, she's my best friend, still my roommate, and I wouldn't have it any other way.'

The elevator finally reached the lobby. The door slid open, and we stepped inside. 'You make it sound like it was fated for you two to be roommates during freshman year,' Colton said.

I pressed the button to my apartment floor. 'Well, when you put it that way, it kinda does sound like it *was* fated,' I said, my tone playful. 'But even if fate did play a role, I know better than to question it. If that was what made me and Nina roommates in the first place, then so be it. I'm just happy that it happened.'

'What about you?' I then added. 'Do you believe in fate?'

I tilted my head his way to look at him, waiting for his answer.

Only to find him already looking at me.

'I didn't,' he said, his voice merely a whisper, 'but I'm starting to think I was wrong.'

His eyes bored right into mine before darting to my lips for a split second, as if it was unintentional—an accident.

It was a second I might have missed, if my attention hadn't fully been on him.

But I caught it.

And I think Colton knew that too.

I took a sharp inhale at the way he was looking at me, only for the urge to kiss him to return in full stride.

I didn't think I was reading him wrongly this time.

And from the looks of it, I *knew* he was thinking the same thing.

But something was holding him back, and I wasn't sure what it was. I don't know how long we stood there in the elevator as it continued its ascent.

'Clara.' I heard him whisper my name, there was a certain tone in his voice that I couldn't fully detect.

It sounded like desire—a longing.

Colton was about to say something. And I knew at that moment, it wouldn't be anything good, at least not in terms of keeping this friendship between us. I was aware we had been blurring lines that night, but once the words came out of his mouth, I knew there was no going back.

'I—' he started.

But the rest of his sentence was cut off when the elevator door opened.

I broke our gaze and exited myself, letting out a sigh of relief, while I still had my back to him.

That was a very close call.

I managed to recompose myself just in time as I felt his presence beside me.

The elevator might have paused the conversation momentarily, but I knew he still had time to voice out the words stuck in his throat. Before he could get another one out, I blurted, 'My apartment is this way.' Immediately, I started walking ahead of him.

Fortunately, my apartment wasn't too far away from the elevator. By the time he caught up with me, I was already unlocking the door.

'Thank you, Colton,' I said, trying to make this quick. 'For everything. I had a great time tonight.'

Seemingly catching what I was doing, Colton let out a deep breath—a closed sigh. 'Me too,' he said instead.

'I'll see you next week then,' I paused before adding, 'partner.'

I could have sworn I saw something like hurt flash in his eyes, but it was gone just as quickly.

'See you next week, partner.' He nodded at me.

Once I finally managed to unlock the door, I opened it and stepped into my apartment. I gave him one final wave before closing and locking in for the night, staying near the door for a minute, waiting for him to leave. When I heard his footsteps slowly fade away, I leaned my back against the door and let out a giant exhale.

'You're back.' I heard someone say. I raised my head to see Nina still sitting on the couch, this time with a bowl of popcorn on her lap. 'How was the date? Did you have a good time?'

Now that Colton was gone, I could slowly feel the panic withering away. I pushed myself off the door and made my way to the living room.

'The date was fine,' I started. 'I—'

'What are you wearing?' Nina gasped.

Her question got me slightly confused, since she had helped me pick out my outfit for the night.

But the confusion quickly turned to horror, when I noticed my cardigan sleeves were in a different colour.

And instead of a cardigan, it was a jacket.

Colton's baseball jacket.

My eyes widened in panic.

My brain must have thought I was still wearing my cardigan, since my arms were covered. If I was wearing Colton's jacket, it meant I had left my cardigan in his car.

But that wasn't why my heart was racing at the moment.

No, the reason for that was the look on Nina's face as she was figuring out whose jacket it was.

'That looks like a baseball jacket.' And I could see the exact moment it finally dawned on her whose it was. 'No way. There's no way. Right?'

I didn't know what else to say. I was pretty sure she had already figured it out. So, instead of saying anything, I just gave her a nod.

It seemed I stunned her into silence. Her mouth gaped at me as she tried to think of what to say.

After what felt like an hour—but was probably only a minute—she said, 'You don't have to tell me anything.

I'm rewatching *Gilmore Girls* and I still have some popcorn. Wanna join me?'

I loved Nina for respecting my space. As much as I wanted to keep the night I had with Colton to myself, it was also the first time that I couldn't wait to tell her about it—even if it wasn't an actual date. Though I did tell her about all those prior to the one that night, it had been more of an active, formal recalling of how the date went, instead of being all giddy about each detail.

But the thing that had been holding me back from telling Nina right then was that I had to make her understand that whatever happened with Colton that night was a one-time thing. It would also mean telling her about the curse, and explaining why Colton and I couldn't be anything more than friends.

I knew that Nina would understand where I came from, but I couldn't help that tiny fear that she would look at me differently after this, once she found out that I was a twenty-year-old who still believed in things as stupid as curses.

'Clara?' Nina said, when she noticed I was still standing there.

Before I could stop myself, the words were already out of my mouth.

'Nina,' I said, so quietly that I wasn't sure she heard me. 'I'm so screwed.'

Chapter Twelve

The Monday after that fateful night, I got a text from Colton.

I was in the middle of my last class for the day, with my phone on airplane mode to avoid any distractions. When the class was dismissed, I took it out of my bag, and turned my phone back online. When I noticed Colton had texted me, my heart couldn't help but flutter a little and yet feel a hint of nervousness when I saw the notification.

We had each other's phone numbers since the first night he had driven me home, but we had never really used it before. Since ASL was a visual language, our assignments and tests weren't paper-based; we only had one test coming in the next few weeks, along with a final at the end of the semester. The rest of the assessments were during class where Mr Albert would randomly pick someone out to quiz them on what we had learnt the previous week. There was, of course, the partnered assignment—the culprit that had brought us together in the first place—but we were yet to be given the guideline for it, so there wasn't much to discuss.

After our first ASL practice at the bubble tea shop, it had pretty much become a weekly routine for us to practice after class. This way, we didn't have to text each other to plan for our next practice.

I was about to open the text, when I noticed more students were coming into the lecture hall for the next class. I figured it wasn't too urgent, so I packed up the rest of my things, and exited the hall, finding a nearby spot to sit. Luckily, there was a sitting area underneath a tree, and those who were sitting there were leaving.

I took a seat at the empty table and put my bag next to myself. Once I inhaled a deep breath, I finally opened the text.

Colton:
Hey. We have an away game this Thursday, and we'll be leaving on Wednesday. So, I won't be attending ASL class.
I guess we'll have to reschedule our ASL practice this week.

I wasn't sure what I had been expecting, especially after whatever happened—or almost happened—on Saturday night, but a feeling of relief came over me reading the text, knowing that it was just him being nothing more than a good partner for ASL class.

Clara:
Got it. Thanks for letting me know! Is there any other time this week that you're free to practice?

It was a little over four in the afternoon. While Colton had told me his practice timings before, they tended to change, based on whether there was an upcoming game. But from what I remember, they usually started at either four or five, depending on the day, so I wasn't expecting a reply from him right away.

I contemplated whether I should wait for Nina's practice to be over and go home together. But thinking I'd be better off doing my work at home, I got up from the seat, picked up my bag, and started my commute back to the apartment.

My phone buzzed as I was re-watching an episode of *Community*.

I quickly picked it up when I saw it was a text notification, expecting it to be from Colton. I couldn't help but feel slightly disappointed to see it was from Nina instead.

Nina:
Have you started dinner yet?

In the first few weeks we had started rooming together off-campus, we mostly cooked our meals on our own, without knowing each other's food preference. But after that midterms week, when I had decided to cook dinner the whole week for the both of us, Nina told me she wanted to cook dinner for us the next week.

Initially, I had rejected the idea, thinking she would usually be late from her training to cook for me, if I wanted to go to bed early. However, she requested for a week's time to prove that I would be able to have dinner before the late hours of the night.

Nina was fully committed to cooking dinner for us throughout the whole week. With the help of meal-prepping and great management skills from her side, she emerged victorious from the challenge. It was then we found out that we were compatible home cooking-wise, and started compromising on who was making which meal, based on our class schedule.

For the past few semesters we had been roommates, we pretty much ate breakfast and dinner at home, and took lunch on our own since our schedules rarely aligned.

And for Monday night that week, it was my turn to cook dinner.

Clara:
Not yet. I just took out the chicken. But I'm not sure how I want to cook it yet.

Her reply was instant.

Nina:
PUT IT BACK IN THE FREEZER. I'm craving some pizza right now. What do you say? My treat!

I couldn't help but laugh at her message. A pizza did sound good.

Clara:
Since you're paying, PIZZA IT IS THEN!

Nina:
YAAAYYY! Any toppings preferences?

Clara:
It feels like a Pepperoni kind of night or is that just me?

Nina:
You know what. You're right, it does feel like a Pepperoni
kind of night.

I'm still on campus. But I'll try to be back in 30 minutes!

Clara:
Take your time! And drive safe.

She must have already started her drive, since she didn't reply to my last message.

I got off the couch and went to the kitchen to put the chicken back into the freezer. Because my phone was on silent, I didn't realize I got a new text message until I sat back on the couch.

And to my surprise, it wasn't from Nina.

It was from Colton.

Colton:
Missing me already?

I read it once.
Then, twice.
And once more for safety measures.
Guess I wasn't hallucinating.

After my mind was officially satisfied that what I was seeing was not a dream, a slight panic came over me.

How am I supposed to respond to this?

But thankfully, I was saved from thinking of one, when the three dots appeared, followed by another text from Colton.

Colton:
I'm not sure what time we'll be back on Friday, and the baseball team wants to hang out that night.

And we have to attend a charity event on Sunday.

What about Saturday?

I quickly went over my calendar on my phone to see what I was up to that day. I was pretty confident of having nothing ongoing. But it seemed that the past-me had already made other plans, when I saw an all-day event titled 'Girls' Day Out!'

Oh right.

Nina, Claudia, Lily, and I finally had a Saturday where we could all hang out together. After that baseball team party, we hadn't gotten around to spending a day with all four of us. But with Nina's training, it meant I had the morning off.

I started texting Colton to tell him I was free on Saturday morning, but stopped before I could finish.

If he's hanging out with the baseball team on Friday night, then he probably wants to sleep in on Saturday.

Clara:

I'm free on Saturday morning! But I totally understand if you want to sleep in, so we don't really have to practice this week. I think we'll be fine skipping a week.

Colton:
Cool.

Cool.

That's it? That's all he has to say?

'Maybe he's not much of a texter', the logical part of my brain pointed out.

I let out a sigh. I didn't really know what I was expecting. But knowing that this might be our only interaction of the week, I couldn't help but feel a little sad by how short our conversation was, even if it was just by text.

This crush with Colton is really getting out of hand.

Deciding not to dwell on it further, I locked my phone. I picked up the TV remote to press play and continue watching my show.

But I was interrupted once again by the buzz from my phone.

It was a new message from Colton.

Colton:
Guess we won't be seeing each other this week. ☹

I couldn't help but smile at his text, with my heart rate increasing just a little faster.

Clara:
And I guess I'll have to walk to get my bubble tea this week.

Colton:
You can't do that. I thought bubble tea is our thing.

My heart skipped a beat.
Our thing.
He probably just meant it as a joke, but my heart didn't seem to want to take it as one.

Clara:
And what's that supposed to mean?

Colton:
It means we can only drink bubble tea when we're together.

I didn't even have the time to question his text, when another popped up, giving me clarification of what he actually meant.

Colton:
Practicing ASL.

Clara:
I mean, it was before you decided to abandon me for baseball.

And I have a weekly bubble tea quota that I require to function.

Colton:
You're breaking my heart here, partner.
I promise I'll make it up to you.

Clara:
And how are you thinking of doing that?

Colton:
I have my ways. Just promise me you won't get bubble tea
this week.

Clara:
Fineeeee, I promise. No bubble tea for me this week then.

Colton:
That's my girl.

I took a sharp inhale upon reading the text. I was pretty sure my heart had just skipped a beat. *His girl?*

Colton:
Anywaaaay, now that you're free for a couple of extra hours on Wednesday, any plans?

Clara:
Not really. I'll probably just head back to my apartment early that day.

What time is your game on Thursday by the way?

The sound of the door unlocking and opening turned my head towards it, and my eyes caught Nina enter the apartment.

'I'm back!' she announced, raising her arm that was holding the pizza box. 'And I brought pizza!'

She set down the pizza on the kitchen island and put her bag on its usual spot on the floor. Then, she went over to the sink to wash her hands, before settling down into her usual seat on the bar stool.

I went over to wash my hands, then opened the fridge to see what drinks we had.

'Do you want a Sprite?' I called out to Nina.

'Yes, please.'

Taking a can for her and another one for myself, I went over to the only other unoccupied kitchen stool. Nina was already lifting the pizza box cover and picking up a triangular piece for herself.

A contented moan came out of her as she took a bite of the pizza.

I helped her crack open her can of soda, pushing it towards her. 'Here you go.'

'Thank you,' she quickly said, before picking it up and taking a gulp.

I couldn't help but laugh at her. 'Slow down.'

I was just about to pick up a piece for myself when my phone buzzed again. I smiled to myself, when I saw Colton's reply in the notifications.

Colton:
2 pm.
Why?

Thinking I could quickly shoot him a text, I sent off my reply before locking my phone, and turned it face down.

Clara:

Just thought I would send you a good luck text before the game.

'What's with the giant smile on your face?' I heard Nina ask.

'Hmm?' I hummed in question, lifting my head to meet her.

She narrowed her eyes at me, a suspicious look on her face. 'Are you texting someone? Who is it?'

I didn't even get a chance to answer her when she let out a gasp, her eyes widening. 'Colton texted you.'

I told my brain to act nonchalant, but it seemed the message got delayed, and my eyes immediately widened at her accusations. My cheeks heated up, as if I was caught doing something scandalous.

My silence was all the confirmation she needed.

'So, you guys are texting now,' she said, her voice filled with excitement. 'Well, what did he say?'

'We just started texting today and it's nothing major.' I shrugged, trying to brush it off as nothing to be excited about. 'He has an away game on Thursday, so he won't be attending class this Wednesday, and we won't be able to practice ASL this week. But it's just one week, so I think we'll be fine.'

Sensing my lack of excitement about the situation, her happiness started to fade too. 'What's wrong?'

I shook my head and let out a sigh. 'Nothing's wrong. It's just that I can't help but be disappointed that I won't be able to see him this week. And I also feel this sadness, you know? Like the sadness you get when you've been looking forward to something only to have it cancelled? And I know for a fact, I wouldn't be feeling this way, if it weren't for this stupid crush on Colton.'

'Well, there's nothing wrong with being disappointed with not getting a chance to see your crush,' Nina replied. 'And what's so wrong about a crush?'

'It's not the matter of a crush, but more of *this* crush.'

A confused look came over her. 'What do you mean?'

When I had returned home last Saturday night, fully prepared to tell her about the curse, Nina quickly stood up from the couch, with a very concerned look on her face. 'Is everything okay?'

Not wanting her to think of the worst things possible, I had quickly reassured her. 'Everything's fine. I had a great time tonight,' I paused before adding, 'but there's something I have to tell you.'

Her eyebrows had narrowed slightly at my request. From the look on her face, I could tell her brain had been trying to decipher what it could be. 'Okay,' she said, her tone suspicious. 'But how urgent is it?'

While I hadn't understood the relevance of her question, I still answered, 'I would say, not too urgent.'

Nina had stayed quiet for a moment, before replying, 'You know you can tell me anything, right?'

I gave her a nod. 'Of course I do.'

Giving me a smile, she had said, 'Look, I'm here if you want to talk about whatever it is you wanted to tell me. But from what I could see,' she paused while making it a point to look at the jacket, 'and from what you said about having a great night, maybe we can save the conversation for another day. You deserve to have a memory of the night without having it spoiled by whatever it is you wanted to tell me.

'We can talk about it now, or we can talk about it later,' she concluded with a shrug.

I might have been ready to lay down whatever it was that had been bothering me about this thing with Colton, but Nina was right. And if that was the only time I would ever get to go on a night out with him, I wanted to preserve it as best as I could.

So instead of me revealing the curse to Nina, we had ended that night with rewatches of *Gilmore Girls*.

But now, it was Monday. A different day.

And I wasn't high on late-night brain fogs or adrenaline rushes any more.

The way I saw it, I didn't really have to talk about it then—or ever. And if I could have it my way, I would have forgotten about it altogether.

But being a hopeless romantic and knowing that she is one as well, I knew Nina would love to hear all about my not-date with Colton. And boy, was I dying to tell her all about it.

And that meant it was time to tell her about the curse.

Here goes nothing.

'You know, how my parents got divorced and Eliza called off her engagement?' I asked.

She nodded.

'Well, there seems to be a pattern in how my parents got together and how Eliza and Nathan did,' I continued. 'Both their relationships had started out by partnering up for something: my parents back in high school, and my sister at her workplace.'

Nina just sat there, slowly taking bites of her food as she took in my words. 'Okay,' she said, giving me a nod, and silently asking for me to continue.

I sighed. 'Another similarity they bore was that there had been an element of the cliché love interest in the relationship. For my parents, it was the bad boy cliché love interest. My mom was what people considered the "good girl" in high school. You know, the one who follows the rules, hands in her homework on time, and rarely gets into trouble. While my dad was the total opposite, he was the "bad boy", breaking the rules and missing most of the classes. And of course, like any love story with a cliché love interest, they got together, got married, and had two kids. They were supposed to live happily ever after.'

'But they didn't,' Nina said.

'But they didn't,' I repeated. 'Instead, they got divorced, and it pretty much fractured my illusion of a happy ending. But then, one day, my sister brought someone home to meet the family. He was a colleague of hers and they had been paired for an assignment together. Sounds normal, but the cliché part? There were work rivals: always staying later than the other person to get ahead. But, of course, as a love story with a cliché love interest, they ended up getting along well and falling in love. When they got engaged, I thought maybe such stories do last. Though that hope didn't last very long, when they decided to call off the engagement three months later.'

I composed myself. 'I know it sounds crazy, but maybe my family is cursed. Maybe we're just not meant to have relationships with cliché love interests.'

'And you're scared of the same thing happening with you and Colton?' Nina asked.

I scoffed. 'I'm paired up with my crush who's the college star baseball player—the cliché writes itself. I mean, technically, the curse wouldn't work if we just stayed friends and it's not like he likes me back. And even if he does, nothing can happen between us. I won't let the curse get in the way of us dooming what we have now. But has that stopped my heart from liking him? Nope. Now, I just have to live with this feeling, and know that we can only ever be friends.'

I continued. 'Why did he tick all the boxes in a checklist I didn't even know I had and also be a star athlete?' I groaned out, putting both of my elbows on the kitchen island, my head between my hands. 'You must think I'm childish to believe in something stupid like this.' I breathed out a laugh, hearing how ridiculous it sounded, now that I was saying it out loud to another person.

I waited for Nina to laugh along with me, but she just stayed silent. As the silence continued to stretch on, I held my breath, scared of what words would come out of her mouth.

But her reply came in the best way possible.

She got up from her seat and put her arms around me, embracing me in a massive hug. 'Thank you for telling me,' she said, her arms gripping me tighter.

'You don't think I'm being ridiculous?' I asked her, feeling vulnerable over the conversation.

I couldn't see her, but I could feel she was shaking her head. 'Definitely not. I think you're right to believe in something like this, especially after seeing what happened with your family. So no, I don't think you're being ridiculous.'

I don't know how long we stayed like that, me just staying in her embrace. When she finally pulled away, I felt lighter than I did before.

'So, what happens now?' Nina then asked.

'I don't know,' I said with a shrug. 'I mean, although Colton and I might never happen, at least, I'll have the memory of Saturday night to hold on to.'

At that, she arched her brow at me. 'So, it was his jacket then,' she pointed out.

A smile automatically appeared on my face at the mention of his baseball jacket. 'Yes, it was.'

And that was how we spent the rest of our night: two best friends at the kitchen counter, a pizza in one hand, and a Sprite in the other, as I giddily recalled the wonderful moments of that fateful night.

After we finished our pizza, we cleared whatever trash we had and went over to the living room to continue our *Gilmore Girls* rewatch from Saturday. I decided to go through my phone while Nina set it up, and I found Colton texted me back about an hour ago.

Colton:
If you do that, I'll make sure to hit a home run.

Just for you.

'Are you ready?' I heard Nina ask from beside me.
'One second,' I answered, quickly sending a text to Colton.

Clara:
Then I'll be sure to send you that text.

Once I made sure it was sent, I locked my phone and said, 'I'm ready.'

We managed to watch two episodes before we got too tired and decided to call it a night. We wished each other goodnight as we headed for our rooms.

After finishing my skincare routine and brushing my teeth, I went to my bed and checked my phone one last time before turning it off.

There was a new message from Colton, sent almost thirty minutes ago.

Colton:
I'll be looking forward to it.

That night, I lay in bed with a smile on my face, the six words floating around my mind as I drifted off to sleep.

Chapter Thirteen

For the first time that semester, I sat in ASL class with an empty seat next to me.

And I wasn't sure how I felt about it.

On one hand, I was hugely relieved that I didn't have to face Colton just yet, when the events of last Saturday were still fresh—at least in my mind they were. Even though we had texted on Monday, conversing with him through a screen was a lot easier than facing him in person.

Because, whether I wanted to admit it or not, I couldn't deny that something had shifted between Colton and me that night. Although, I would have loved to just write off that night as a wonderful memory and never bring it up again, I wasn't sure if Colton felt the same. So, if his absence meant I could postpone the inevitable conversation, I couldn't help but feel grateful for it.

But on the other hand, I was sad that he wasn't there that day, along with the fact that we wouldn't be able to practice ASL the same week.

While our ASL practices had started off as a necessity for the class, it became something I looked forward to each week. That might have more to do with the person I was practicing with, than *actually* about practicing ASL.

When the class was dismissed, I slowly packed up my things. From what I remember, there wasn't any class after that, and I was not in any rush to leave just yet. I had some homework that needed to get done, and the library seemed like a good option. As much as I wanted to go home right away, I knew the ambiance in the library would make me more productive.

The library was, thankfully, not too full. Considering it was a little over two in the afternoon, most people were probably still in classes, but my guess was the space would slowly start to fill, once people finished their classes after four.

Making my mind up to stay until at most 3.45 p.m., I pulled out my laptop and started my work. I put my phone on airplane mode, and started on the questions, with music flooding through my earphones being my only companion.

When I hit the thirty-minute mark, I gave myself a break. I turned my phone back online to check my notifications and saw one completely standing out among the rest.

It was a text from Colton.

Colton:
How's my partner doing this week without me?

I could sense the smile appearing on my face as I read his text.

Clara:
Great! It's been a while since I got this much peace on
a Wednesday.

Colton:
🙁 🙁 🙁
Have mercy on my heart here, partner.

I couldn't help but laugh at his reply, but stopped right away when people started shooting me with sharp looks.

I forgot I was in the library there for a moment.

Clara:
Just kidding.
To be honest, it feels a little weird. I didn't realize how much I look forward to our ASL practices.

Or maybe, I was just looking forward to my weekly bubble tea.

Which I could have still gotten today. But UNFORTUNATELY, someone made me promise to not get it this week. 🙄

I knew Colton was aware that I was just teasing about actually getting one because, like him, I saw getting bubble tea as our thing. Something we did together. And getting it alone just didn't feel right to me for some reason.

Colton:
You'll get your bubble tea this week.
I promise.
Are you at home?

Clara:
Nope, in the library. Trying to get some work done before I go home.

Are you already on the road?

Colton:
Not yet, still on campus.

We're squeezing in one more practice before we go.

Clara:
Well, I don't want to keep you. And I have to get back to my work.

I was about to lock my phone, but something stopped me from putting it away just yet.

Maybe because it was the first Wednesday where I didn't get to see him since our first ASL practice, and I just wanted to talk to him a bit longer than this.

So, I shot him a follow-up text.

Clara:
Text me when you leave?

Partner?

Colton:
You got it.
Partner.

His next message came at a little past 6 p.m., while I was lounging around the couch with my book.

Colton:
Just loaded up our things. Road trip starts in ten minutes.

Along with the message was an attached selfie of him next to the college baseball team bus.

Clara:
Finaallly! How long is the drive?

Colton:
Around two hours. But we're getting dinner on the road, so we might be arriving at the hotel around nine.

What are you up to?

Clara:
Nothing much. Just reading.

Colton:
What book are you reading?

I was still reading *You Deserve Each Other* by Sarah Hogle, mostly because I wanted to take my sweet time with it. I only had fifty pages left, and I was trying very hard to pace myself, so it wouldn't be over too soon.

This wasn't the first time Colton had asked me about the book I was reading. It had been a recurring question since the week after we started practicing ASL together.

I remembered how hesitant I was when he first asked me this question. It was right after we had finished our second ASL practice session. I hadn't realized I'd taken out my copy of *It Happened One Summer* as I was rummaging through my bag for my pack of tissues, when Colton's eyes caught the book cover.

I mean, I wasn't ashamed of my love for romance books, but there was something unnerving about sharing something that you love with someone else who might not understand. So, when he asked about it, I just answered him with the title of the book, thinking he would end the conversation then and there.

But Colton surprised me, asking about the details of the book, and whether or not I was enjoying it, with a look of genuine interest on his face. Over time, it had just gotten easier to talk about them with him.

I never brought it up myself, but Colton never failed to ask me.

Clara:
I'm reading You Deserve Each Other by Sarah Hogle. It's a romance book.

Yet again.

Colton:
As it should.

Is it good? Do you like it so far?

Clara:
It's my all-time favourite book, so it's fair to say I like it A LOT.

Colton:
How is it your all-time favourite book when you're still reading it?

Clara:
This is my third time reading it.

Colton:
You must REALLY like it then.

Clara:
I love it. This book has my whole entire heart and soul.

His next reply came in another image.
It was the book cover.

Colton:
Is it this one?

Clara:
Yup! That's the one.

Colton:
I'm gonna have to read it then.
So please refrain from telling me the details of this particular book.

His texts made me pause for a moment. Colton might have shown interest in the books I was reading, but he never said anything about wanting to read them.

> Clara:
> Why?

Colton:
You mean, why don't I want you to spoil this book for me?

> Clara:
> Well yes.
> But also, why would you want to read it in the first place?

> I mean, it's a romance book.

Colton:
So?

> Clara:
> Wouldn't you rather read something else?

> Like a book from a different genre maybe?

Colton's reply was instant.

Colton:
Because it's your all-time favourite book.

That's all the reason I need.

I tried coming up with a response, but I couldn't think of what to say.

And Colton must've caught on to it, because he sent me a message a few minutes later.

Colton:
And we're off!

The next message was a selfie of him sitting in a window seat of the bus, grinning widely, with a peace sign.

Clara:
About time!

So what's the ABBA album of choice for this road trip?

Colton:
Good question.

It's definitely a Super Trouper kind of road trip.

I let out a chuckle at his answer.
My eyes darted to the time on my phone, seeing that I would have to get started on preparing dinner.

Clara:
Nina is coming home soon, so I have to start cooking dinner.

Text me when you arrive!

Colton:

I headed to the kitchen with my phone in my hand, opening Spotify to see what playlist I should listen to while I prepared dinner.

But it seemed my mind had already been made up, when my fingers started typing the search bar and wrote ABBA. Clicking on the discography, I scrolled to the *Super Trouper* album and played the first track.

I quickly took a screenshot of the Spotify player and typed out a message. Without thinking twice, I sent it to Colton.

Clara:
My cooking album of choice for tonight! Now you can pretend I'm listening to the album with you.

In case you miss me.

I was about to lock my phone when the three dots appeared, and his reply came.

Colton:
Guess I'm playing this album on repeat until I see you again.

I had a love-hate relationship with Thursdays when it came to my class schedule.

Although my first class of the day started at 10 a.m., an hour later than the previous three days of the week, Thursday was also the day I had to stay on campus the longest, with my last class finishing at 5 p.m.

I was on my way to my second class of the day after having lunch with Claudia.

Just as I was about to sit on the bench outside the lecture hall, while I had been waiting for the ongoing class to finish, students started piling out of the door. I quickly pulled out my phone and checked the time, thinking I wrongly estimated my time. But the time on my lock screen told me my class was starting in ten minutes. Hence, their lecture must have ended early.

When the number of students exiting the hall decreased to one or two in between interval gaps, I finally made my way inside the lecture hall. Quickly scanning the seats, I opted for the one in the middle.

Once I took out everything I needed for the class, I let myself scroll through my phone before the lecturer got there. A few notifications were up on my phone, but none I was looking for.

My text chain with Colton kept getting longer the previous night, with him updating me on his latest whereabouts and the occasional photos from the road trip, including one of Miles sleeping on his shoulder that I immediately showed Nina.

The conversation finally came to an end after an exchange of goodnight texts before I went to sleep.

But as of that day, he hadn't texted me yet.

And my heart couldn't help but feel a little sad about it.

I mean, there wasn't any harm in me texting him first. But since the first time we texted, Colton had always been the one to initiate the conversation, so I couldn't help but find it a bit nerve-wracking to be the one to send the first text.

Plus, friends text each other, right?

It wasn't as if I was doing anything that was out of the ordinary for a friend to do.

And I really wanted to send him that good luck text.

Even though Colton's game was starting at 2 p.m., they would most likely be on the field before to get ready. Sending it an hour earlier seemed like the most optimum time.

'It's just a text,' I muttered to myself.

I started typing out the message, and immediately sent it before I had a chance to back out.

> Clara:
> Good luck with the game today! 
> There's my text, now you owe me a home run.

A few minutes passed and he hadn't replied.

Was I too late? Are they already on the field?

The lecture hall started to fill up with more students, and before I knew it, the lecturer had already entered, preparing his slides on the computer.

I was about to turn my phone on airplane mode, when his reply came just in time.

> Colton:
> Hit a home run for you?

> You got it, partner.

✦

The lecture ended exactly at 3 p.m., and I had a free hour before my last class of the day. Usually, I would head to the coffee shop to get some reading, but as I stepped out of the lecture hall to its open outdoor space, I was greeted with a soft breeze and the afternoon glow of the sun.

Fortunately, my next class was close to a shaded sitting area under a tree, and it seemed the universe was on my side when there was an unoccupied table. Settling into one of the seats, I took out my planner to go through all the assignments that had a next-week deadline.

I had managed to stay on top of my work that semester—at least by then, I had. Moreover, I had already started both the assignments that were to be submitted soon, one of them was even halfway done. My initial plan was to finish both the day after, since I didn't have any classes, but I could try to get ahead with this free time.

Thinking I could get some work done while waiting for my next class, I took out my laptop and opened the Word document.

One minute.

Then, two.

And now, five minutes had passed, and I was still staring at the same document.

Adding nothing, cutting nothing, the only movement was the cursor blinking, as it waited for me to pour out my words. But it seemed my brain was already locked in on me facing this assignment the next day and nothing came to mind.

I let out a sigh. Might as well have continued my binge of *Schitt's Creek,* and just enjoy the leisure since I already had my laptop out.

But just as I was about to click on Netflix, a better idea came along.

I went to our college's website to look at the baseball team's fall exhibition games schedule. Seeing who they were battling up against that day, and then searching for the opposing team's Facebook page.

Bingo.

They had a live stream for the game.

I took out my earphones from my backpack, and plugged them into the laptop before clicking on the stream.

I wasn't sure which inning the game was in, but from what I could see, based on the colours of their jerseys, it was then the other university's turn to bat. The stream was taken from a wide-angle shot, so you could see everything, which made it hard to identify who was who. But I knew that Colton played first base, so I tried my best to seek him out, based on his position on the field.

As time passed, I immersed myself in the game as the other team managed to score a point, until, finally, a third player was struck out and we were starting a new inning.

When it was time for the next player to step up to bat, I quickly checked the time on my phone and realized that my next class was starting in fifteen minutes.

That was my cue to turn off my laptop and get ready for class.

But just as I was about to exit my browser, I heard the commentator announce, 'And up next to bat is Colton Reed.'

And there he was, stepping up to the plate.

I quickly estimated how long his turn might take, and if I could still make it to class on time after watching him bat.

'I have time,' I muttered to myself.

With my decision made, I gave my full attention to the game.

Once both players were prepared, it was time for Colton to bat.

The pitcher threw the first ball.

Colton didn't swing.

But fortunately, the ball went above the striking zone.

And that's 1-0 on the ball-to-strike count.

The ball was tossed back to the pitcher, then it was thrown the second time.

Colton swung.

He missed.

Strike one for Colton.

The ball was back into the pitcher's glove as both players prepared one more time.

Then the third throw came, and Colton swung again.

And this time, his bat managed to hit the ball.

Perfectly positioned and timed with the throw, redirecting the ball as it flew to right field. And continued to fly over the fence. It was a home run.

'Ahhhhhhhhhh!' I shrieked in excitement, as Colton jogged his way around the infield.

I wasn't aware of how loud I was being, but at the same time, I didn't care. I was filled with joy from having to witness such a moment, and no one was going to take it away from me.

When the next batter stepped up, I quickly, but gently, shut my laptop before sprinting to my last class of the day.

I was once again in a battle with the cursor on the Word document, as I was fighting my procrastination and willing my brain would churn out words.

It was Friday afternoon, and after a day of isolating myself in the apartment—moving from the desk in my room to the kitchen island, and finally ending up on the couch—I was left with one final part of the assignment. But trying to complete two assignments in a day finally caught up to me, as I began to struggle to write the conclusion.

For a second, I thought about just finishing it off later that night, and just take a break to recharge. But at the same time, I was left with one small part to complete the whole thing.

'You can do this,' I told myself.

Just as I was about to type, someone knocked at the front door.

At first, I thought I must have misheard it, and continued typing when I heard the knocks again.

I grabbed my laptop from my lap and put it on the coffee table, standing up to see who it was.

I wasn't really expecting anyone, and Nina had her keys. Usually, she would text me in case she had forgotten to bring them and asked if I was home. Or it might be Lily or Claudia popping in for a surprise visit as they like to do occasionally.

But when I finally opened the door, it was the last person I expected to see.

Chapter Fourteen

'Eliza?'

'Surprise!' my sister exclaimed with her arms open wide, anticipating a hug.

I blinked once.

And again, to make sure my tired brain wasn't imagining her there.

Once I finally got over my shock, I let out an inhumane screech and went straight into her arms. She engulfed me in a bone-crushing hug, and I hugged her back with just equal fondness.

Despite our six-year age difference, Eliza and I had always been close, with her being my go-to person whenever I needed some advice. But it wasn't until our parents' divorce that we truly became inseparable. While I was going through my emotions of anger, confusion, and betrayal towards my parents as an eight-year-old, Eliza became solace for me to vent out my rollercoaster of feelings—without me feeling scared of being judged by her or to justify myself.

When she had started applying to colleges during her senior year of high school, one of her top priorities in choosing one was how close it was to home—to me, so we wouldn't be too far apart whenever I needed her, especially when the wound from the divorce was just starting to heal. But knowing my sister as well as I did, I knew what her dream college was, and how hard she had worked ever since she made up her mind about going there and majoring in journalism. I wasn't going to stand in the way of that, especially not when I saw how happy she was when she got accepted into her dream college.

I remember the day when she was listing down the pros and cons of the few colleges she was considering—chosen from her pool of acceptance letters, all of them not too far from home.

'What are you doing?' my then eleven-year-old-self had asked, sitting down on her bed.

'Just researching colleges,' she answered.

'Why?'

'Because I'm trying to figure out where I should go, silly,' she said.

'I mean, why are you considering other colleges? I thought you got into Northwestern?' I asked, slightly confused. Northwestern was her dream college, why was she thinking of going elsewhere, if she had already gotten in?

Eliza was silent for a moment, before she said, 'I'm not going to Northwestern.'

'Why not? Going to Northwestern is all you could talk about ever since I was old enough to understand what college is,' I said, my tone exasperated.

'Well, things change.'

'Things change?' I repeated. 'What do you mean things change?'

'I just—' she broke off. 'I just changed my mind.'

I stayed quiet for a few moments, gathering up enough courage to speak my mind. 'Liar,' I finally said, calling out her bluff.

Eliza stopped whatever she was writing and turned to me. 'What did you say?'

'I said, liar,' I repeated. 'You and I both know how badly you wanted to go to Northwestern, how badly you still want to go there. You wouldn't have applied there in the first place, if you didn't want to go.'

'You don't know what you're talking about,' she said in a slightly harsh tone, her shoulders tensed. 'I was just trying to see if I could get in. I wasn't planning on actually going there.'

'Please,' I scoffed. 'Northwestern has always been the only choice, more so now that you got in. Why are you even considering other options?'

'Clara—'

I cut her off. 'I'll be fine, Eliza.' My voice was soft, finally addressing the real reason why she was listing off alternative colleges in the first place. At that moment, I could see her internal struggle: choosing whether to follow her dreams, or be the responsible older sister she had always been.

'It's too far, Clara,' she sighed, giving in to the fight. 'I can't just leave you behind like that.'

'And I can't let you say goodbye to your dream college for me.'

'You're much more important to me than my dream college,' she said, her voice just as soft. 'You know that.'

'I do. But I also know how hard you've worked to have come this far,' I told her. 'I can't let you do this, not for me.'

The room was silent as the words we had just spoken lingered in the air.

I opened my mouth and said the last part of the unspoken truth that I knew she needed to hear. 'The divorce wasn't your fault, Eliza. You shouldn't have to bear the consequences of it for my sake.'

'I had six more years with them together than you did, Clara. Me not going to Northwestern is a small price to pay,' she replied.

I rose from her bed and went over to her, wrapping my arms around her. 'I'll be fine, Eliza,' I repeated, trying to make her—and myself—believe the words.

She patted my arms as she said, 'I know you will.'

And we just stayed like that, wrapped in each other's arms, taking comfort in one another.

It still took a lot of convincing on my side to reassure Eliza that I would be fine on my own, and that she wasn't selfish for choosing Northwestern for the next chapter of her life.

I won't lie, though I was happy she ended up going to Northwestern, there were moments during her college years when I wished she was just a two-hour drive away, instead of a two-hour flight away—moments when life got a little too much. But it also gave me the space that I needed to grow on my own.

While Eliza might not be there physically, she was always one call away. Since starting her freshman year in college, Eliza had made sure to always block out time from her full schedule each week to give me a call and for us to catch up, with our conversations ranging from big announcements to small daily occurrences.

And her coming down to visit me was definitely something I would've remembered if she had told me.

'Come in!' I invited her, after we pulled away from our hug. 'What are you doing here? And how come you didn't tell me you were in town?'

'Well, it wouldn't have been a surprise if I had told you,' she said. 'And it was a last-minute thing. There's a conference here and one of the journalists who was supposed to come withdrew her place because she got sick, so I thought I would fill in.'

She then added, 'Plus, it's an all-expenses paid trip to see you for a weekend. I couldn't possibly say no to the opportunity.'

I laughed at her. Leave it to Eliza to fully optimize all the opportunities sent her way.

'Where's Nina?' she asked as she made her way to the living room, settling herself on the couch.

'Training,' I answered back while rummaging through my fridge for some beverages. 'Do you want anything to drink?'

'Water, please.'

Taking out a glass from the kitchen cabinet, I filled it with water before heading toward her.

'Here you go.' I handed her the glass and took my seat beside her.

'Thank you.' She instantly took a huge gulp, her eyes catching the open Word document on my laptop. 'What are you doing by the way?'

'Just some assignments.' I shrugged. 'I'm almost done though; I just need to do my conclusion.'

'Well, I'll tell you what. You finish this up and I'll treat you to dinner as a reward.'

I arched an eyebrow. 'You mean, you weren't planning on taking me out to dinner?'

'Of course I was,' she said, putting down her glass on the coffee table. 'But at least this way, you're motivated to finish the assignment and not procrastinate.'

'Oh, come on,' I whined. 'I only have one part left; I can finish it tonight.'

'Nope,' she said, shaking her head. 'We're not leaving until you finish.'

'Ugh, fine,' I groaned before picking up my laptop and started getting to work. My brain rejuvenated with the promise of good food as the reward.

As I was finishing up the last paragraph, I heard another knock on the door. I was about to get up and see who it was when Eliza stopped me.

'I'll get it,' she declared, standing up to greet whoever was at the door.

Letting Eliza handle the distraction, I continued my work, my attention laser-focused on finishing this up, as I was getting closer to the end.

I was typing out the last line when I heard Eliza call out to me. 'Clara! There's someone here to see you.'

I wrote out the last word and the final full stop, and saved the document. Standing up from the couch, I headed to the front door to see who it could possibly be.

My eyes widened in surprise when I saw who it was.

It was Colton.

'Colton,' I exclaimed. 'What are you doing here?'

From my peripheral vision, I could see Eliza's eyes darting between Colton and me. 'I'll let you two talk,' she told us. When she passed me, she whispered, 'He's cute.'

I quickly shushed her, scared that Colton might've picked up on what she said.

Eliza just let out a small laugh. My gaze followed her as she went back to her spot on the couch, leaving me and Colton alone at the door. Once I was sure she was out of ear range, I let out a small exhale before turning to face the unexpected guest at the door.

Colton greeted me with a beautiful smile and butterflies immediately started erupting in my stomach.

I missed that smile.

'Hey, partner,' he said.

I gave him a big smile of my own in return. 'Hey, partner.'

I couldn't help but start fidgeting, not really knowing where I should put my hands.

After spending so much time with Colton, I had gotten pretty comfortable around him. But the last time we had seen each other was for the not-date previous Saturday, and this was the first time we were seeing one another since. I was just fully unprepared for his unexpected arrival—in my apartment of all places.

I tried coming up with something to say, when it hit me that he might have just gotten back in town from the away game. 'Did you just arrive back in town?'

'Yeah,' he nodded. 'Just a little over an hour ago.'

'Oh! And congratulations on winning the game by the way,' I continued, as I remembered them winning against the opposing team. 'I know I already texted you, but I thought I would say it in person.'

When I had finished my class the day before, the first thing I did was look up the score of the game. Seeing that they had won, I immediately sent a text to Colton congratulating him. His reply came only a moment later, with him telling me they had just finished the game, and were making plans to celebrate the win while they were still in a different town for another night.

That day's conversation had been initiated by Colton, with a little good-morning text. But with me trying to finish up my assignments to free up my weekend, I had told him I wouldn't be able to reply to his texts as much. The last one that I had read from him was him telling me they were on their way back. I hadn't looked at my phone since then, so I wasn't sure if he had texted me again.

'Thanks,' he replied shyly, before playfully adding, 'And just to let you know, I *did* hit a home run.'

I let out a small laugh. 'Yeah, I know.'

At that, a questioning look covered his face. His eyebrows furrowing at my words.

Then, it was my turn to be shy. 'I had a free hour, and I googled the team you guys were competing against to see if they had a live stream of the game. And they did, so I thought I would tune in while I waited for my next class,' I explained. 'And you just so happened to hit that home run during the time I was watching.'

Colton stayed quiet upon hearing my admission, his mind seemingly caught elsewhere.

'Colton?' I gently prompted, calling him back to me.

'You watched the game,' he murmured.

I gave him a nod. 'I did.'

'And you saw me hit a home run.'

'Yeah.'

A tender look came across Colton's features, his tone soft as he asked, 'Sounds like it was fated, don't you think?'

I smiled at him. 'Who knows? Maybe it was.' I shrugged, my voice teasing when I added, 'I mean that home run *was* for me, right?'

A small but genuine smile made its way to his face. 'Yeah, it was.'

'Anyway,' I said, snapping out of the trance Colton's attention seemed to bring me to. 'What are you doing here?' Noticing that he had both his hands behind him, I arched an eyebrow at him, teasingly. 'And what are you hiding back there?'

He gave me a massive grin in return as he brought his left arm to the front, his hand grasping the handle of a bag. He held it up to me, the look of excitement on his face urging me to take it from him.

I gave him a suspicious look before grabbing the handle of the bag and sneaking a peek to see what was inside.

It was bubble tea.

Not one, but two of them.

'What is this for?' I asked, slightly confused.

'Well, I did promise you that you'll get your bubble tea this week,' he answered. 'And this is me delivering on my promise.'

'But why are there two of them?'

'You didn't think I would get one for you without getting one for myself, did you?' he said, a teasing tone accompanying his words. 'And like I said, bubble tea is our thing, so the other one is for me. But if I had known your sister was here, I would've gotten an extra one, so your sister can have mine.'

I snapped my eyes back to him. 'Colton, you don't—'

'It's fine, really,' he reassured me.

'Thank you,' I said with a smile on my face. 'But you really didn't have to do this.'

'That's not all.' He stopped me, as he brought his other arm forward, revealing his other surprise. 'I also got you these.'

Gripped in his hand was a bunch of flowers, enveloped with a cellophane wrap and strapped together by the stems with a rubber band.

Flowers.

Colton got me flowers.

And they weren't just any flowers.

They were pink flowers.

In not just one kind but a variety of them, different shades of pink from different types of flowers, all wrapped together. 'Flowers,' I breathed out, stunned by the gesture. 'You got me flowers.' My hand reached out to receive the offered gift.

'I know that you usually get them after our weekly ASL practice. Since we didn't get to do that this week, I thought I would get them for you,' he explained, his voice getting a little quieter towards the end. 'I figured you might have gotten them today instead. But even if you have, these are still yours.'

I continued admiring the beauty I was holding in my hand, before glancing up at Colton, my lips tilted up when I realized the tips of his ears were a light shade of red.

'Well, you're in luck because I completely forgot to get them,' I told him, trying to ease away his nervousness. But it was true, it had completely slipped out of my mind to get flowers this week.

'They're beautiful, Colton. Thank you,' I then added, my voice faint. I tried to think of more things to say. 'Thank you' just didn't seem enough to convey my appreciation for how thoughtful these two gifts were.

But it seemed like I didn't need to. The soft look on Colton's face told me he knew exactly what I couldn't voice out. 'You're welcome,' he replied, his low tone matching mine.

We just stood there for a moment, looking like two fools who were smiling at one another. I snapped out of my daze when I realized I hadn't even invited him into the apartment. 'Crap. I didn't even ask you to come in.'

'It's okay. I just came by to quickly drop those off,' he quickly reassured me, gesturing to the two gifts he had just given me. 'I was just about to get going actually. I'm hanging out with the baseball team tonight.'

'Oh, right,' I said, trying my best to disguise the disappointment in my voice.

But of course, Colton caught it. The spark of joy radiating from him diminishing by the second.

I didn't want to make him feel guilty over this small thing, he shouldn't be. I could sense that he was starting to. Before he could linger in that feeling any longer, I quickly added, 'Have fun with the team tonight. Guess I'll see you next Wednesday in class?'

With the promise of seeing each other again, his smile came back. 'Next Wednesday it is.'

I thanked him one more time and waited for him to walk down the corridor to the elevator. He waved me goodbye as he went into the elevator hall. Once I was sure he was out of sight, I closed the front door and stepped into the kitchen, my hands bringing up the flowers to my nose as I breathed in its floral scent.

I was so stuck in my own little bubble that I completely forgot Eliza was there.

'So, who was that?' she asked, bringing my attention to her.

'Just a friend,' I answered, trying my best to avoid eye contact with her. I placed down the flowers and the bag of bubble tea on the kitchen island, while I opened the fridge, clearing up some space to put the two new drinks I just received.

'A friend who brings you flowers,' she pointed out, eyeing the abundance of pink petals. 'And is this bubble tea?'

Once I was sure I cleared up enough space for the drinks, I took both bubble teas from the bag and put them inside the fridge. 'Yeah. One is for you by the way. He got one for himself, but he wanted you to have it instead,' I explained.

'Well, isn't that sweet of him?' she asked. 'But why is he bringing you bubble tea and flowers?'

'It's a long story,' I told her, wanting to steer away from having to talk about Colton.

Despite our weekly phone calls, I was yet to bring up Colton in any of our conversations. I pretty much told Eliza everything, even the most mundane things. But, for some reason, I had refrained myself from talking about him, and I wasn't sure why. I definitely wasn't planning on telling her any time soon, but it seemed that plan had gone off the rails the second Eliza opened the front door with Colton on the other side.

'Well, good thing we're heading to dinner, and you can tell me all about it,' she proclaimed. Her tone told me I wasn't getting away that easily.

I let out a sigh, already knowing I was fighting a losing battle. 'Fine. Give me thirty minutes to get ready.'

Chapter Fifteen

Eliza sat across from me in the restaurant—the one she had fallen in love with, when she came to visit me last semester. Our table was seated in the corner, allowing us a bit of privacy over the tables that were scattered all around.

I texted Nina before we left the apartment and invited her to join us when she finished her training. Her reply came ten minutes later, saying that the track team was heading to dinner, and she was just about to ask me if I wanted to join them. We ended the conversation by saying that we'd see each other back in the apartment.

After a quick peruse of the menu, we ordered our food, and the waitress left us.

And the moment I dreaded most has finally arrived.

Eliza took a sip of her water and placed her glass back on the table before settling her gaze on me. 'Start talking.'

I let out a sigh. *Might as well just get this over with.* 'His name is Colton and he's my partner for the ASL class I'm taking this semester.'

'And why is he bringing you bubble tea and flowers?' she asked, arching her brow.

'We usually practice ASL after the class at the bubble tea shop nearby,' I answered. 'And afterward, we head over to the shop across the street, so I could get flowers for the apartment. But since he had an away game this week, we didn't get to practice. So, this was his way of making up for it, I guess.' I shrugged. Picking up my own glass, I took a sip of the iced tea I ordered.

'An away game?' I heard Eliza ask.

'He's on the baseball team,' I clarified.

'Is he now?' Eliza exclaimed, clearly enjoying this. Especially when she knows all about my streak of crushes on school athletes. 'Is he any good?'

I gave her a sour look. 'How would I know? I don't watch all of their games,' I said, trying to deflect her questions.

'But I thought you attended all of the home games.' Eliza tilted her head, her voice all innocent. I shot a glare her way, knowing she was anything but innocent especially when she was interrogating me.

'Ugh, fine. Yes, he's a really good baseball player,' I admitted. Considering he had hit a home run at almost all the games I had attended, I would say that was an accurate description of him.

'Good to know,' Eliza said, a knowing smirk plastered on her face. 'So, what's been going on between you two?'

'Nothing,' I stated, point blank. 'We're just friends.'

Eliza gave me an amused look. 'Friends don't stop by your apartment just to drop off bubble tea and flowers.'

'Good friends do?' I said, phrasing it more like a question than a statement.

Eliza just arched a brow at me, then took another sip of her water. 'Speaking of the baseball team, what happened to your other crush who was also on the team?'

Eliza might be the most ambitious person I knew, but deep down, she was also a hopeless romantic just like me.

And that's when I realized why I hadn't told her about Colton.

After seeing that first game during my freshman year, I remembered our phone conversation that week, when I had told her about Colton: how I might have started developing a crush on him that day, and how it just continued growing bigger and bigger with each game I went to. But I was always cautious of never giving out his name, only referring to him as 'my crush', without ever putting a name or a face to it. This was just so I could keep the fantasy of crushing on the baseball player, and the happily-ever-after of it all alive, whenever I talked to her.

But fantasy was easy to keep, when you're separated by a whole campus, not when it showed up at your front door with bubble tea and flowers.

My inner turmoil must have brewed longer than I thought, when I heard Eliza let out a massive gasp as she pieced out the puzzle herself.

'It's him, isn't it?' she exclaimed. 'Your baseball player crush is Colton.'

Sighing, I nodded. No use in trying to hide it any more. 'Yes, it's Colton,' I confirmed.

'Well, aren't you a lucky gal,' Eliza laughed. 'I should be taking notes from you on how to get guys.'

'Get guys?' I murmured before speaking up, 'You're getting ahead of yourself here. We're *just* friends, Eliza. That's all we are and that's all we will ever be.'

'You seem pretty confident about that,' Eliza said, tilting her head. 'Did he say anything about only staying friends?'

'I mean,' I trailed off. 'Technically, he didn't. But how do you move forward to being more than friends, when he hasn't asked me out yet?'

'Fair enough.' Eliza nodded.

Our food arrived a few moments later, and we ate silently through the first few bites, savouring our meal. Eliza offered her plate for me to taste her food, and I did the same with mine.

I thought the whole Colton conversation had come to an end, but I realized I was completely mistaken, when Eliza asked me her next question. 'So, what you're saying is, the only thing that's holding you back from being more than friends with Colton is that he hasn't asked you yet.'

'Pretty much,' I shrugged.

'Okay. But what if he does ask you out?'

'Doesn't matter, since he didn't,' I quickly answered.

'Humour me then. Think of it as a hypothetical situation.'

Her words made me pause. I already knew what my answer would be. But knowing Eliza, a simple no wouldn't suffice. And that meant telling her about my stupid beliefs over something so childish.

Before I could think it through, the words were already out of my mouth. 'I would probably say no,' I confessed.

Eliza looked taken aback by my answer, surprise evident on her face. 'How come? If you like Colton and he asked you out, why wouldn't you say yes?'

'Colton and I just can't happen, Eliza,' I admitted. 'It's just better off this way.' I directed my eyes to the food in front of me, trying my best to ignore her heavy gaze.

'What is it you're not telling me, Clara?' I heard Eliza ask, her voice soft.

I let her words hang in the air, as I tried to muster up the courage to talk about the curse and my stupid notion of it.

'Did you ever notice a similarity between the story of how Mom and Dad got together with how you and Nathan got together?' I started, letting my eyes finally meet hers.

Her eyebrows furrowed at my question, a look of confusion on her features. 'And what exactly is the similarity?'

'It started when you were paired up for something. Mom and Dad were partners for that class assignment back when they were in high school, while you and Nathan were partners for that work assignment.'

'Okay,' Eliza trailed off. 'Well, that's just a coincidence.'

'But that's not where the similarities end,' I continued. 'Another thing I noticed was how both of your relationships followed the whole cliché love interest story. You know, how in every romance story, the main character always brushes off the idea of ever being with the cliché love interest, because they're convinced it's never gonna happen,' I said, putting up air quotes for the last three words.

Eliza raised her eyebrow in amusement at me. 'I see where you're getting at. So, you're saying Dad was the cliché love interest because he was the bad boy?'

'And Nathan was your work rival, which is another type of cliché love interest,' I continued.

'Fair point,' Eliza said. 'And Colton fits into this whole category because he's a college athlete?'

'Star athlete,' I corrected her. 'He's one of the best players on the baseball team.'

'And now you're also partners for a class.' Eliza slowly nodded, seeming to understand where I was going.

'Exactly.'

'But why do these similarities have to do with you saying no to Colton asking you out on a date?' Eliza then asked.

'You're going to think I'm ridiculous.'

'I will never think that,' she answered truthfully.

I let out a tired sigh. What's one more person to share my childish beliefs with? 'I think our family is cursed, Eliza.'

Her head jolted slightly at my words. 'Cursed?'

'See,' I exclaimed. 'I know you'd think I'm being ridiculous.'

'No, you just took me by surprise, that's all,' she quickly reassured me. 'And what is the curse exactly?'

'Cliché love interests are only meant for stories, that's why people can't stop writing them, and why we can't stop reading them. But that's all there is to it. They only sound good in fiction, stories of make-believe. But when it comes to real life, it just doesn't last. At least for our family, it doesn't.' I shrugged.

'Oh, Clara,' Eliza said. 'You can't possibly believe that.'

'How can I not, when I saw it happen in front of me?' I said. 'First with our parents' divorce, then with you and Nathan calling off the engagement three months later. It's all there, Eliza—the same pattern. I think I have enough reasons to be justified in believing this'. I quickly directed my eyes back to my plate, trying my best to avoid Eliza's gaze on me.

'Clara.' I heard her say, her tone pitiful.

'I know you're thinking about how ridiculous I'm being. Hearing all of this.'

'I didn't say that,' Eliza said. 'Nor do I think that.'

Her soft voice made me brave enough to meet her eyes. And all I could see was understanding, no judgment whatsoever.

'I just feel so stupid saying all this out loud,' I admitted. 'It's just that I used to think Mom and Dad's love story was the best of all time. How beautiful it was for having started with a cliché love interest, then actually living in their "happily-ever-after" with us by their side. I thought it was always going to be the four of us, together. I never knew there would be an end to happily-ever-after.'

I continued. 'And when it did end, it just shattered this illusion I had of love stories with a cliché love interest and how maybe there wasn't such a thing as a "happily ever after" after all. But then you and Nathan came along, a story straight out of any workplace romance I had read. Seeing you so happy made me believe that maybe there was something to the romance of it all,' I told her.

Once I realized the weight of my words, I quickly added, 'I don't want to make it seem like I'm pinning this on you.'

Eliza simply shook her head. 'Not at all. Go on.'

'I looked up to your relationship a lot. I remember how shocked I was the first time you brought Nathan home; I couldn't believe there was actually someone out there who had managed to capture the heart of *the Elizabeth.*'

Eliza let out a small laugh.

'And I was so happy for you, because you deserve all the happiness the world has to offer. I was glad that the person who would be giving that to you was Nathan. The day you called to tell me that he proposed to you was when I had started to believe that maybe there was something to falling in love after all—that maybe there was a thing such as a "happily ever after".'

'But we called off the engagement,' Eliza continued for me instead.

'You guys called off the engagement,' I repeated. 'And you were a wreck, Eliza.'

Another similarity between my parents' and Eliza's relationship with Nathan was that they had both ended mutually, but at two very different speeds. While my parents' divorce was caused by years of build-up, Eliza and Nathan's cancellation of engagement was sudden and abrupt. But that didn't mean the hurt wasn't there. I remember during the early days, once the divorce was finalized, how sadness lingered in the house, an awkward tension between my parents when we had our family dinner together.

When Eliza's engagement was called off, she returned home for two weeks. Within those days, I remembered passing by her room and hearing her soft sobs through the door. My hand would reach out to the doorknob before I pulled it back, figuring she wanted to be by herself.

While Eliza did end up moving to New York City, she was alone.

'And I just remembered thinking, "What's the point of falling in love when it won't last?"' I confessed. 'When it just ends in pain and heartbreak?'

Eliza just gave me a small smile. 'There really isn't one.'

'What?' I said, confused by her answer.

'I think the point of falling in love is to fall in love. It's this strange but beautiful thing we want to experience, a natural feeling. It's also this strange occurrence that we can't help but search for, because that's just how we are,' Eliza explained. 'Well, of course, there's more to it once you get deeper into the relationship. But in the early days? It's getting to know someone more each passing day, and just letting the feeling come to you.'

The sounds in the restaurant surrounded us as Eliza's words lingered. We had never really talked about love and relationships—at least not in depth. Of course, I would call her up with details of the dates I had, and she would do the same when she and Nathan started dating. But after they called off the engagement, I hadn't brought up anything related to dating, which might also explain my gatekeeping of Colton—the real Colton—from her.

To keep it as a fantasy for both her and me.

'Can I ask you a question, though?' I asked instead. 'About Nathan?'

'Sure.'

I hesitated for a moment, contemplating whether I should ask her this. Eventually, I decided to just let it out. 'Would you still have gone out with Nathan when he first asked you out, even if you knew how the story would end?'

Eliza got quiet, taking her time to ponder over my questions. 'If you were to ask me when we first broke off the engagement, I would have said no. I don't think I would've gone out with him if I had known. I mean, getting over him was the hardest thing I ever had to do,' she confessed. 'But now, my answer would be yes. I would still have gone out with him. And I would still have wanted to live through everything we did, even though I knew the end was nearer than I hoped it would be. I know relationships end for a multitude of different reasons, and sometimes, people might even wonder why they started it in the first place—that they'd be better off not having been in it before it got to a certain point. But I got lucky with Nathan, and I truly believe what we had was special. It was something I will always cherish, even if we're not talking any more. I will forever feel grateful to have had him in my life.'

'I'm glad to hear that,' I said, truthfully.

'At the same time, I didn't know it was going to end; I thought we were forever. We were going to get married after all,' Eliza continued, her voice turned sombre now. 'But that's the thing about being in a relationship with someone, you know? When you start to fall in love with them, you don't know when it will end. That's why it's called falling—not fall, fell, or fallen—because it's a continuous thing. Though, keep in mind my only relationship ended in a failed engagement, so take it for what you will,' Eliza added the last part teasingly.

I let out a light laugh, glad that the tension from the whole conversation was starting to ease up.

'But if there is one thing I've learned about falling in love,' Eliza then said, 'is that it's a choice. While we might not be able to control our feelings, I do believe we get a say in who we fall in love with. And most of the time, the choice isn't really anything momentous. Sometimes it's as small as saying yes to going on a date with someone. Though in order to start falling, you first have to be brave enough to take the leap on your own,' she said.

'So, my advice is to find someone who's worth taking the leap for,' Eliza concluded.

I let her words sink into me, slowly letting them imprint into my mind. 'But how would you know when to take that leap?'

'Well. That's up for you to decide.' she shrugged. 'There's no rush in figuring it out. And you don't always have to justify your emotions, you know?' I tilted my head up to her, meeting her eyes.

'It's okay to let yourself have feelings. We're humans, and emotions are what make us real,' Elizabeth continued. 'I still remember the day when Mom and Dad told us they were divorcing, while I had already started to shed some tears, you were just sitting there, trying to understand all the emotions you were feeling. You kept it to yourself for so long. And it wasn't until I saw you sitting on the couch one day, looking through our family album, that you finally decided to let the emotions out.'

I remembered that day like the back of my hand. I hadn't wanted to bother anyone about me, when they all had their own set of problems to deal with—the after-effects of the divorce. Mom and Dad had already started to live separately at the time, so we didn't get to see them together any more, the idea of a picture perfect family remained only a memory.

I wasn't sure what had come over me that day, but my mind was on a reminiscent mode as I flipped through our old photos. Everything I had concealed up to that point just burst out of me like a broken dam—the tears, the screams, along with every pent-up emotion.

I hadn't noticed that Eliza was watching me, until I felt her arms wrapped around me. I tried stopping the tears, but she just kept holding me tighter, a silent message to just let it all out: all the sadness, the anger, every single emotion I had kept to myself.

The next few months—years even—were spent not only navigating the physical aspect of the divorce, but also its emotional aspect, understanding why my parents' marriage ended in that way, while also acknowledging how I felt about it, instead of pushing it aside.

And every time I felt confused on having certain emotions, Eliza had always been there to reassure me that it was okay, that vulnerability wasn't a weakness, but a strength.

I did end up rebuilding my relationship with both of my parents, and even opened up to them on how I felt about the whole situation and how it had affected me emotionally. The first step of it all was to have enough courage to let myself be vulnerable to people.

It's still something I struggle with even today, but I've been blessed to be surrounded by people who were patient enough with me through it all.

And it's all because of the person sitting across from me.

'Hard to believe that it was more than a decade ago,' I told her.

Our conversation took a pause when the waitress came back to our table at that moment, asking us if we wanted desserts. In between bites of the cake we ordered, Eliza said to me, 'But I do have another question though.'

'What is it?'

'If I'm understanding correctly, the thing that's holding you back from going out with Colton is the whole Colton being a cliché love interest and the curse thing,' Eliza stated.

I gave her a nod, taking another spoonful of cake.

'So, what if that wasn't a factor? What if Colton wasn't the star athlete, would you go out with him?'

There it was.

The million-dollar question.

The question I had avoided each time my mind started to wonder about the curse and the what-ifs.

I stayed quiet as I contemplated her question. All this time, my reasoning on why I couldn't be with Colton was because of the cliché of him being a star college baseball player. Since that was unchangeable—at least in the foreseeable future—I had never entertained the possibility of a situation where it didn't play a role.

'I don't know,' I said, shocking myself with the answer, as I admitted it to myself for the first time.

I always thought my immediate answer would be yes, that the only reason why Colton and I couldn't be together was because of the curse. I never thought there would be something else that was holding me back from fully saying yes, and I couldn't help but wonder what it was.

But based on the look on Eliza's face and the familiar smile on her lips, it looked like she knew the reasoning behind my confusion. 'It seems like the curse might not be the only thing holding you back then.'

'Even if it wasn't, there's no point in thinking about it, when the reality is he's still the star baseball player,' I pointed out.

'Okay, okay,' Eliza said, her voice teasing as she put her hands up in mock surrender.

I pinched my eyebrows at her. 'What's with that look on your face?'

'What look?' she deflected, trying to look all casual.

'That one,' I replied, pointing my spoon in her direction. 'You have this look on your face. Do you know something I don't?'

'Maybe.' She shrugged.

'Well, tell me.'

'Nope,' Eliza shook her head. 'You need to figure this out on your own.'

I groaned. 'I hate it when you do that.'

'I know. But you still love me.'

'Unfortunately.'

'And for what it's worth. I really like Colton.'

I snorted at her statement, but failed to keep the smile away from my lips. 'You're just saying that because he gave you his bubble tea.'

'Maybe,' she shrugged. 'But you can't prove it.'

I just laughed at her, grateful to have her company that night and finally letting her know what had been on my mind regarding this whole thing with Colton. While I was glad I could tell Nina about it, telling Eliza—the person I could fully confide in—was something I didn't know I had been wanting to do. I also couldn't help but think that her unexpected visit may have been a blessing in disguise after all.

'I'm glad you're here,' I told her once she scooped up the last bit of cake left.

She gave me a smile—a familiar smile that assured me she understood what I truly meant by those four words. 'Me too.'

Chapter Sixteen

The weekend was shaping up to be great.

Eliza stayed over just long enough, until Nina got home on Friday night, and promised to meet up with us again the next day, since her flight back to New York City was early on Sunday.

Saturday was spent hanging out with the girls as we shopped, got manicures, and simply caught up with each other. We finally met up with Eliza for dinner, before heading back to our apartment and watched *Bridget Jones's Diary*, wine glasses filled with rosé in our hands—thanks to Eliza—as we fawned over Mark Darcy. We were up until early dawn, before finally succumbing to our battle against sleep.

We slept in through Sunday. The next morning, I was greeted by the sweet aroma of coffee and pancakes, along with the voice of Taylor Swift, as Lily and Claudia busied themselves in the kitchen making breakfast—or brunch, considering it was almost 11 a.m.

There seemed to be an unsaid rule to our sleepovers: whoever was sleeping over must make breakfast the next day. I would've been fine helping them, but they completely blocked me from trying to do so the first time they stayed the night. So, I just took my seat at the kitchen island, sipping my coffee while the duo prepared our meals.

Nina woke up just in time as Lily scooped up the last batch of pancakes. We switched locations to the living room instead, turning the TV to a random show on low volume. That was how we spent the next hour: indulging in our food, occasionally chiming in to make random remarks, and conversation starters.

Our time together officially came to an end when Lily and Claudia packed up their things, hugged us goodbyes, as they brought their things out of the door, and headed back to their own apartment.

With the amount of time spent socializing that weekend, I knew I needed to recharge my social battery. Thankfully, Nina was catching up with her homework in her room, leaving the living room all to myself.

I was finally done with my reread of *You Deserve Each Other* and was pondering on which book I should read next. I eventually decided on *Bringing Down the Duke* by Evie Dunmore. There's nothing better to read on a lovely Sunday afternoon than a story about a duke falling in love with a commoner, and doing whatever it takes to have her.

Fifty pages into the book, I decided to take a break, and headed to the kitchen to get some water. When I retook my spot on the couch, I picked up my phone to see if there were any new notifications. It was only when I saw the text that I realized how much I was hoping to see it.

I quickly clicked on the message sent from Colton.

Colton:
Guess who I met today.

An attachment followed the text of a picture of a boy—seemingly eleven or twelve years old, with a huge grin on his face as he fiercely hugged Colton who wore an identical grin on his own.

Colton:
IT'S PHILLIP!

It took me a few seconds to recall someone named Phillip, until I finally remembered who he was.

Clara:
PHILLIP?
AS IN THE PHILLIP WHO MADE YOU WANT TO TAKE
ASL CLASS?

I didn't know if he was still at the event, so I wasn't expecting a quick reply. But to my surprise, his reply was immediate.

Colton:
The one and only.

Clara:
How did it go?
Did you sign with him?

Colton:
I did!

Our conversation only lasted for a few sentences
though, before I asked for a notebook for us to continue
communicating like we did last time.

But the smile on his face when I signed him 'what's your
name?' and asked him if he remembered me, I don't think I'll
ever forget it.

Clara:
Awwwwwww.
Well, I'm glad to hear ASL class is paying off.

Colton:
It sure is.
I'm just glad I managed to meet Phillip again today.

Clara:
So, you can impress him with your beginner ASL skills?

Colton:
Rude.
But no, there's another reason why I was happy to see
him today.

Clara:
And that would be?

Colton:
As cheesy as it sounds, I wanted to thank him in person. For
making me want to take the ASL class.

I don't think I would have considered the class if it wasn't
for him.

And then I wouldn't have met you or been partners with you.

Although I can do without the whole bubble tea
obsession thing.

But I'll let it slide.

I let out a laugh at his last text.

Clara:
Says the guy who is equally as obsessed with it.

Colton:
Well, you got me.
What are you up to?

Clara:
Nothing much. I just started a new romance book.

Colton:
How is it so far? Is it any good?

Clara:
I'm only fifty pages in, but it seems very promising.

Colton:
Well, let me know what you think about it in the end.

I miss hearing you talk about the books you're reading.

I could already start to feel the blood rushing to
my cheeks.

Colton:
And who knows? If this becomes your new favourite book,
then I'll have to read this one as well.

His text made me pause for a moment.

As well?

Does this mean he actually read the last book I told
him about?

Don't be ridiculous, I thought to myself. *He's just trying to
make conversation; it probably doesn't mean anything anyway.*

Clara:
I'll make sure to let you know my thoughts once I'm finished.
Anyway, what about you?
What are you up to?

Colton:
I am currently grocery shopping.
Spending some quality time with the roommate.

The text was followed up by a selfie of a grinning
Colton, joined by a confused Miles in the background,
holding up two different brands of sauce in each hand.
It seemed like he was struggling to pick out which one
to get.

I let out a small chuckle at the photo, knowing I was
going to show it to Nina later.

Clara:
Aren't you two roommates goals?
I'll leave you to it then.
I'll see you on Wednesday then, partner?

Colton:
See you on Wednesday, partner.

As I put my phone down and picked up my book once again, I couldn't help but recall the events of that weekend, and smile at everything that had happened: from my sister coming to town, Colton showing up unexpectedly at my door with bubble tea and flowers, spending time with my best friends, and my latest text conversation with Colton.

'This really was a great weekend,' I muttered to myself, verbalizing my thoughts to tattoo this beautiful weekend into my memory, before thrusting myself back into the world of historical London in the book I was reading.

I was sitting cross-legged on the grass, while Colton leaned against the tree trunk with his legs stretched out in front of him, the shade from the tree protecting us against the afternoon sun.

We were sitting at 'the spot', as I liked to call it. Two bubble teas sat a bit crookedly—courtesy of the uneven ground—in the space between us.

I had an assignment due on Friday and I was only almost halfway through it. I had asked Nina the day before if she was going home straight away after her training, since I was planning to hustle my way through the assignment in the library once my practice session with Colton was over. She had told me she was, and we promised to meet up in the conjoint parking lot of the baseball stadium and the track field at 7 p.m.

That also gave me and Colton the opportunity to practice at 'the spot'. I suggested the idea to Colton, and he immediately agreed to it, and that's how we ended up here once again.

My notes from our ASL class that day sat across my lap as I tried to recall all that we had learned in the past two weeks. I tried my best to revise last week on my own, since Colton was out of town, but there was only so much you could do by yourself when it came to ASL.

The leaves started falling one by one in different shades of brown as the trees welcomed the fall season. The air was starting to get a little chilly, and I seemed to have underestimated the weather with my clothing. I gave a slight shiver, when a gentle breeze passed by.

While going through my notes, Colton's eyes were closed as if he was in a deep slumber. I glanced up at him, seeing his face void of any stress—just calmness and serenity. Seeing him like that brought me back to the first time we came there together, the first time I had ever seen him that relaxed, and how much I wanted to capture this version of him.

For a moment I thought about taking a photo of him, something for myself once we say our inevitable goodbye at the end of the semester. However, I felt I was intruding by doing so.

Nonetheless, it seemed that unwanted thought was slowly winning, and before I could stop myself, I quickly took out my phone, hoping to sneak some shots in.

But the scandalous act I was attempting was short-lived, as the rebellious sound of the shutter button gave me away.

I immediately froze in place.

I must have accidentally turned the sound button on, I cursed to myself.

Thinking I could still save myself from the embarrassment, I quickly put my phone down and turned off the sound setting. But it seemed I was a tad bit too late, when Colton peeled one of his eyes open, a teasing glint shining in it, accompanied by an equally teasing smile that was slowly appearing on his face.

'Trying to sneakily take my picture, partner?' he teased, both of his eyes closed once again but his smile was still there.

'No,' I said without missing a beat, clearly lying.

His smile grew into a grin. 'That sounded 100 per cent believable.'

'Because it is 100 per cent the truth.' I knew he was trying to provoke me, but I wasn't going to let him win that easily.

'Whatever you say, partner. At least now you have something to look at when we're not together,' shrugging as he added, 'you know, in case you miss me.'

'You seem very confident in that. How are you so sure I'm gonna miss you?' I asked him, my voice teasing.

'I won't,' he said, finally opening both of his eyes, his gaze searching before it locked in on mine. 'But I hope you do, because I know I'd miss you.'

I immediately felt my cheeks flush at his words, with warmth spreading through my whole body. Cold weather be damned, when there was Colton making me blush in an instant.

I broke our gaze and looked back to my notes. 'Anyway, are you done with your nap? I think it's time we get started.'

'I know you're just mocking me about taking a nap, but if I were to lie elsewhere on campus, it would most likely be here,' he explained.

'You really like it here, don't you? This spot I mean.'

'I guess you could say that,' he shrugged. 'I don't know what it is, but I just feel a lot calmer whenever I'm here.'

'Do you ever come here before games?' I remembered Colton telling me he would occasionally come by, but he never really specified when.

'Sometimes, mostly when we're up against another competitive college team.'

'Like the team you're competing against next week?' I asked. Their last off-season game was happening next Saturday, right there on campus. The team might have won the last Men's College World Series, but they hadn't gotten that far without a few near misses, winning by only a point against the other team. The team they were battling against next week was one of those others.

He gave me a nod. 'I know it's only an exhibition game, but I want to do well.'

'You will,' I said, giving him a genuine smile.

'Thanks,' his voice was a little shaky from his honest admission. 'Are you coming to the game?'

I thought of teasing him about my potential absence, but the vulnerability in his voice quickly dissolved that idea.

Instead, I thought about something else to liven up the mood. 'Yes, I am. I heard part of being a good partner is attending the other partner's home games.'

'Really? How come I never heard of that before?'

'It's an exclusive rule. It only applies when your partner is a star athlete.'

Colton's laugh burst out of him, and it was so contagious that I started joining along.

'Okay, enough chit-chat. Time to get to work,' I said.

We were in the questions phase of our ASL class, meaning it was starting to get a little difficult. The things about asking questions in ASL are the movements of your eyebrows, and how different the structure of the sentence is, compared to the English language.

For example, for wh- questions, instead of signing them as the first word of the sentence, they are signed at the end, and you have to make sure your eyebrows are down when you ask the question. As a beginner, it takes some time to understand how to sign correctly as you rearrange the words from English to ASL.

We started with simple questions, such as 'what is your name?', 'where are you from?', and 'where do you live?', before moving on to yes or no questions.

When it comes to yes or no questions in ASL, you don't have to sign the first part of the question, such as 'are you' or 'do you'. Instead, you just have to make sure your eyebrows are up in order to signify that you're asking a question, then continue signing exactly as you would, when making the usual sentence structure in ASL.

We slowly worked our way down the list from 'do you like ice cream?', 'are you a student?', and 'is it cold here?'. We each took turns signing the questions, while the other tried to guess what was being signed.

It was Colton's turn to sign, and it seemed my brain was starting to get overloaded.

'Wait, can you do that again?' I requested.

He signed it once more, but I couldn't seem to remember one of the words from the question he was asking.

'What's this?' I asked him, repeating the hand motion of the word that I couldn't quite recall.

'It's ASL for date,' he said, signing it again. 'Date as in a romantic date.'

'Oh,' I nodded. 'Can you sign the question again?'

He signed the question one more time, and after his third attempt, I finally understood the question.

'Do you want to go on a date with me?' I guessed.

'You got it,' he said with a fond smile on his face.

I quickly flipped through my notes to see if I had written it down somewhere, when Colton asked me another question.

'So do you?'

'Do I what?' I asked distractedly.

'Do you want to go on a date with me?'

My hand halted its movement as my entire body froze.

He's not asking what I think he is, right?

'What?' I asked him again, silently praying I heard him wrong.

But it seemed my prayers were left unanswered.

He asked the question once again, only this time in ASL. Then, once more vocally to give me full clarity. 'Do you want to go on a date with me?'

I hadn't heard him wrong.

He was actually asking if I wanted to go on a date with him.

But instead of answering him, I asked him another question. 'Why?'

Colton's eyes widened slightly in surprise, with confusion written on his face at my question. 'Because I like you. And I want to take you out on a date.'

And there they were.

The three cursed words.

My worst fear, coming to life.

The expression on my face must have been alarming, when Colton's face started to look concerned. 'Are you okay?'

'Yeah, I'm fine.' I quickly looked down at my notes, trying my best to not meet his eyes. A part of me was hoping that he would drop the question. But since he had already asked me numerous times, the best thing I could do was give him an answer.

'I can't,' I finally replied, my voice much smaller than it was a moment ago.

'I mean, we don't have to do it this week, if you're not free,' Colton answered instead. 'I have a game next Saturday, but Sunday should—'

'Colton,' I cut him off, my voice louder and clearer this time, looking him in the eyes. 'I can't.'

His eyebrows narrowed in confusion as my words sink in. 'I don't understand.'

'I can't go on a date with you, Colton. I just can't,' I clarified.

I could tell Colton was waiting for me to offer up an explanation, but I didn't know what to say, or how to explain the reason, without it sounding nonsensical.

Instead, I just looked back down at my notes, pretending to peruse through them, silently willing Colton would forget about what just happened.

Once again, we let the silence surround us. Only this time, tension accompanied us instead of comfort.

Colton was the one to break it.

'What are you hiding from me, Clara?' he asked, his voice soft.

For a moment, I thought about coming up with a story or a random lie, but as I brought my head to look at him, I just couldn't do it. So, I took a deep breath and said the words out in an exhale. 'You're a cliché, Colton.'

His head jerked back at my admission, not expecting the words that just slipped out of me. 'I'm a cliché? What do you mean?'

'Do you know how in every cliché love story, there's that one guy that the main character will never consider ever having a relationship with? A cliché love interest?' I started explaining. 'Maybe it's the work rival or the school bad boy?'

A look of confusion came over him, and his eyebrows furrowed. 'And what does that have to do with me?'

'You're the star athlete. Everything about that screams cliché love interest.'

'I don't necessarily think that's true.'

I snorted. 'Tell that to the whole sports romance genre.'

'Wait,' he then said, his open palm hanging in the air. 'So let me get this straight. The reason why you can't go on a date with me is because I'm the star athlete?' he asked. I could tell by the tone of his voice how idiotic he found it to be.

'Look, I know it sounds stupid. But—'

'You were the last person I thought to see me as just a star athlete, Clara,' Colton admitted.

I snapped my head toward him, seeing his face looking down on the grass, avoiding my gaze.

'I don't just see you as a star athlete,' I said. 'You don't really think that, do you?'

'Really?' he scoffed. 'Because from what you're telling me, the reason you can't go on a date with me is solely based on the fact that I'm a star athlete, which just so happens to be one of the traits of a cliché love interest.'

That's not what I'm doing. Right?

'Colton, you don't understand,' I said, exasperated.

'Then, make me understand.'

'My mom and sister fell in love with cliché love interests too, okay?' I blurted out. 'And you know how their relationship ended? My parents got divorced, and my sister called off her engagement. Maybe it sounds ridiculous to you, but I just can't help but think that my family might be cursed, that maybe we're just not meant to be with these cliché love interests. And I just won't doom myself the way they did. I just can't, Colton.'

Colton was silent as minutes—or maybe it was just seconds—flew by, the words I just said dangling in the air between us. I darted my eyes away from him, trying to think of something, anything to say that could dissolve this unwanted tension away from us. But Colton beat me to it.

'You're being really unfair right now.'

I braved myself to face him, only to find him looking ahead, instead of at me. 'What do you mean?'

He took a deep breath before he turned to me, his eyes on mine. 'You're being unfair to me by already making up your mind about me without even giving me a chance. Heck, you're not even being fair to yourself for not even trying to see what this whole thing between us could lead to.'

I shook my head. 'That's not true.'

'But it is, and you know it is,' Colton said, his tone firm. 'Clara, you can't let the outcome of other people's relationships define your own potential relationship with other people. It isn't fair for anyone—even if the relationship is the one between your own parents or your sister's. But that's just an excuse for the real reason, isn't it?'

I just stayed quiet, unsure of what to say.

'You're scared,' Colton continued, his firm tone turning soft. 'Of whatever this is.'

'I don't know what you're talking about,' I said, quickly brushing him off.

'You know exactly what I'm talking about, and it doesn't have anything to do with clichés and curses. Maybe I'm getting over my head here, but I think you like me too. But you're scared. You're scared because you don't know how this will play out; it isn't something you can just read about, knowing it'll end well. You love to read about it, but you're scared to actually do it, to actually pursue something with a person,' Colton explained. 'But Clara, you can't let that hold you back forever.'

'That's not what this is,' I replied, my tone defensive. 'Just because I don't want to pursue something with you, doesn't mean I don't want to pursue it with somebody else.'

He arched a brow at me. 'But you won't date me because I'm a cliché love interest. And falling in love with one is a curse?'

'Yes.'

'Then, answer me this. Would you go on a date with me if I wasn't a star athlete? If I was just a normal college student that asked you out. Would you have said yes?'

There it was, the same question Eliza had asked me, not too long ago—the question my head often went to, whenever the idea of being with Colton came to mind.

But just like what I told Eliza, I answered him the same way.

'It doesn't matter,' I told him, my voice a faint whisper. 'Because you *are* a star athlete, a cliché love interest. And I won't allow myself to tempt the curse, not with you.'

A look of hurt flashed over Colton's features, but he quickly masked it away. Giving me a nod, he said, 'Good to know.'

I opened my mouth to say something, yet nothing came out. I don't think anything I could say would soften the blow of whatever I had just said.

'I think we're done practicing for the day. Don't you?' Colton said, putting a smile on his face—though it was nothing like his usual, but a tight-lipped one, that didn't reach his eyes.

I didn't know what else I could do in this situation, so I just went along with it. 'Yeah. You should probably go if you don't want to be late for practice.'

We started packing up our things and cleared up the space. Colton stood up first, his hand holding out to help me get up. But he quickly clenched it into a fist and dropped it to his side. He probably thought I didn't see it, trying to play it off as being nonchalant.

But I did see it. And I don't know why I felt a painful tug in my heart at something so small.

'I should get going,' he said, his backpack strapped to his shoulders as he nudged his head to the baseball stadium. 'I'll see you next Wednesday then.'

I gave him a nod. 'See you next Wednesday.'

Colton waved me goodbye before heading his way. I decided to give him a head start, thinking we would be better off walking separately this time.

Once I couldn't see his outline any more, I started my walk to the library, carrying my heavy heart with me.

Chapter Seventeen

The next couple of days were filled with dark clouds and heavy rain.

Normally, I would have welcomed the rainfall with open arms and be happy to have it accompany me as I finish up my work in the apartment, rewarding myself afterward with some reading time.

But this time, the weather was only amplifying my already sad mood.

With the heaviest of rain falling on Thursday—the one day of my week that was filled with classes—I opted to hitch a ride with Nina to go to campus, extremely thankful for not setting an alarm for a later time that morning.

Being on the track team meant Nina had a 9 a.m. class every weekday. On days that I had one too, she would be happy to give me a ride. On Thursdays, however, I would go to campus on my own, wanting to enjoy an hour of the morning to myself, since my first class started at 10 a.m. But with the heavy rain, arriving an hour earlier than I would have liked was a much better option than having to do my normal commute on buses and walk through this stormy weather.

Throughout the day, there seemed to be a dull ache in me that I simply couldn't shake. My spirits were lower than normal, but I simply dismissed them by blaming it on the moody weather, along with the fact that I was stuck on campus ground, instead of the comfort of my own room to fully appreciate the atmosphere.

On Friday, I woke up to the sound of heavy rainfall hitting the ground and splashing against my window. The sweet scent of coffee Nina had made before she left greeted me as I made my way to the kitchen to make my breakfast, before locking myself in my room to get started with my assignment. Thankfully, I didn't have much left, and decided to finish it off, adding a few final touches and submitting it right away—way before the 11.59 p.m. deadline that night.

After completing my main priority of the day, it was time to reward myself as I picked up *Bringing Down the Duke* and made my way to the living room, curling up on the couch. The sound of rain outside and the smell of the candle I just lit, slowly filled the living room.

It sounded like just what I needed to lift my dampened spirits, but it seemed even reading about a broody duke wooing a commoner wasn't enough to cheer me up.

Deciding to go with a different approach, I reached over to the coffee table to pick up the remote. That's when my eyes settled on the vase filled with pink flowers I had put in the centre. I knew that no books, movies, or television shows could help me soothe the slight ache in my heart.

After going our separate ways at 'the spot' a couple of days ago, Colton and I were yet to see each other, and hadn't texted one another since. I wouldn't consider it to be a big deal, since we had started our semester by only seeing each other once a week and only recently did we start texting. But with how we left things off on Wednesday—at the place where he found the most comfort—I couldn't help but worry.

I thought about texting him the day before, just to see where we stood after that conversation—that is, if we were still okay. But every time I did so, the memory of the hurt on his face put on by my words never failed to remind me of its existence.

I locked my phone immediately before even typing a single word.

It had been a week since Colton got me these flowers, which meant it was about time to get fresh new ones. But the weather didn't seem to be providing me with that option, and I was not looking forward to walking in this heavy rain just to get some flowers.

As I drowned myself in my melancholia, the sounds of keys jamming in the lock brought my attention to the front door. I turned my head and saw Nina come into the apartment.

'Hey,' she greeted me when she entered the kitchen, dropping her backpack on one of the stools at the kitchen island, along with a bag of what I assumed was groceries.

'Hey,' I greeted her back. Standing up from my couch, I went over to the counter and took out the items from the bag, while Nina put them away. It was then I noticed that a bunch of sunflowers sellotaped together by the stem propped on the side. 'You got flowers?'

'Yeah, I know you said you'd get them today but since I was already at the store, I figured I would just get them there,' she shrugged. 'I didn't know which ones to get, so I just went ahead and got sunflowers.'

'They're beautiful,' I told her. 'And thank you for getting them.'

'No problem.'

I went over to the coffee table to pick up the vase, placing it on the kitchen island, before I slowly took out the flowers one by one.

'Are you feeling okay?' Nina asked, once all the items she bought were in their rightful place.

'Yeah,' I shrugged, feeling a bit sombre than usual. 'It's just one of those days, I guess.' I kept my focus on the flowers, but I didn't need to look at Nina to know she had a concerned look on her.

'Well, do you want to talk about it?' she asked.

I let out a sigh, contemplating it for a moment. In the end, I just decided to let it out. 'Colton asked me out.'

'Oh,' Nina voiced out. She was quiet afterward, the pitter-patter of the rainfall being the only sound in our apartment. Once I took out all the flowers, Nina took the vase to the sink and threw away the water before refilling it. Meanwhile, I prepared the newly bought sunflowers to be put into the vase.

Her next question came as I was trimming the stems. 'What did you say after he asked you?' she asked.

'I told him I can't,' I answered her.

'So, you told him no?'

I shook my head. 'I told him I can't, because he was a star athlete which makes him a cliché love interest and that's why I can't date him.'

'And how did he react to that?'

I thought about all the things he had said, about my unfairness, about me not giving us a fair shot, and using the outcome of other people's relationships to predict my own.

'He asked me whether I would have gone on a date with him if he wasn't a star athlete,' I told her. 'And I told him, it wouldn't have mattered, because he was a star athlete, and I wouldn't allow myself to be with one, not even him.'

Nina let out a wince. 'That sounds a bit harsh.'

'You should've seen the look on his face.' The memory of his face crossed my mind once again, along with his words that kept haunting me.

You were the last person I thought to see me as just a star athlete, Clara.

'So, technically, you didn't actually give him an answer,' Nina said after a moment of pause.

'That's the thing. I didn't.'

And that was what had been bothering me.

On top of this sadness I felt over what happened with Colton, there was also confusion over the last question he had asked me. In short, it was a simple yes-or-no question—nothing more, nothing less. And yet, I couldn't seem to pick an answer between the two options.

It had been easier to brush off when Eliza brought it up, since we were discussing a hypothetical situation where Colton was asking me out on a date.

But when the question came straight from Colton, I couldn't help but ponder over it.

Was Colton being a star athlete the only thing that was holding me back, or is there something else?

I thought back to what Colton said, about me being scared of whatever was happening between us.

Was he right?

'I should've just given him a no when he asked, instead of telling him why I can't,' I groaned. 'Then, I wouldn't have to deal with all this confusing shit and avoided this whole mess. We could've just gone back to being the way we were before.'

Back to being friends.

Just friends.

My heart clenched at that thought.

'Are you sure that's what you want?' I heard Nina ask.

I kept my gaze on the sunflowers, trying to come up with an answer. 'I don't know,' I finally said. 'But I think we would've been able to get past this if I did say no, without letting this whole thing come between our friendship.'

Nina was quiet once again, seemingly letting my words sink in before she said, 'Then, tell him no.'

'What?' I said, whipping my head over to her.

'I mean, from what you're telling me so far, you only told him the reasons why you couldn't date him. But you haven't yet rejected his date offer,' Nina explained.

'You think that's what I should do?'

'I think you should do whatever you feel is right.'

I let out a sigh.

Nina was right: I could still somewhat salvage the friendship and write it off as a rough patch in the road.

But why did the thought of giving a definite no to Colton hurt?

The rain started to slow into a drizzle on Friday night and fully came to a stop as the sun came up the next day, leaving behind a cool breeze in the air—allowing everyone to take advantage of the weekend outdoors before we started a new week.

My Saturday was spent deep cleaning the apartment with Nina. After she came home from training and we had lunch together, it was time for us to conquer our main task of the day. Each of us started from our own room before heading to the kitchen and finishing off in our living room. The day ended with us ordering takeout and watching *Clueless*.

While Saturday was spent being productive, on Sunday we indulged in rewarding ourselves as we both slept in, tired from the previous day. We spent the whole day chilling in the apartment, only leaving our humble abode for a last-minute dinner plan with Claudia and Lily.

Having all four of us together was always enough to cheer me up out of whatever sadness I was feeling, and for a while it did work. But as we headed home and I lay in my bed that night, I couldn't help but feel the ache still lingering there.

Still no text from Colton, and none going out from me either.

I knew I would still see him eventually; we were still partners for ASL class after all, and we still had a fair number of weeks in the semester left.

I truly believed we could still go back to being friends, despite what had happened.

But why did I have this feeling that might not be the case?

Monday and Tuesday passed by in a blur, and the next thing I knew, I was already on my way to ASL class.

As I got settled into my seat, a feeling of nervousness rose within me. I scrolled through my phone, while I waited for the minutes to tick away until the class started, with my eyes occasionally snapping up to the door every time I heard the sound of it opening.

The seats in the classroom started filling up one by one, but the seat beside me remained empty, even when Mr Albert entered the classroom and our ASL class began for the day.

It was unlike of Colton to be late to a class. After that first one, he had been on time ever since, but I wouldn't put it past him to have a mishap and be late again today.

But as the minutes started to tick by, the nervousness I was feeling slowly switched over to confusion with a touch of sadness.

Five minutes.

Ten minutes.

Fifteen minutes.

And as the clock struck half-past the hour, it finally dawned on me what was happening.

Colton wasn't late; he wasn't coming.

The realization hit me so hard that I couldn't even focus on the rest of the class. I was so over my head that I didn't even notice the class was over and students were already leaving their seats. I quickly packed up my things before leaving the classroom, searching for an empty sitting area somewhere for me to gather my thoughts.

I know I am an overthinker, though I was trying really hard right then to not jump to conclusions headfirst. But the fact of the matter was, Colton had missed the class that day, the first class held after what went down last Wednesday at 'the spot'.

There was no use in me dwelling on this any further—coming up with reasons on why he wasn't there that day, not when I could ask him straightaway.

Plus, even if he did miss the class, he hadn't said anything about cancelling our practice session that week, which seemed like a solid enough reason to text him first.

I took out my phone and opened our text chain, trying to think of what to say and the best way to word it.

Clara:

Hey! You weren't in class today and I was wondering if everything is okay?

And if we're still practicing ASL today?

I didn't have much else to do that day, other than my classes, and practicing ASL with Colton, so I just watched another episode of *Schitt's Creek* on my phone while I waited for his reply.

But as the episode came to an end, his reply never came.

I opened our text chain just to make sure I sent the message, and I had.

Our practice session usually lasted for about an hour, and technically, we still had about thirty minutes left. But from the looks of it, I didn't think he was coming. Maybe he had a reasonable explanation, but as it stood right then, he wasn't there, and he had neither informed me about it.

In the end, I picked up my bag and made my way over to the bus stop, feeling disappointed at how things had turned out.

Colton's reply came as I was getting ready for bed.

I let his message remain unopened unintentionally, as I was finishing up my skincare routine, only seeing the notification once I retrieved my phone. But I continued ignoring it consciously, wanting to serve him a little payback for his late reply.

I held out for as long as I could, but my itch of curiosity got the better of me—leading me to finally open his message.

Colton:
I AM SO SORRY.
One of my classes got cancelled, so I went home and
decided to take a nap just now.
And I overslept.
The next thing I know, I had to go to practice.

After weeks of getting to know each other and spending time together, Colton had shown me that he was worthy of my trust. Though I couldn't help but question him at that very moment.

Colton had never given me a reason to not trust his words, but if he were telling the truth, then why was he only informing at that moment? It seemed like something he could have told me earlier than 10 p.m. Baseball practice had been over hours before, and I was pretty he had the time to hold his phone since then.

I believed him for the most part, but there was a part within me that thought it was just an excuse. The reason why he had taken so long to reply was that he needed time to think of a plausible reason to not want to see me.

I snorted at my train of thought. I was definitely reading way too much into this.

Clara:
Hey.
Thanks for letting me know.

And don't worry too much about our practice session this week. I know you have a game on Saturday, so I think we'll be fine skipping another week.

I'm gonna head to bed soon. Goodnight!

The three dots appeared not long after I sent my last message, then disappeared again.

The motion kept repeating for a minute or so, before Colton finally decided on a reply.

Colton:
Goodnight.
Partner.

Chapter Eighteen

Thursday came around, and I was back in my usual spot at my favourite coffee shop on campus. The afternoon sun illuminated through the windows, giving off a warm ambience as I immersed myself in my book.

Everything about that moment was perfect. But it seemed my heart wasn't fully on board with it.

Colton's messages from the previous night kept floating in my mind. Though it might not have been at the forefront, it still stood at the sidelines, occasionally reminding me of its existence, whenever my mind started drifting during class.

I was waiting for my next class, with a book in my hand to distract me from reality, but it wasn't working as well as I had hoped. As I tried reading the start of a new page for the third time, I heard footsteps coming toward me and coming to a stop near my seat.

My traitorous heart started speeding up, holding out to the hope and ridiculous notion that it might be Colton.

But the glimmer of optimism instantly burnt out, when I titled up my head to see who it was. I instantly switched over to confusion as my eyes registered the person actually standing in front of me.

'Miles?' I called out.

He gave me a sheepish smile followed by a small wave. 'Hey. I'm not bothering you, am I?' he asked, noticing the book in my hand.

'Not at all,' I shook my head, closing the book. It wasn't as if the words were entering my head anyway, so I didn't really mind the interruption. 'How have you been?'

'So far, so good,' he shrugged. 'I was wondering if I could talk to you for a bit?'

'Oh, sure,' I said, surprise lacing my voice at his request. I quickly picked up my backpack that was occupying the seat across from me, and gently placed it next to my seat before gesturing to the now empty spot to Miles, 'Have a seat.'

'Thanks,' he said, putting down his backpack by his legs as he got himself settled.

The next minute was filled with silence as I waited for Miles to start the conversation. But as more time passed, I decided to take initiative.

'So, what did you want to talk to me about?' I voiced out, leaning forward and picking up my coffee from the table between us. I couldn't help but be curious as to why he had decided to approach me. Other than the time when Colton invited me to the party and at its venue itself, Miles and I had rarely crossed paths, so I wasn't sure what he wanted to discuss with me.

He took a moment to collect himself—as if he was working up the courage to voice out his words. From the way he kept fidgeting, my suspicions started to arise as to what it might be about.

Another beat passed along with an exhale from Miles, when he finally said what was on his mind.

'It's about Colton,' he confessed, confirming my suspicions.

'Is he okay?' My spine straightened instantly, slightly alarmed. *Did something happen to him?*

'Yeah, he's doing all right,' he replied.

'Oh, that's great,' I breathed out, relieved to hear that he was fine.

My words hung between us, and the silence started to stretch once again. I thought about asking questions about the baseball team to fill the silence—it was slowly getting awkward—but Miles beat me to it.

'Colton didn't ask me to talk to you by the way, in case you were wondering,' Miles said.

My head jerked back upon hearing his words. That thought had not crossed my mind. 'Okay?' I said, my confusion making it sound more like a question.

'I just wanted to tell you that he really did oversleep yesterday. From his nap, I mean; he barely made it in time for practice.'

'Okay,' I repeated, my tone still confused. 'But I still don't see why you're telling me this. He already told me about it yesterday.' *Well, texted me more like it.*

'And he apologized to you for missing your ASL practice, right?'

At that, I narrowed my eyes at him. 'He did apologize, but how did you . . .' I trailed off.

Miles let out a sigh. 'When Colton arrived at practice yesterday, he was disoriented and out of focus. You could tell his mind was elsewhere. Once we had a break, I decided to ask him what was wrong. It was then he told me he missed you guys' weekly ASL practice session.'

'And the class too,' I added.

'And the class too,' Miles parroted. 'But that wasn't what he was panicking about. I couldn't ask him to elaborate more, since we were still practicing. Only after it was over, I could finally corner him about it. That's when he told me he had missed the practice session, and about how you texted him about it, and how he hadn't replied to you yet, because he didn't know what to say.'

'Why would he panic? I would've understood,' I said.

'He was scared.'

'About what?'

'That you wouldn't believe him considering what went down last week between you two,' he answered.

It took me a moment to figure out how Miles could've found out about what had happened the previous week between us, until I realized how simple the answer was.

'He told you.'

Miles winced slightly at my accusation, but he gave me a nod. 'He did. But you can't blame the guy, he was just venting out his emotions. Anyway, he was freaked out over what to do. He didn't want you to think he was some kind of an asshole that ditched you, just because of a small disagreement. He freaked out even more, because he should've just replied to you straight away, instead of waiting.'

The picture materialized in my head before I could stop it: the look of frustration on Colton's face as he told Miles about his mistake of not texting me right away, the look of confusion on how to fix this, and the look of hurt as he recalled what happened at 'the spot' a week ago.

While I mostly believed the reason he had given me the day before, I couldn't help that tiny part in me—the one that was guilty—that doubted his honesty. So, it was nice to hear it from someone else—his best friend, no less, to be reassured that he was, indeed, telling the truth.

'Okay, so he overslept,' I said. 'But I still don't understand why you're telling me all of this.' I paused, before continuing. 'Is that why you're here? How did you know I was here?'

At that, he blushed. 'I texted Nina and asked if she knew where you were. She told me this coffee shop would be my best shot.'

Of course she did.

'I just wanted to tell you that Colton is a nice guy and the whole situation yesterday just happened at the wrong time, that's all. Colton wouldn't have just left you hanging, when he knows how important the class is to you even after what happened between you two.'

'Well, I'm glad—'

'And I think Colton deserves a chance if you're willing to give him one,' Miles cut me off.

That caught me off guard. 'A chance?'

'I know it's your choice, and I'm not trying to force you to do anything,' Miles replied. 'But Colton is a great guy.

He just happens to be a star athlete, instead of the other way around.'

It was my turn to let out a wince, recognizing my own words being thrown back at me. 'He told you about that as well.'

'Yeah,' Miles trailed off, his hand coming up to his hair and messing it up.

'I don't understand,' I expressed. 'If Colton didn't ask you to be here, then why are you trying to win me over his good side?'

'He's happier on Wednesdays,' Miles said without hesitation. 'If you exclude the two recent ones.'

'And how does that apply to me?' I argued. I knew where he was heading with this, but I wanted to make sure I wasn't over my head with my imagination.

'I think you know exactly how it applies to you,' Miles argued back. 'Don't get me wrong, Colton has always been an all-around happy guy on most days. But ever since the start of this semester, I've noticed there's one day of the week, when he looks happier and lighter than usual. No matter what our coach puts us through, it doesn't get to him as much as it would on any other day,' Miles continued. 'He did tell me about the practice sessions you guys were having, and how he'll meet up with his partner for ASL class every Wednesday before baseball practice, but I never thought much about it. It wasn't until we ran into you outside the baseball stadium that it finally hit me.'

He went on.

'It was *you*,' Miles stated, point blank. 'The reason why he looks so happy every time he arrives for baseball practice on Wednesday, was because he just got back from spending time with you.'

The sounds of the coffee shop became the only ones I could hear as I took in his words, which I wanted to believe in so badly. But what if Miles was wrong? What if he was just making things up from his perspective?

'Well, I think you're wrong, Miles,' I protested instead.

'I might be, if he hadn't told me himself,' he countered. 'I put two and two together, once I saw how he reacted to you. And right after he invited you and Nina to the party, I decided to tease him about it in the car. But turns out, that was the nudge he needed. Because after that day, all he could talk about was you.'

My heart gave a tiny squeeze.

'Look, I know it's up to you if you want to go on a date with him,' he said. 'But if the only thing that's holding you back is that he happens to be great at baseball, then I truly think you're missing out. He's so much more than that star athlete reputation.'

I didn't know what else to say, because I did know that. While I liked my star baseball player fantasy version of Colton in my head, I liked the real Colton—the one I had gotten to know in those past few months—more, a lot more. But those weren't the words I wanted to say out loud just yet, especially not in front of his best friend.

So, instead, I said, 'You're a great friend, Miles.'

He gave me a smile. 'That I am. I mean, I'm already his roommate and best friend, so I figured why not try being his wingman for once.'

His last two words caught my attention. 'For once? What do you mean?'

The look on Miles's face told me I knew exactly what he meant, but for some reason, I wanted to deny what he was implying. 'By for once, you mean you didn't have to wingman him before, because he always gets the girl on his own, right?'

Miles shook his head. 'By for once, I mean there has never been anyone else. Until you came along.'

And there it went, my last out.

My last chance of wanting to find a reason to validate my decision of not wanting to go out with Colton other than the fact that he's a star athlete.

I didn't have time to ponder over that new thought, when the alarm from my phone sounded off, alerting me that my next class was starting in ten minutes.

'I gotta go. My class is starting soon.' Putting my forgotten book in my backpack, I quickly got up and hooked the strap to my shoulder.

I tried to think of what to say before I took off, but Miles came to my rescue. 'Are you coming to the game this Saturday?'

Right. Their home game.

This was the game I had promised Colton I would be attending, just minutes before things went wrong. I still had more to think about before I could decide on whether I should go to the game. Since I couldn't give Miles a definite answer, I finally decided to settle on 'Maybe.'

'Well, I'll see you there if you are. And if not, then I'll see you around.'

I gave him a nod. 'See you around.'

I quickened my pace and exited the coffee shop, arriving at my class with a couple of minutes to spare before it started. I made it right on time, when the lecturer entered the hall just as I got settled into my seat.

Thankfully, the class was one that I was interested in, offering me a welcome distraction from my conversation that had happened with Miles.

I knew I had a lot to think about, and I couldn't ignore it forever, but if I could postpone the inescapable for a couple more hours, then you bet that was exactly what I would be doing.

I was back in my apartment a few minutes before 6 p.m. It was Nina's turn to cook dinner tonight, and after a full day of classes, my brain was too drained to do anything academic. So, reviewing my lecture notes was not on my to-do list that night.

I browsed through Netflix to see if there was anything I could watch to pass the time, but nothing seemed interesting to me.

I let out a frustrated groan.

With nothing left to distract me, it was time to face the inevitable music.

I knew there was no going around it, but I also needed someone to vent this out to. Nina wouldn't be back for at least another hour, and I had texted Eliza while I was on my way back to the apartment to check if she was free for a phone call. Unfortunately, she had a meeting to attend, followed by a dinner with her co-workers.

There was one final option. My thumb was already hovering over the call button as I hesitated on whether I should press it or not.

Taking a deep breath as I gathered my courage, I pressed it and put it on speaker.

The call line rang three times before it got picked up.

'Hello?' My mom's gentle voice came out from the other side.

'Hey, Mom,' I answered.

While Eliza and I had a scheduled phone call for each week, my catchups with my mom come at the most spontaneous times: whether it be when she was driving home from work, or when I was getting ready to leave the apartment for class.

My parents made sure that the divorce would be an easy transition for us, and they did—never failing to remind us they would always be there for us, no matter what.

The hardest part of the divorce, personally, was not having the whole family under the same roof any more, and understanding that I would have to live with one parent at a time. It also meant I had to choose which parent I would rather stay with for the most part.

But I hadn't wanted to choose. I loved both my parents equally.

So I didn't. I let Eliza decide for me.

Wherever she would go, I would follow, especially since our time together was on the clock with her going off to college soon.

Eliza ended up picking our Mom to stay with during the weekdays and my Dad for the weekends. Even so, our father made an effort to see us during the weekdays too, by having dinner with us a couple of times a week. During the early years of the divorce, I focused on spending time with Eliza as much as possible before she left and started a new chapter of her life.

It wasn't until she left that I truly started bettering my relationship with my parents individually. With me staying at Mom's most of the time, she got to hear everything about my high school experience—which included all the friendship drama, way too much homework and, of course, me reaching the age where I had started to go on dates.

Eliza might have gotten details through our phone calls as I recounted my dates, but it was my mom who had the first-hand experience of seeing me go there, and hearing how it went right away once I got home.

It was nerve-wracking the first time in high school, but it eventually got less awkward over time. Though I couldn't help but feel nervous to tell her about Colton and my reservations about him.

'How have you been, sweetheart?' I heard my mom ask.

'Good,' I answered her. I started playing with the rings on my finger that I hadn't taken off, just so I could have something to do with my hands to get rid of my nervousness.

'Is everything okay?'

I let out a quiet exhale. 'Yeah, everything's fine.' After a beat, I added, 'A guy asked me out.'

'That's great!' Mom replied with a note of enthusiasm in her tone. 'So, when is the date? Are you excited?'

'Actually,' I started. 'I haven't said yes yet.'

'Oh. Why not, honey? Do you not like him?'

'It's the opposite actually,' I said. 'I really, really, really like him.'

'Then, what's the matter?'

I stayed quiet for a while, trying to muster up enough courage in myself to finally voice it out. I wanted to let it all out, all that had been hanging over my head all that time, but never wanted to admit it out loud.

'Clara?' My mom's concerned voice filled the living room.

'I'm scared, Mom.' And there it was. The real reason. The very thing that Colton accused me of.

Because what Colton said was true.

I was scared. I always have been.

I was scared of opening up my heart to someone else. I was scared of giving someone a chance—a real chance, not the one that I convinced myself into thinking is one. Even though I had been on dates since I was a high school senior, they never went past the first one, because every single time, a strike count was ready at the back of my mind. It would go off each time I found something— any random excuse that assured me we won't match well—which could fill up all three counts, to justify my decision of not going on a second date with the same guy.

But then Colton came along, and everything changed.

Maybe it was because we never went on an actual date before. But I don't think that was it. I think, deep down, I knew that if we did go on one, I would just want more dates with him, and the strike counts wouldn't matter any more.

Heck, all semester long, as I fell deeper into my crush for him, I had been waiting for him to slip up, for any kind of reason that will slowly diminish my feelings towards him over time. But every time I tried to find one—why he decided to take the ASL class, his late reply to my text the day before—it backfired. Instead, my crush on him grew bigger and bigger.

The curse wasn't real, I was aware of that. Of course. I knew that this curse was just a fabrication and a coping mechanism for me to keep my guard up—specifically against those whom I could see myself easily falling for, someone like Colton.

But it had never applied to anyone else before, not when the rose-coloured glasses of their allure were snatched off immediately once I *actually* got to know them.

And I didn't expect it to apply then.

I kept waiting for the same effect to happen to Colton, something to wake me from this daydream, but it never came.

And after trying so hard to search for other reasons as to why him and I couldn't step out of the friendship territory—and failing miserably each time I thought there was one—the only thing I could cling to was the curse. My only lifeline.

And now, if you took that curse away, I had nothing left. No more excuses. Everything was leading me in Colton's direction and to agree to his date offer, to explore this thing between us.

Yet, I couldn't find it in me to say yes.

'Oh, honey.' I heard my mom say. 'What exactly are you scared of?'

'I don't know exactly,' I started. 'I think I'm scared of what happens afterward. Like, what if the date goes well? And what if I want to go on a second date? I have never been on second dates before.'

No one knew about my strike counts, but I was pretty sure Mom had caught on to it, since I never went on second dates with the same guy and relayed to her the details of why we wouldn't work together.

'Then, you go on the second date. And if that goes well too, you go on a third one,' my mom explained fondly, as if I was a curious child asking about the simplest of things.

'And what happens after that?' I asked her.

'Well, that's for you to decide,' she replied. 'It's okay to be scared. There's nothing wrong with guarding yourself against getting hurt. Your heart is a precious thing, it deserves to be protected. Allowing your heart to fall in love can be a scary thing, and it's okay to feel that way.'

'Then how do I get over it? This fear?'

'You don't,' Mom answered. 'At least not right away. You just have to take it one step at a time each day. But the first move is to actually take that leap of faith with someone. If you're lucky enough to find that person, hopefully, that leap will look a little less scary than it did before.'

Listening to her words reminded me of Eliza's advice—how similar they were, and how well they complimented one another. Both Mom and Eliza had found someone that was worth taking the leap for, but were they ever scared to take that jump? I couldn't really ask Eliza about it—at least not right now, but I could ask my mom.

I must've been stuck in my head for a while, when I heard my mom's voice snapping me back to reality. 'Clara?'

'What about you and Dad?' I blurted out, deciding to just voice out my thoughts. 'Were you scared of falling in love with him?'

Silence stretched out for a moment. I couldn't help but feel slightly awkward by asking her such a question, for we had never really talked about such things before. Just as I was about to brush off the topic, Mom's voice stopped me.

'I wasn't actually,' she started. 'Scared to fall in love with him, I mean. But that might have to do with the fact that we were high schoolers when we started dating, and that it was a different time,' she chuckled. 'But what I will say is, your dad made it easy for me to fall in love with him, or at least made it easy for me *to see* myself doing so. While the relationship didn't end the way I had hoped, I will always cherish what we had and what we do have, because it brought me you and Eliza. You'll always be the world's greatest gift to me.'

I could feel my eyes start to tear up at her words. 'You're gonna make me cry.'

'Well, I didn't expect us to have such a sentimental conversation today.' I heard her laugh, but the scratch in her voice told me she was shedding a few tears. 'I might not know who the guy is, but if he's got you to admit this to yourself, then maybe he deserves a shot. And if things don't work out between you two, then that's okay too. But just make sure you don't let that fear hold you back from giving the right person a chance.'

I let her words hang in the quietness of my apartment, as I took each one of them to heart.

'Thanks for the advice, Mom,' I finally said, breaking the silence.

'You're welcome,' she answered. 'Anyway, I actually have to get ready for dinner. But will you be all right?' Her voice got quiet towards the end, with the concern evident in her voice.

'I'll be fine,' I told her. And it was true, I still had a lot to think about after our conversation, but I would be fine. 'Enjoy dinner!'

She bid me goodbye, and we ended the call.

The soft sounds of cars on the street below accompanied me in the comfort of the living room as I reconvened everything my mom had just laid out for me.

The way I saw it, there were only two ways to go, when it came to me and Colton. To either let my fear hold me back from taking that step—to take that leap of faith with him, or embrace it, along with all its uncertainty.

And I thought I did want to take the leap; I had been for a while. All semester long, I had received nudges from the people around me: Nina, my sister, and heck, even Miles.

Now, all that was left for me, was to take that final step.

But after everything that had happened between us, Colton might not want anything to do with me. We could possibly just remain friends and be civil enough, while still being partners for ASL class for the rest of the semester.

Either way, I had to let him know what I felt about him, and be vulnerable with him just as he had been with me.

No more hiding.

If overcoming this fear meant taking it one step at a time, then that moment would start off with sending one simple text.

With my phone still in my hands, I opened my text chain with Colton and typed out my message.

Clara:
Hey. Can we talk?

Chapter Nineteen

Colton:
See you tomorrow.

My eyes stayed locked on Colton's last text as my mind pondered how rude it would be on a scale of one to ten, if I were to come up with a random excuse to avoid this confrontation, less than fifteen minutes before he got there.

Our conversation the previous night had barely lasted a few messages. After asking him if we could talk, I had quickly followed up with another text, saying that we could meet up at 'the spot' if he was free the next day.

It was officially the next day, and here I was, sitting with my legs folded, and my back against the tree trunk.

I wasn't nervous per se. Well, that's a lie. I was a nervous wreck; it got to a point that I ended up arriving thirty minutes earlier than we had decided on. This was just to give me ample time to work up the courage on what I wanted—no, needed—to say to Colton.

I wasn't leaving until I got my words out to him.

But that didn't mean I was looking forward to it.

Breathing out a sigh, I locked my phone and put it on top of my backpack, my hand accidentally brushing against the plastic bag containing two bubble tea cups.

Two bubble teas from our usual place.

I don't know why I had decided to get them. But the moment I stepped out of the apartment, my feet were already heading to the bubble tea shop, before my mind could even register it. And now, here it was next to me, the plastic sticking to the cups caused by the condensation.

My hand itched to put a straw into one of them and take a sip, just so I had something else to focus on. But something about that just didn't feel right. Ultimately, I decided to go back to my usual method to distract myself from the world.

Reading romance books.

Taking my copy of *Bringing Down the Duke* out of my bag, I willed it to whisk me away.

It did work for a moment, and I didn't even realize someone was there until I heard a question being asked.

'Is that a new book you're reading?'

My head snapped up towards the sound of the familiar voice, the one I didn't know I had been missing.

'Colton,' I called out, my voice soft. I quickly put down my book and tried to stand.

Seeing what I was doing, Colton held out his hand in front of me.

My eyes went to his offered hand, and to his face, which had a warm smile greeting me. His gesture made me pause, remembering the last time he wanted to offer me his hand, and from the look on his face, he seemed to be thinking the same thing. But before I could give him a chance to pull his hand back, I placed one of my own in his. His eyes widened slightly at our clasped hands, before he slowly helped me up, his hold gentle.

And now here we were, standing face to face, as we let the silence envelop us.

Nervousness started to creep up on me once again as goosebumps prickled my arms. But it was the soft brushes on the back of my hand that helped me stay grounded and kept the fear at bay.

Bringing my eyes to our joined hands, I was met with the source of the gentle touches—Colton's thumb. I didn't even realize I was still holding his hand.

'Do you want me to stop?' he said, noticing what I was looking at.

I shook my head at him. 'No.'

Colton eventually did stop, but he didn't let go of my hand. From the delicate way he was holding it, I knew what he was trying to say.

He was letting me decide whether I wanted to continue holding his hand or drop it.

Making my decision, I gave it a gentle squeeze, letting my hand linger in his.

And because it was Colton, he got my message, and he gripped my hand even tighter.

'Hey, partner,' he then said, a small smile on his face.

'Hey, partner,' I repeated with a smile of my own, matching his.

We let the quiet surround us once again, as we held on to the comfort of one another.

Colton was the one who broke the silence. 'I got you these, by the way.'

It was only then that I noticed that his other arm was tucked behind him, hidden from me, until he pulled it forward, showing me what it was.

It was a bunch of pink flowers: a variety of them, wrapped with cellophane wrap and tied together at the stems—the same way it had been the last time he gave me flowers.

Using my unoccupied hand, I reached out to them, accepting his wonderful gift.

'Thank you,' I held it closer to my nose and inhaled its floral scent. 'But what's the occasion?' I teased.

'I guess you could say they're apology flowers,' he shrugged. 'I felt bad about what happened on Wednesday. And I know giving you flowers doesn't make up for the fact that I missed our ASL practice, but I don't know,' he continued, his voice shrinking towards the end, 'giving you flowers just felt right to me.'

Upon hearing his words, my eyes immediately shifted to meet his, only to find them looking at the ground instead, as if in embarrassment of his sweet gesture. But he shouldn't have, and I realized I needed to let him know that.

'Colton,' I called out, willing him to look at me. And when he finally did, I said, 'Thank you.'

A small hint of a smile appeared on his face. 'You're welcome.'

'And plus. The flowers in my apartment were starting to wilt, so this couldn't have come at a better time,' I said, lighting up the tension from what the weight of his words had left behind.

He let out a small laugh. 'Glad I could help.'

'And oh! I got you something too,' I exclaimed, remembering I had brought gifts of my own. I pulled my hand away from his, and went to put the lovely flowers on top of my backpack. Grabbing the handle of the plastic bag, I offered it to Colton. 'Here you go.'

Surprise flickered on his face as his hand reached out for the plastic bag, and he peeked to see what was inside.

'Bubble tea,' he stated, seemingly needing no explanation for it but I gave him one anyway.

'Think of it as a peace offering,' I explained, 'for what happened between us last week.'

'But why are there two of them?'

'You didn't think I would get one for you, without getting one for myself, did you?' I said, my voice teasing as I repeated the words he had said to me not too long ago. The smile on my face was evident as I voiced out the next sentence. 'Plus, someone once told me that bubble tea *is* our thing.'

Emphasizing the 'is'—present tense.

His lips tugged into a small smile. But the glow of happiness started to dim slightly, as his smile was replaced by a frown. 'I feel like I should be getting you bubble tea since I messed up.'

'You already got me flowers,' I reassured him.

'I could've gotten you both.'

'Colton,' I said softly. 'You didn't—'

He cut me off. 'Can I say something first?'

I let out a heavy exhale, preparing myself for what he had to say. 'Sure.'

Putting down the bag of bubble tea next to my bag, Colton took a deep breath once he stood back up. He made sure to put all his attention on me.

'I know what I did—or accidentally did—on Wednesday was a jerk move. I just want to explain what happened on my side,' he started. 'I've been pulling a few all-nighters lately with some of my assignments, and when one of my classes on Wednesday got cancelled, I thought I would take a nap and catch up on some sleep. I just didn't realize how tired I was, when I slept through my alarm. Unfortunately, it led me to miss the ASL class and our practice session.'

Now that he pointed it out, I did notice the circles under his eyes were slightly darker than when I had seen him last. My heart clenched a bit at the sight, for he really did look tired.

'I know it sounds like a lame excuse, and I should've texted you earlier than I did about it. But—' Colton broke off. 'Shit, I just panicked, you know? We were already not on good terms, and the whole thing just came at the worst timing possible. I can only imagine how it must have looked from your side. Basically, what I'm trying to say is, I'm sorry for what happened on Wednesday. Regardless of what happened the last time we were here.' His eyes wandered to our surroundings. 'We're still partners for ASL class, and I won't take that for granted.'

I stayed quiet as I let his words hang in the air between us, understanding the hidden meaning of what he was trying to say. Colton was offering me one final out, to let our last in-person conversation become just a memory. He didn't say it out loud, but I knew what he meant. He promised not to bring it up again, and that we could go back to being what we were before this rough patch in our friendship.

Back to safe territory.

Back to being friends.

All I needed to do was step back.

But I was done hiding.

'Can I talk now?' I said.

He gave me a nod. 'Sure.'

'I kept thinking about what you said,' I started, 'the last time we were here—about me being scared of this thing between us.'

He winced. 'I was completely out of line saying that.'

'I mean, you *were* a little bit out of line,' I agreed sheepishly. 'But you were right. I am scared. I always thought I was open to the idea of love and relationships, but that's not true. I keep finding reasons to push people away, before anything serious can happen. But when it came to you, I couldn't find it in me to look for one, because even if there was any, it wouldn't have mattered. That scared me,' I told him, my voice shaky.

'I like you, Colton. A lot. And I know I hurt you the last time we were here, but I think that was just my defence mechanism kicking in, before I even realized what it was,' I said. 'And I'm really sorry for hurting you the way that I did. You are a star athlete, but you're also so much more than that to me. And I just wanted you to know that.'

I kept my eyes on his face throughout my monologue. But the heavy look on Colton's face was just too much for me to handle after everything I had laid out. I darted them to the baseball field behind him instead, then to my shoes—anywhere but his face.

'So, does that mean you'll go on a date with me?'

My eyes immediately snapped up to his upon hearing his question.

'What?' I said, thinking I heard him wrong.

He gave me a small smile and signed the question to me, the same way he asked me the last time we were here. He voiced it out loud again, 'Do you want to go on a date with me?'

I knew I should give him an answer, but all I could say was, 'But why?'

'Because I like you, and I want to go on a date with you,' he reasoned with me, his words the same. And at that moment, I learned just how complicated I had made everything out to be, when it really should have just been that simple.

'You still want to go on a date with me?' I asked instead. 'Even after everything I said to you last time?'

'Yes, I do,' he answered. 'I can't change the fact that I'm what you call a "star athlete", his fingers mimicking air quotes at the two words, 'but we're still partners for ASL class for the rest of the semester. I was hoping that it'll give me enough time for you to see past that part of me, when I asked you out again once the semester ended.'

My eyes widened at what he just said. 'What? You were planning to ask me out again?'

'I mean, if there's one thing athletes do have in common, it is how they never give up. Also, you didn't really give me a direct answer.' He shot me a teasing look. 'I might've come a bit too strong earlier, and I'm really sorry if any of the words I said last time hurt you in any way; it really wasn't my intention. And come to think of it, those flowers were definitely not enough for my apology,' he continued. 'I mean, buying you a house seems like a good idea, but that seems a little bit excessive.'

I furrowed my eyebrows at him. 'Buy me a house? Why would you?' I trailed off.

And then, it hit me.

You Deserve Each Other. My favourite romance book. The scene where Nicholas bought Naomi a house to save their relationship.

My eyes widened in realization.

He couldn't have.

'Did you read the book?' I voiced out. '*You Deserve Each Other?*'

He gave me a nod. 'I did.'

'But why would you read a romance book?'

'Because it's your favourite book,' he simply answered, as if that was reason enough. And maybe for Colton, it really was.

From all the months I got to know him, Colton had only ever been straightforward with me: telling me exactly what was on his mind, leaving me no room to doubt him.

I knew that I didn't owe Colton anything, even if he did read my all-time favourite book. I could still say no to his date offer, if I wanted to.

But I did owe it to myself to see where this thing with him could lead, if I stopped letting this fear hold me back.

I was scared; I continued to be. And I knew overcoming that wasn't going to happen in a snap of a finger.

But as my eyes looked at Colton, his gaze locked in mine with his heart on his sleeve. I felt a spark of something else lighting within me.

It was the desire, the want, the longing to experience all those romantic notions I had read about in all the romance books. And not just with anyone, but with Colton.

The boy who continuously insisted on driving me home whenever he could. The boy who had ABBA CDs in his car, because it brought back good memories. The boy who brought me flowers and bubble tea. The boy who could make me laugh, and with whom, I could share a comfortable silence.

I knew the fear would linger, but that didn't mean it couldn't coexist with desire.

And while I had already decided with my whole heart to give Colton a chance, I couldn't help but need one final nudge. Only this time, it was from Colton himself.

'So, what do you say?' he asked, breaking off my inner turmoil. 'Go on a date with me?'

'I will,' I answered him, before quickly adding, 'but on one condition.'

A twinkle of mischief appeared in his eyes, recognizing the times he had uttered the same words to me, asking me to put my trust in him. 'And what's that?'

'Hit a home run for me,' I stated, 'at tomorrow's game.'

A beaming smile broke on his face once he heard what I said. As he repeated the same words he had texted me the last time he promised to do the same thing, he said, 'Hit a home run for you? You got it, partner.'

Chapter Twenty

Saturday evening came around a bit too slow for my liking, or maybe that was just my excitement over finally getting to watch a live baseball game again.

But it might have more to do with the fact that a certain boy was playing later.

Either way, I had spent the whole day running errands. From getting groceries to taking out the trash, I did anything I could to distract myself from how mind-numbingly slow time was moving.

Heck, I even managed to finish *Bringing Down the Duke,* and I was already a quarter into a new book.

Eventually, the anticipated event was starting in a few hours, and I could *finally* start getting ready at a reasonable time.

For a minute I thought about dressing up for that day's game, just because it was the first and only home game that semester. No other reason. But in hindsight, I decided to prioritize comfort, if we were going to be there for at least a few hours.

Knowing how packed it was going to be, especially parking-wise, Claudia and Lily decided to meet us at our apartment before we booked an Uber to go to the stadium together. Nina heated up some leftovers from last night, just to pan off our hunger throughout the game, since we planned on getting dinner later.

'Everyone ready to go?' Nina said after putting the last of the dirty plates in the dishwasher.

'Yup!' Claudia shouted at the same time as Lily exclaimed. 'Ready!'

'Me too,' I replied. 'Just let me grab my things, and then we can leave.'

I made my way back to my room and went to my closet to pick out a jacket. The weather wasn't too cold thankfully, but the game was starting at 5 p.m. and would last into the early night.

I was about to reach for my denim jacket, when I noticed the one hanging beside it.

Colton's baseball jacket.

After the not-date with Colton—as I liked to call it—I had immediately hung it inside my closet, instead of having it laid around my room. I did so because, one, to take care of it, and two, to let myself get rid of the memory and the desire to want more. I knew if it was placed somewhere I could see, I would just be reminded of what I couldn't have.

But that was before I had decided to give him—give us—a chance. And maybe, there was a part of me, even back then, that just didn't want to give it back to him just yet.

'Clara!' I heard Nina call out. 'The Uber is coming in three minutes.'

'Coming!' Without further hesitation, I unhooked his jacket and placed it on my arm. Grabbing my tote bag from my desk chair, I joined the girls at the front door before we headed for our ride downstairs.

It might have been just an exhibition game, but when your college team is as celebrated and renowned as ours was, every game that you can catch in person is a big opportunity you shouldn't miss. That also pretty much meant that the shared parking lot between the baseball stadium and the track field was filled to the brim, along with all the empty parking spots that were within walkable distance to the stadium, just as we had expected.

It seemed not only the whole college, but the whole town had the same idea of how to spend their Saturday evening.

We told our Uber driver to drop us off at the library instead, so he could avoid the ongoing traffic.

As we walked along the path, talking about who we were most excited to see play today, I took my phone out to see if Colton had texted me back.

After our conversation the day before, we had both gone our separate ways. Colton had to meet up with his team, and I had to head home and start prepping dinner. I had a new recipe I wanted to try out, and thus needed extra time, in case I messed it up.

But that only meant our conversations continued through text instead, and I hadn't realized just how much I missed talking to him. It didn't go too late into the night, since I knew he needed his sleep for the game.

We didn't text as much that day, other than a good morning text, and him telling me he was going to be in the stadium all day with the team and their coach to discuss the strategy for that night's game.

My last message wished him good luck for the game, but I wasn't sure if he had seen it, since I only texted him on the Uber ride.

Our short walk finally came to a stop, as we approached the entrance to the stadium. The game was starting in half an hour, but it seemed like all the good seats were already taken.

Luckily, we managed to find four seats between the home plate and first base, somewhere in the middle of the numerous rows. It gave us a pretty good view of the game.

I settled into the furthest seat to the right, with Nina sitting next to me. A playlist of the day's latest hit songs blasted the speakers as we waited for the game to start.

I unlocked my phone to see if there were any new notifications.

There were none.

I couldn't help but feel a little upset at not sending the text a bit earlier. Not that he needed it, but I'm sure he would've appreciated it.

'Are you wearing what I think you're wearing?' I heard Nina ask next to me.

I tucked my phone into the jacket. 'What?'

'It's Colton's jacket, isn't it?'

I was yet to update Nina on what had happened with Colton the day before, only because I didn't want to have her hopes up just yet, since Colton had a condition to fulfil to earn his chance of a date with me.

'Yeah, it's his jacket,' I told her and left it at that. But the smile on my face pretty much told her everything she needed to know.

She gave me a smile of her own. 'You'll tell me when you're ready?'

'Always,' I said, putting an arm around her and giving her a side hug, silently letting her know how grateful I was for her.

The song that was currently playing through the speakers slowly faded out. It was replaced with the sound of trumpets, followed by our college's own sports commentator announcing the game was about to begin.

'Welcome folks to another exhibition game during this off-season! And this time, we'll be playing in the home of last year's Men's College World Series champion, our very own Dust Devils!'

The crowd gave a massive cheer for our beloved team, while they waved around for us as they got ready in the dugout.

'Today's game will be against another one of college baseball favourites, the Raptors!'

Applause sounded all over the stadium for the away team.

As the crowd started to settle down, our college baseball players started making their way to the field and got into position. It seemed that the away team was batting first.

My heart couldn't help but speed up seeing Colton taking his place right in front of our stand at first base.

His eyes started to dart across the stadium—from his right side, before coming over to the left.

My side.

For a moment, I gave in to the temptation of the fantasy that he was looking for me.

But it seemed my fantasy wasn't far off, when he went a little over from where I was sitting, before bringing his eyes back to me.

Remembering that he might not have read my text, I thought of the next best thing I could do, while I still had his attention.

'Good luck!' I signed to him.

A massive grin instantly appeared on his face. He tipped his hat at me before signing a little 'thank you' back, not wanting to alert anyone who might have perceived it as Colton giving a flying kiss to someone in the stands.

He turned his attention back to the game as the first batter from the opposing team stepped up to home plate.

And so, it began.

The game kicked off to a good start with our team leading, managing a score of 2-0 in the first inning. But the other team was starting to catch up to us, which led to a tie score of 4-4.

A slight strain of worry filled the air in the crowd at the score, though it didn't last too long as Jack, our team's pitcher, managed to pull three strikeouts in a row. Soon, we were back to being the batting team. As each player managed to swing a good shot, we now had all three bases loaded. While that didn't necessarily bring in points, it did mean things were starting to look up for us.

But as the next couple of batters got struck out, the tension was back in the atmosphere. Everyone started to feel nervous again, since we were only left with one last player to bat, if we wanted to take advantage of the loaded bases. The nervousness instantly switched to excitement, when we heard the name of the next batter being called out.

'And next up to bat is the star player himself, Colton Reed!'

I immediately leaned forward in my seat. I'm pretty sure I heard Nina chuckling at my actions, but I wasn't sure. My mind was solely focused on Colton.

'Colton has managed to hit a home run at every single exhibition game the team has had so far this off-season. Let's see what he can do for them tonight!' the commentator announced enthusiastically.

My right knee started bouncing as Colton prepared himself to bat. 'Come on, come on,' I muttered to myself.

Once Colton was in his stance, the rival's team pitcher let out an exhale, demonstrated by the rise and fall of his shoulders, before throwing a fastball that was within the strike zone.

Colton swung.

And he missed.

'Strike one for Colton,' the commentator declared.

Stepping away from home plate, Colton rolled his shoulders and readjusted his gloves. When the ball was back in the pitcher's glove, he stepped up, his hands gripping the bat handle as he got back into position.

The pitcher threw another fastball, only this time it was towards first base in hopes of eliminating another player. Thankfully, Miles managed to get back just in time and was saved.

The voice of the commentator filled the speakers. 'I see the pitcher decided to pull a little trick, but it seems Thompson saw right through it and is still in the game.'

Colton prepared himself once again as the pitcher did the same.

And the ball was tossed.

Colton swung again.

Missing once more.

'Oooof. And that's another strike for Colton,' voiced the commentator.

'Damn it,' I grumbled.

The crowd was once again filled with agitation, with everyone sitting at the edge of their seat as we were left with one last strike, before we had to switch the batting team. The effort of having all bases filled was going to be wasted.

Colton readjusted his gloves once again, as he let his eyes wander around the stadium. When they landed in my direction, I signed to him, counting on the off chance that he might see me, 'You got this, partner.'

And it seemed like he did see me, if the nod he sent my way was any indication.

Stepping up to the plate once again, Colton prepared his stance.

The ball was hurled out of the pitcher's glove and another fastball headed towards Colton.

He swung.

And this time, the sound of the ball hitting the bat filled the stadium, as the ball continued to fly right into left field and flew over the fence.

Everyone in the stand was already up on their feet. Wild cheers echoed throughout the stadium as the four players made their way to home base.

He did it.

He hit a home run.

'What a beautiful hit from the Dust Devils' finest player!' cheered the commentator. 'The star player not only added another home run to his list of accomplishments, but also a grand slam for the whole team! With four points added to their score, the Dust Devils are once again in the lead tonight.'

After completing his run of the infield, the other players immediately attacked Colton with a group hug and pats on the back as he made his way back to the dugout. Once they finally let him go, Colton turned his way to my side of the seats and signed, *'That was for you.'*

I couldn't help the grin on my face, and it only grew bigger when he added, *'partner.'*

The game lasted for another hour. As Jack managed to strike out the third batter of the other team, the match came to an early end, with a score of ten points for the Dust Devils and seven points for the Raptors, giving our baseball team a victory to celebrate that night.

'And that marks the end of tonight's game as well as the last game with the Dust Devils this off-season,' the commentator announced. 'Hope to see you folks again next year, as our team goes into battle to defend their Men's College World Series champion title. Goodnight, everyone!'

With his bid of farewell, the crowd started to make their way to the nearest exit.

'You guys okay with waiting for everyone else to go first?' Nina asked as the people around us were getting out of their seats.

'I don't mind,' I answered.

'Sure,' Lily said.

'Fine by me.' Claudia shrugged, settling back into her seat. There were still a lot of people in the stadium, so we could have been there for a while. 'I forgot how fun it was to watch live baseball again.'

'Right? I can't wait for the world series to start again next semester,' Lily agreed enthusiastically, just as her stomach let out a growl. 'Ugh, I'm starving. What are we having for dinner?'

'I was thinking we could go to that Chinese restaurant. We can take an Uber and go there straight away or—' Nina's suggestion was cut off, when her phone started vibrating with notifications.

'What is it?' I furrowed my eyebrows.

'Miles texted me,' she said, a slight blush appearing on her cheeks at her admission. 'They're throwing a celebratory party tonight at the baseball team's house. And he invited us.'

'I mean, I'm not saying no to free booze,' Claudia said.

'I'm down but I think we should head for dinner first before we go,' Lily suggested. 'What about you, Clara?'

I thought about it for a second. I mean, I would have loved to go and hopefully hang out with Colton there. But at the same time, I wasn't really looking forward to being in another tightly packed space filled with people that soon.

'I don't think I'm in the mood for it,' I admitted. 'But ask me again after dinner.'

The crowd had finally started to decrease to a smaller amount, giving us enough space to leave the stadium without having to squeeze through.

'I'm gonna head to the bathroom first before we leave,' Lily announced once we reached the entrance.

'Oh wait, I wanna go with,' Claudia replied, hooking her arm with Lily's.

'We'll just wait for you two out here,' I told them.

Lily gave me a nod while Claudia said, 'Got it.' Turning her head to Lily, she added, 'Let's go.' And off they went.

The crowd might have lessened, but that didn't mean the cars had too. Honks sounded everywhere in the parking lot, as everyone was impatient to leave and go back home. The noise eventually died down once the cars started moving again.

We ran into some of Nina's friends from her class, and I stood on the side while she talked to them, enjoying the quieted noise on my own.

But the clamour of sounds was only replaced by the racket of the college baseball team that was high on the adrenaline of winning that night's game.

I automatically looked down at the ground to avoid eye contact with any of them, until I heard his voice, and my head tilted up immediately hearing it get louder. My eyes finally found him among the other players, with Miles walking right beside him, talking animatedly.

Colton was laughing at what Miles just said, with a massive smile plastered on his face. As if he could sense my eyes on him, his head turned to where I was standing.

His eyes immediately lit up when he saw me.

I'm pretty sure mine did too.

His tall frame started making its way to me, stopping just a few steps in front of me.

'Hey,' he breathed out.

'Hi,' I greeted him back, my voice soft. 'Congratulations on winning! You guys were great out there.'

'Thanks,' he answered sheepishly, a bit shy from the compliment.

His hair was still slightly wet from the shower he had after the game, I presumed. Whatever parts that were already dry were a mess—just like during those brief moments I saw him without a cap or a helmet on, when he was on the field.

And it looked *so soft*. Without even thinking about it, my hand went up to his hair, my fingers slowly untangling it.

My unexpected intrusion caused Colton to freeze for a beat, and my eyes widened in horror as my brain finally realized what I was doing.

I was about to pull my hand away when he reached up his hand and gently wrapped it around my wrist.

For a second, I thought he was going to drop it at my side. But, instead, he slid my hand lightly across his cheek, before giving a soft kiss in the middle of my palm.

My stomach instantly erupted with butterflies at his sweet gesture. It continued as he slid his hand the rest of the way and intertwined it with mine, his thumb softly brushing the back of my hand.

'Is this okay?' he asked nervously.

'It's perfect,' I replied.

He gave me a small smile in return, continuing the gentle strokes. A look of confusion appeared on his face as his eyes started to wander up the sleeve of my arm.

'What's wrong?'

He shook his head. 'Nothing. Just that . . . is that my jacket?' His eyes were laser-focused on my outerwear.

A blush rose to my cheeks at his question. *I definitely had not thought this through.*

'Yeah,' I answered sheepishly, my eyes darting everywhere that wasn't his face. 'I forgot I still have it with me. I'll give it back once I—'

'Keep it.'

My eyes snapped up to his. 'What?'

'Keep it,' he repeated, his voice just as confident. 'I like seeing you wear it.'

I was pretty sure my cheeks couldn't get any more scarlet than they were right then. 'Are you sure?'

'100 per cent,' he reassured me. 'Plus, we're getting new ones for the new season. And I don't need two jackets,' he then added, his tone light. But I knew what he was trying to say, even if he wasn't saying it out loud.

'Well, thank you,' I answered, grateful for his unexpected gift. 'It is really comfortable though.'

He let out a small laugh. 'I'm glad it is.'

'Yo, Colton!'

Both of our heads turned to the sound of the voice, seeing Miles coming toward us. When his eyes landed on me, he gave me a nod of acknowledgment. 'Ah, Clara. Good to see you.'

'It's good to see you too, Miles,' I said, mimicking his nod. 'Congratulations on winning by the way.'

'Thanks. It's all thanks to this one hitting that homerun and giving us a lead,' he said, while nudging his arm at Colton's side. 'Anyway, just want to let you know that we were about to leave. Are you coming to the party?' Miles asked, his attention on me.

'Umm, probably not,' I replied. 'One social event is enough for me today.'

'You're not coming?'

My head turned towards Colton at his question, a disappointed look on his face at the indication that I wasn't going later.

'I'll give you two a minute.' I heard Miles say, before he walked away to give us some space.

My eyes followed him as he left, and once I was confident he was out of earshot, I turned my head back to Colton. 'I'm sorry.'

'Don't be,' he said softly. 'I mean, you don't have to come if you don't want to. It's just . . .' His voice trailed off near the end.

I scrunched my eyebrows at him. 'It's just what?'

'I wanted to spend time with you,' he admitted, his voice nervous. 'I don't know . . . I miss talking to you, so I thought we could hang out for a bit.'

There it was again, that squeeze in my heart that seemed to only happen with Colton.

'I would love to hang out with you too,' I told him truthfully. 'I just would rather not do it while I'm in a place with a hundred different people tonight.'

Colton was quiet for a moment, his eyes narrowed as if he was mulling over something.

'But if you want me to go——' I started.

Colton was quick to cut me off. 'Then, we don't have to go to the party, we can go somewhere else. Just be with me tonight. What do you say?'

Yes. Yes. Yes.

But the words I voiced out were: 'You don't want to celebrate with your teammates?'

He shook his head. 'There's only one person I want to celebrate with,' he said, his gaze locked on mine. 'So, hang out with me tonight?'

A beaming smile spread across my face when I answered, 'I'd like that.'

'Colton, you ready to go?' I heard Miles shout from behind me.

'You guys have fun without me,' Colton announced, just as I turned around to look at Miles. I was greeted by the sight of him having his arm swung around Nina, both of them wearing the same smug look on their faces.

'I thought so,' Miles said.

Nina gently pulled away from Miles and gave me a hug. 'I'll text you when I get back. He's a good one, Clara. Don't let him slip away.'

I gave her a squeeze in return before letting her go.

'Call me if you need a ride home,' Colton said to Miles.

'You got it.' He gave a mocking salute and joined the other baseball players.

I was so stuck in my little bubble with Colton that I didn't even realize Claudia and Lily were already back.

Just as I was about to make my apology, Claudia interrupted me. 'I guess I'll see you when I see you then,' she said with a knowing smile on her face.

'I guess so.' I gave a light laugh, internally grateful that they weren't mad I was ditching them. 'You girls have fun tonight.'

'Oh, we definitely will,' Lily said.

We hugged each other goodbye, before they joined the rest of the baseball players.

'Where do you want to go?' Colton asked me once the rest of the team had left.

'Honestly, I just want to grab some dinner and head back home,' I told him. 'We can hang out in my apartment if that's okay with you?'

Giving me a small smile, he answered, 'That sounds perfect to me.'

Chapter Twenty-One

Colton and I decided on getting pizza as we made our way to his parked car. I wanted to just have it delivered to my apartment, but Colton suggested that we could just get it ourselves, saying that we might get our dinner faster that way. It was a Saturday night, after all; the pizza place might be busy with more deliveries than usual.

'But we can have it delivered if you want don't to,' Colton told me as he started the engine of his car.

A song instantly started playing on his radio and the very familiar chorus of 'Mamma Mia' greeted my ears, reminding me of the first time he ever drove me home—the night that led me to the decision of letting this boy into my life.

'Getting it ourselves sounds better,' I started. 'But only if you let me pick which ABBA album we'll be listening to.'

He let out a chuckle. 'By all means.' He was reversing the car out of the parking space when he said, 'the rest of the albums are in the glove compartment.'

Opening it, I took out all five albums he had. When I found the one I was looking for, I ejected the CD from the music system. I placed it back into its respective case before inserting the one that I chose.

I could see the moment Colton's face lit up, as the intro to 'Waterloo' blared out from the car speakers. He immediately started singing along to the song, taking the same parts as he did the last time we sang together on that fateful night a few Saturdays ago at his aunt and uncle's bar.

The night I realized something had shifted between us.

Up until then, I had always thought of Colton's presence in my life with the romantic notion of him breaking down the walls around my heart through its little cracks that I needed to patch up. But, as I looked at the boy sitting next to me, happily singing along to a Napoleon metaphor song about surrendering to love, I realized that wasn't it at all.

Colton wasn't trying to take it down.

He just kept waiting at the gate, persistently making his presence known and patiently waiting to be granted entry.

As I joined him with my parts of the song, and we sang the last chorus together, I couldn't help but be hopeful that the after-events of the duet this time around would be different than the last time. In a good way.

And I was very much looking forward to it.

The funky sound of the second track started to play, and I joined the band as they sang out the words.

Colton's eyes widened as he stole a glance in my direction, before returning his focus to the road.

I burst out laughing at his reaction. 'What?'

He shook his head. 'Nothing. I'm just a bit surprised. I don't think this song was in the *Mamma Mia* movie.'

'It's not,' I agreed. 'It's not in the second movie either.'

'Then, how . . .' he trailed off.

'So, there's this really handsome guy that I like, who *loves* ABBA,' I started. 'I'm talking having their physical albums kind of love. It's the cutest thing ever. And I don't know, I thought I would expand my ABBA music knowledge and listen to their other songs that are not in the *Mamma Mia* movies.'

After that night, when I had played the *Super Trouper* album to prepare dinner, I started listening to their other albums, and actually went through all the songs on each of them, instead of just skipping to the ones I knew. I remembered rationalizing to myself that I was just listening to the songs from a very beloved band. But I think, deep down, I knew that the main reason for it was the person sitting next to me.

With that being said, it didn't mean I would ever be bold enough to admit this to him out loud. But after having Colton reveal to me how he had read my favourite book, just because it was my favourite book, I figured it was worth the potential embarrassment.

Colton didn't say anything as the song continued to play. Just as I was starting to feel mortified, he reached his hand across the console to grasp mine that was settled on my lap.

I looked over at him and saw a genuine smile on his face as he gave my hand a gentle squeeze before pulling it away to switch gears.

But that gesture alone was enough for me to convey what he meant—the things that couldn't be expressed through words.

I gave him a smile of my own—even though he couldn't see it—before turning my head to the open road. We sang along to the rest of the songs as Colton drove ahead.

Unlocking the door with my keys, I twisted the door handle and let myself into the apartment. Colton followed closely behind me with a large box of pizza in his arm.

'Welcome to the apartment,' I said to him. 'This is the kitchen, that's the living room and that's where the washer and dryer are. This one is Nina's room and that's mine.' My fingers pointed out each of the spaces and the door to mine and Nina's rooms respectively. 'Do you want to eat at the counter or in the living room?'

'Living room sounds good.' Colton made his way to the living room, placing the pizza box on the coffee table.

I headed to the kitchen. Placing my tote bag on the island, I opened the fridge to see what drinks we had. 'Okay, so you have two options for drinks,' I called out. 'Do you want water or chocolate milk?'

'Chocolate milk?' I heard him ask.

I closed the door of the fridge partly to look at him. 'Too old for chocolate milk?' I arched a brow, slightly offended by his remark.

'Definitely not,' he answered without missing a beat. 'Just a bit surprised, that's all. I'll have the chocolate milk, please.'

Pouring him a glass and one for myself, I brought them with me as I headed to where he was standing right next to the TV, holding up a framed photo of me and Nina in our old dorm room during freshman year.

'Here you go.' I handed him a glass.

'Thanks,' he said, taking it from me with his unoccupied hand. Raising his other one with the framed photo in my direction, he asked, 'when was this taken?'

'Freshman year, second semester,' I answered. I still remember the day we took that photo. There wasn't anything special about that particular day: no birthdays, no achievements to celebrate, nothing worth commemorating. Nina and I were just chilling in our room, catching up on our work, when I randomly realized we had never taken a picture together in our dorm room before.

We had immediately enlisted the help of Claudia and Lily to help us take the photo.

The photo was nothing more than me and Nina with our arms around each other. No cute outfits and our slightly messy room, just two best friends, standing in a place where their lives intertwined with one another. But there was always something endearing about that photo, and when we moved in together for sophomore year, Nina had surprised me by having it printed and framed. And then, it sat proudly next to the TV.

'You look cute here,' Colton pointed out.

A blush rose to my cheeks.

That, I agreed with; I did look cute in that photo, and Nina did too—which was why, it was a mutual favourite from the bunch that we had taken. Or I didn't think Nina would have it printed out, much less have it framed.

Colton placed the photo back in its original spot as he turned to me. 'So, pizza?'

'Sure.' I nodded. 'You can wash your hands in the kitchen, I'm gonna go change first.'

Picking up my abandoned tote bag on the kitchen island, I headed to my room and set it on my desk chair. After I *carefully* hung Colton's baseball jacket, I reached through the rest of my closet, searching for an oversized t-shirt and some sweatpants.

Once I was done changing, I returned to the living room and found Colton sitting on the right side of the couch, scrolling through his phone. I washed my hands on the kitchen sink before joining him, folding my legs together once I sat down.

Colton leaned forward to put his phone on the coffee table, the screen facing down. Opening the pizza box, he picked it up and brought it towards me. 'Your dinner, milady,' he said, not forgetting the head bow as he uttered the words.

I shook my head at his dramatics, amused laughter coming out of my mouth. 'Why thank you, milord,' I said, picking up a slice of the pizza.

He gave a playful grin and took a slice of his own before placing the box back on the coffee table.

We both ate in silence, content with our food of choice for the night. I was only halfway through my slice, when Colton reached for his second one. As I sat there eating pizza with Colton in my living room, I couldn't help but think of the other male figure in my life and our little pizza tradition.

Without even second-guessing myself, the words were already out of my mouth. 'My dad and I had a baseball tradition while I was growing up.'

'Yeah?' Colton said as he started on his second slice.

I nodded. 'We used to attend those little league games when I was in middle school, and we would get pizza afterwards. It wasn't something we did intentionally, but the more games we went to, it sort of just became a routine—a tradition. When the divorce happened, we sort of stopped doing it for a while.'

'What happened then?'

'We started it again, only this time, instead of eating pizza after going to a baseball game, we ate it while we were watching a live baseball game on the TV. It didn't matter which team was playing, I would just go to his house every Sunday, and he would already have the pizza ready for us. Sometimes he would even make it himself.' I couldn't help but laugh at the memory. 'It took a few tries, but he eventually got the hang of it. And now, whenever I go to his house to watch a game, the delicious smell of pizza never fails to greet me.'

'Was your dad a big baseball fan?' I heard Colton ask.

I shook my head. 'Not really. I think he liked watching the sport, but wasn't a big enough fan to follow it religiously. Anyway, what about you? Did you have any family traditions related to baseball, or family traditions in general?'

'I do actually,' he started. 'To be honest, I never really thought of it as a tradition before, just something we did. But when I just started playing baseball, my whole family and I would go celebrate at this ice cream shop we had in my hometown if my team won. My usual order was a chocolate sundae.'

'And what happens if you lose?'

'I also get an ice cream sundae.'

'So, you mean, you'll get one either way? Whether you win or lose?' I asked him, my voice teasing.

'Yeah,' he broke off, the tips of his ear going slightly red. 'They just went about it differently. Like if I win, then it's a celebration and if I lose, then it's to cheer me up. I think my family thought it was just a hobby when I was younger, so it didn't really matter much. But once I started taking it seriously, we just stopped doing it any more.'

I took another bite of my pizza, tucking this piece of information about Colton into my mind, and adding it to the list of things I knew about him. But this particular story reminded me of another trait from that list—one of my favourite things about him.

'Is that how you got your sweet tooth?' I pointed out.

Colton pondered over my question for a moment. 'Now that you mentioned it, I think so. But hand to heart, that shop had the best chocolate ice cream sundae I ever had.'

'When was the last time you had it?'

'The week before I came back for the new semester,' he answered, as his hand reached out for another slice of pizza. 'It's sort of like a little farewell gift for me before I head off.'

'It really is that good, huh?' I teased him.

'I'll take you there someday and you can decide for yourself.'

My breath caught up in my throat at his words, anticipating a feeling of fear to creep up on me, but it never came. Instead, I felt excited at the prospect of it, of seeing the town Colton grew up in, and the legendary sundae that created his sweet tooth.

Giving him a smile, I said, 'I'd like that.'

We continued exchanging stories from our childhood to our life in high school, trying to one-up each other on who had more funny stories, as we rated each one on a scale of one to ten.

The pizza box eventually emptied up. Colton ended up eating five slices, while I ate three—the perfect balance for us. Once we were done, Colton insisted on helping me throw the pizza box through the garbage chute in the hallway, so I went ahead and wiped the coffee table. I refilled our glasses of chocolate milk and waited for him in the living room. The sound of the front door closing signalled his return not moments later. He went to wash his hands before reclaiming his spot on the living room couch.

'So . . .' Colton trailed off.

'So . . .' I parroted.

'I hit a home run today.'

'You did.'

He gave me a small smile. 'So, what happens now?'

'I mean, a deal is a deal, right?' I shrugged.

At that, his smile faded away. 'Clara, you don't have to do this, if you don't want to. If you need more time to decide, I'm willing to wait for you.'

I frowned at his words. It never crossed my mind that Colton would second-guess my decision to let him take me out on a date. But given my track record of pushing him away, it wouldn't be too far off to assume that I made the condition just to reject him again.

After the reassurance he had given me the day before, I thought it was time to reciprocrate.

I scooted closer to him and grabbed his hand, enveloping it with both of them as I rubbed my thumb on the back of his hand. Seeing what I was doing, Colton turned his body to face me and moved closer.

From two ends of the couch, we met in the middle.

I placed a soft kiss on his knuckles before lifting my gaze to meet his. 'I like you, Colton. I like you so, so much. And I don't blame you for thinking I made the home run condition in the hopes that you won't meet it. In some ways, it's my fault for making you feel that way. I'm sorry for ever making you feel that being a star athlete is a bad thing, because it's not. It shows so much character than just being a dumb trait that cliché love interests have. The deal—or the condition, or whatever it was—didn't actually matter. It never did,' I told him. 'But for what it's worth, I was confident you'd actually hit one and I was right.'

The edge of his lips tilted up slightly.

'And if you were to ask me again, I'll give you a straightforward answer this time. No more confusion,' I added.

'You promise?'

I nodded. 'I promise.'

'Good.' The palm of his other hand met the back of mine, as he asked, 'Clara Healy, do you want to go on a date with me?'

There was only one answer. 'Yes, Colton Reed. I would love to go on a date with you.'

The look on Colton's face was one I knew I wanted to store in my mind forever. His massive grin reached all the way to his eyes, and before I knew it, Colton had his arms wrapped around me and picked me up. He settled me into his lap as he rested his head between my neck and shoulders, my legs straddling him.

I pulled away just enough so I could see his face. 'I am still scared, though—of whatever this is. So, we might have to take this slow, and you're going to have to be real patient with me.'

'Don't worry about having to take it slow. We can go at whichever pace you want,' he reassured me. 'And I'll be there with you every step of the way. You just make sure you'll let me be there with you, okay?'

'Okay,' I whispered. I rested my head sideways on his right shoulder as he gave me gentle rubs on my back.

We settled into a comfortable silence, both of us just breathing in the other person's presence as we were entangled with one another.

The quietness didn't last too long when Colton decided to speak. 'You know. You haven't apologized to me for one other thing.'

I raised my head, facing him. 'What other thing?' I arched a brow.

'For shamelessly gawking at me shirtless.'

'Shamelessly gawking?' I trailed off, recalling all the times we had spent together as I tried to remember if I ever saw him shirtless.

And then, it hit me.

No way.

There was just no way.

The incident, I thought to myself.

There was no way he was referring to *the incident*, right?

'So, you *do* know what I'm talking about,' Colton said in a proud mocking tone.

This is a joke, right?

'You're not talking about—'

He cut me off, or to put it more accurately, he finished it off for me. 'The bathroom at the track field.'

He *was* referring to *the incident.*

I was mortified.

I don't think I had ever been more mortified than I was at that moment.

I immediately brought my hands up to my face, placing my covered face back on his shoulder, shielding myself from him.

I could hear and feel Colton's amused laughter rumbling through his body in this position. While I was mostly hiding from my own embarrassment, a part of me was using it as an excuse to stay this close to Colton for a little bit longer.

When I finally gathered enough courage to look at him again, I immediately laid playful slaps on his very hard chest.

'How long have you known it was me?' I exclaimed in between slaps.

'The first day of ASL class.' He shrugged.

My eyes widened in horrific embarrassment. *He's known it was me for that long?* 'Why are you only telling me this now?'

'You remember the day you asked me if I believed in fate?' he asked instead.

I furrowed my eyebrows at him, slightly confused at his question but still giving him a nod. 'Yeah. You said you didn't believe in it but you were starting to think you were wrong.'

A small smile appeared on his lips, as if he was remembering the memory of that night as well. 'After our encounter in the bathroom, I actually went back to the track field for the next few days, hoping I might bump into you again.'

'You did not.'

'Oh yes, I did,' he countered back. 'But I wasn't so lucky. Then I tried going on Wednesdays instead. But again, my efforts were in vain. So, eventually, I gave up. I thought that was it for me, and for the pretty girl who seemed to like watching me put my shirt on.'

A blush rose to my cheeks.

'Fast forward to a month later, the baseball team decided to throw a party at the team house,' he continued. 'I wasn't actually planning on going since I'm not the biggest fan of parties, but my teammates were blowing up my phone, asking me to come. And someone had to drive them home.'

'Always the responsible one,' I pointed out.

He gave me a sheepish smile. 'Well, someone had to take care of them. But anyway, I did end up going, and at one point in the night, I was talking to Miles in the kitchen, when I saw someone very familiar standing in the corner. Can you guess who it was?'

'You're joking.'

He shook his head. 'It was you. And just as I wanted to approach you, another one of my teammates—one of the seniors we had last year—started talking to me, so I couldn't really say no. But once we were done talking, I tried to see if you were still there, but you were gone. I thought you might have gone elsewhere around the house, but I couldn't find you, so I'm guessing you went home.'

I knew exactly the moment he was talking about. It was just minutes before the girls and I had headed home, and Lily and Claudia were in the bathroom, while Nina went to say goodbye to her friends. My social energy had drained for the night, so I just waited for them in an empty corner.

I gave Colton a nod. 'I did. The crowd was getting a bit too much, so we decided to leave.' There was a chance that Colton might have mistaken me for someone else, but his timeline fit mine, and from what I remembered, the team only threw one party that month. 'I didn't know you were at the party; I didn't catch a glimpse of you all night.'

A teasing smile appeared on his lips. 'Were you looking for me, sweetheart?'

I playfully slapped his chest again, and a deep laugh came out of him as a response, while I tried to fight the scarlet from entering my cheeks a second time. 'Shut up. I wanted to save myself from the embarrassment in case you remembered me from our little encounter.'

'Oh, I remember you, all right,' he deadpanned. 'You've been on my mind ever since.'

That tug in my heart made an appearance once again at his words. 'Well, what happened next?'

'For a while, I thought about asking the people at the party if they knew who you were, but something held me back. I couldn't really explain what it was; I just had this gut feeling that I'll run into you again someday. When the time is right,' he continued, 'and it turns out, I was right. Because the next time I saw you was at our first ASL class. Imagine my surprise when I found the only empty seat was next to yours. I couldn't believe it. The girl I had been looking for was right there, in front of me.'

I tilted my head to the side. 'And what were you planning to do about it?'

'To be honest, I don't know,' he answered truthfully. 'I never actually thought about it that far ahead. I thought about bringing up the bathroom incident to break the ice—to see if you remember me, but I figured that wasn't really something you could just casually bring up to a total stranger. When Mr Albert had us partnering up, I thought it would be a good opportunity to get to know you. But you were pretty apprehensive about us working together,' he explained. 'It was never about me being too busy, was it?'

I shook my head. 'I mean, I knew you were going to be busy, but that had nothing to do with me not wanting to be partners with you.'

'I thought as much.' Colton nodded. 'Anyway, when we did eventually become partners, I thought about just letting the whole thing go. I wanted to brush off whatever gut feeling I had as some nonsensical thing I had made up, and the fact that I kept missing you at every turn was just nothing more than a coincidence. But then, we had started spending time together and I realized that maybe there was something to this whole thing, after all. I kept finding myself wanting to know more about you and just wanting to constantly hang out with you. I was crushing on you so hard,' he let out, pausing momentarily before saying his next words.

'I wasn't lying when I said I didn't believe in fate before, but I couldn't ignore the events that led me to you. Whether or not there is such a thing as fate, I'm just glad it brought me you. In some sense, I didn't realize I was waiting for you. I've waited for you all this time, Clara. And I'm willing to wait however long it'll take, so don't worry about taking it slow, okay?'

But how does one want to take it slow, after hearing *all of that?* Because now all I wanted to do was kiss him until I was of breath. It seemed like the perfect moment for it.

At least, that was what all the romance books had told me.

I had never actually kissed someone before.

How does someone even initiate a kiss?

And do you actually kiss until you're breathless?

'Hey, are you okay?' I heard Colton ask, taking me out of my inner turmoil.

Shaking my head, I tried to brush off my thoughts. 'I'm fine,' I told him.

Colton kept his eyes on me, a concerned look on his face. 'What's going on in that head of yours?' he said, tucking a strand of my hair behind my ear.

Kissing you.

'Oh, nothing,' I quickly said, trying my best to hide the blush on my cheeks. But with how close we were, I was pretty sure Colton could feel my whole body warming up.

'Come on. What is it?' he persuaded me. 'You can tell me.'

'I want to kiss you,' I blurted out, my eyes widening in horror once I realized what I just said out loud.

An amused smile slowly took over Colton's face. 'Do you, now?'

'Please don't make fun of me,' I said, covering my face with my hands once again.

I could feel Colton's hands gently wrapping around my wrists, slowly prying my hands away from my face.

'Hey. Hey,' Colton lifted my chin, so my eyes were looking into his. 'For what it's worth, I want to kiss you too. I've been wanting to kiss you for quite some time now,' he reassured me.

'Yeah?'

'Yeah.'

'I just,' I broke off. 'I don't want to give you any more mixed signals. I mean, I just said I wanted to take things slow, and now I'm telling you I want to kiss you, when we haven't even gone on a date yet,' I explained.

'Well, what do you say about having a free pass for tonight?'

I furrowed my eyebrows at him. 'What do you mean?'

'We'll let ourselves kiss each other tonight and just go back to normal tomorrow.'

I took a moment to think over his suggestion. But to be honest, I didn't need to, as my mind was definitely on board. 'Will you be okay with that?' I asked instead.

'Not gonna lie, I do like the idea of kissing you. Hell, I've been wanting to kiss you since that night at the bar,' he confessed. 'And it'll be torture not doing it again for a while after tonight. But yes, I will be okay with that. So, what do you say?'

'A free pass sounds great. But I do have to warn you though: I have never actually kissed anyone before, so I don't really know what I'm doing,' I admitted, my voice shaky at my confession.

I wasn't ashamed of having never been kissed before, but saying it out loud to someone else made me feel exposed—especially saying it to the boy who you wanted to be your first kiss.

But Colton just gave me his small, familiar smile. 'Then, we'll take it slow.'

'But I have read a lot of romance books, so you have a lot to live up to, mister,' I teased him, pointing an accusatory finger into his chest.

'You wouldn't have deserved anything less,' he said.

I had wanted to kiss Colton for a while, specifically since that night at the karaoke bar when we almost did kiss—the same night he just admitted to wanting to kiss me too. But things were different that night, I was high on an adrenaline rush—along with a glass of margarita—and we were slow-dancing to a love song so, of course, all my mind could focus on was just wanting to kiss this boy I had long been crushing on.

Whereas right then, we weren't surrounded by a romantic atmosphere. It was just him and me, with both of our hearts on our sleeves, and I couldn't help but feel slightly nervous.

I tried to shake it off, thinking there was nothing I should be worried about, but that was easier said than done.

As if sensing my nervousness, Colton cupped my cheeks with both of his hands, pressing his forehead to mine. 'Breathe with me, okay? Inhale.' He took a deep inhale, then slowly exhaled it, making sure I was following his patterned breaths.

'Good. One more time.'

Inhale. Exhale.

'Last one.'

Inhale. Exhale.

The pulse in my heart was still quick, but now it was fluttering with excitement instead.

'There's nothing to be nervous about,' Colton said, his voice a whisper. 'It's just me.'

He started leaving kisses all over my face. My forehead. My cheeks. My chin. Two kisses on each corner of my lips.

And finally, he kissed me.

Ever since I convinced myself of the curse that had fallen upon my family, I knew that I wouldn't get—or allow myself—to live my own romance story with a cliché love interest, just like my mom and sister had. So instead, I had decided that I would, at least, have a cliché first kiss story. It would be as dramatic as the ones I had read in books and watched in movies.

I didn't think I would have settled with having my first kiss on a couch in the living room of my college apartment.

But as Colton's arm slipped around my waist, and as he pulled me closer to him, my hands tangled in his hair, I realized I didn't give a fuck about having a dramatic first kiss any more.

Because right then, all that mattered was I was kissing Colton. It was worth more than my thousand dramatic ideas of having a cliché first kiss story. Nothing beats kissing the right person.

I pulled back once I realized how breathless I got, gently pressing my forehead against Colton's.

'How was that?' he asked, his breath in a steadier rhythm than mine.

'Eh, it was okay,' I teased. 'I think you have to kiss me again for me to be sure.'

A grin made its way to his face. 'Don't worry, sweetheart. We have all night after all.'

We spent the next few hours talking about anything and everything, with the occasional kisses in between. We didn't realize how late it had gotten, until Colton received a text from Miles, telling him that my friends needed a ride home.

When we reached the baseball team's house, all of them were already waiting outside. I left the passenger seat for Miles, while I squeezed in with the girls at the back. They were all only slightly tipsy at that point and were craving some ice cream, so we decided to do a midnight trip to Creamsicle Corner.

And that was how I spent the next hour hanging out with my three best friends, the guy whom I had a massive crush on, and his best friend, whom I was very happy to form a bond with.

Colton dropped Claudia and Lily at their apartment first, before driving me and Nina back to our place.

Parking his car at the drop-off spot, both guys got out of the car, with Miles opening the car door for us.

I thanked him and was met by Colton as he waited for me on the sidewalk, his hand held out to me. Once my hand was in his, Colton lifted it to his lips and gave me soft butterfly kisses on each of my knuckles.

I giggled at how cute he was being, feeling him starting to smile across my skin.

'I had a great time with you tonight,' I told him once he stopped, still holding my hand in his.

'I had a great time with you too,' he said. Leaning closer to me, he added in a light whisper, 'One last kiss before we call it a night?'

I stole a glance to see if Nina was looking. When I saw that her full attention was on Miles, I gave him a nod, 'Yes, please.'

Bending down his head, Colton pressed his lips to mine. My arms instinctively wrapped themselves around his neck, pulling him to me. I couldn't help but smile through it, slightly interrupting the kiss, though I could feel him smiling too. I felt one of his arms wrapped around my waist as he lifted me closer to him, making me stand slightly on my tiptoes. And with one more peck, we both pulled away, his other arm joining the one that was still on my waist.

'Text me when you get home?' I said.

'Will do, sweetheart,' he answered, sealing the promise with a kiss on my forehead.

I hugged both Colton and Miles goodbye, wishing them a safe drive home, before Nina and I entered our apartment building and waited for the elevator to arrive at the lobby.

'How was your night?' Nina asked as we got into the elevator. I was pretty sure she saw Colton and me kissing, but I still appreciated her attempt to act casual about it.

I didn't even try to stop the grin from breaking out on my face. There was only one word to describe it. 'Magical. I'll tell you all about it tomorrow.'

Once the elevator reached our floor, we made our way to our apartment. We said goodnight to each other as we headed straight to our rooms, both worn out from the long night.

After taking a much-needed shower and finishing my night routine, I finally looked at my phone and saw a new text message that was sent twenty minutes ago.

Colton:
Just got home.
All safe and sound.

Clara:
Good to know you're back safely.

Thanks again for tonight. ♡

I'm gonna go to sleep now. It's been a long night.

Goodnight, partner.

Colton:
Goodnight, partner.

Placing my phone on my nightstand, I laid my head on my pillow.

And just like that first night Colton drove me home, I slept with a smile on my face.

All thanks to the star athlete I got partnered up with in ASL class.

Epilogue

The soft warmth of the sun woke me up from my sleep and dreams of the night before. The sight of a beautiful Sunday morning greeted me as I opened my eyes, courtesy of the drawn curtains.

I slowly started to sit up, taking in the gentle sunlight as I reached for my phone on my nightstand to check the time. A smile curled up on my lips—as it always did—once I saw my lock screen. It was a photo I took of Colton from our first late-night Creamsicle Corner run, the one of him flexing his arm. It was one of my favourite photos of him.

My smile only grew bigger when I noticed a glass of water sitting on the nightstand as well, covered with a lid. One of the first things I always do in the morning is drink a glass of water. Normally, I would've had to go to the kitchen to do so, but it seemed *someone* caught on to my little habit and brought the water to me instead.

I chugged the water as quickly as I could before taking a quick detour to my bathroom. Once I was done, I tried my best to be quiet as I opened my bedroom door, my eyes immediately set toward the kitchen, knowing that a certain someone was there.

I was met by the sight of my boyfriend cooking spaghetti, swaying on-beat to an ABBA song that was playing from the radio CD player I got for him as his Christmas present last year.

I still remember how hard it was trying to find a gift for him. We were still *just* friends at the time—friends who had already been on two dates with each other. While I was confident that we were entering into the relationship territory soon, I didn't want to get him something that was too much. But at the same time, I knew I wanted to give him a meaningful gift that he would love.

I didn't realize how hard it was navigating the area of dating, when you're toeing the line between friends and something more.

But as soon as I saw a radio CD player being advertised when I was Christmas shopping for my family, I knew it was the perfect gift for him.

He usually kept it in his apartment that he shared with Miles. And it followed him as he moved to the baseball team's house. I remembered him contemplating whether he should move or not. On one hand, he loved having his own space, but now that he was made the team captain, he figured it was better to live with the team.

The radio CD player has its special spot in his new bedroom. But on the few occasions that he slept over at my place, he always brought it along with him.

Nina went back to her hometown for the weekend for a family celebration, leaving the whole apartment to me and Colton.

He was spinning around when he finally caught me watching him, momentarily caught off guard, before a grin made its way to his lips. 'Good morning, my beautiful partner.'

Matching his grin with one of my own, I said, 'Morning, my handsome partner.'

I made my way over to him, intending to kiss him on the cheek, only to have him greet me with a passionate kiss on the lips instead.

A small squeak of surprise escaped me, which was quickly replaced by a contented sigh, as my arms immediately wrapped themselves around his shoulders. I pulled him closer to me, taking him in.

We both eventually leaned back from the kiss, both of us breathless—me more than him. Colton kissed me one more time, a sweet and gentle one, before fully pulling away. 'Have a seat, breakfast will be ready soon.'

Pouring myself a cup of coffee, I took a seat on one of the kitchen stools and just admired my boyfriend preparing our morning meal.

After that night we had hung out in my apartment for the first time, Colton and I were back to what we were before: friends. Meaning, there was no kissing involved. But that didn't stop him from reaching his hand out to grab mine, his thumb softly rubbing the back of my hand, occasionally giving it or the middle of my palm a light kiss.

And I think most of the time, he didn't even realize it. It was just pure instinct.

It was clear that we were more than 'just friends' at that point.

I couldn't fully put the blame on him either, not when he had given me every opportunity to stop him.

But I never did. I didn't want to.

Colton stayed true to his words of taking this newfound thing between us at my pace. He even asked me whether I wanted to go on the date after the whole semester ended and we stopped being partners for ASL class.

The logical thing would be to say yes—in case our first date backfired, and we weren't as compatible as I thought we would be. But that was the fear talking, and I was done letting it hold me back.

So instead, I chose to trust Colton.

I chose to believe in us.

And so, our first date happened just a week after our first kiss, with a second one following two weeks later. At the end of our third one—a week after winter break— Colton asked for him to be mine and me to be his.

We've been together ever since.

But that didn't mean we stopped having our ASL practice sessions. Every Wednesday, we would still get our bubble tea and practice at 'the spot'. When the semester came to an end and we entered a new one, we held on to the tradition of hanging out there at least once a week. With it officially being baseball season, it was hard sticking to the Wednesday part of the tradition as Colton's schedule was packed with games and practices. But he always made sure we didn't go a week without spending time there, two bubble teas sitting next to us.

Sometimes, we talk and catch up. Sometimes, we brush up on our ASL. But my personal favourite is when Colton lays his head down on my lap, taking a much-needed nap after a few long days, while I read a romance book, occasionally playing with his hair.

Because, sometimes, no talking is necessary; our presence was enough.

Our ASL class also gave me the opportunity to meet the reason why Colton had joined the class in the first place.

You guessed it, I got to meet Phillip.

The partnered-up assignment that Mr Albert gave the class was to meet up with the Deaf community and converse with them; it didn't matter which age range it was. We decided upon meeting with the younger kids, and that was when I got to meet the sweet boy who was the catalyst for bringing Colton into my life.

Seeing the eyes of the kids lit up as we introduced ourselves in ASL was something I'll never forget, and I knew I wanted to continue learning, which was how I ended up taking a class at the Deaf centre the next semester and levelled up when I entered my senior year.

It's been one of the best decisions I've made. On par with the other decision that was currently serving up breakfast for me.

Once he was done, Colton placed a plate of spaghetti and meatballs in front of me. He put his plate next to mine, before settling into the only other kitchen stool in the apartment.

We both ate our breakfast in comfortable silence, as we always do in the mornings when he comes to stay over the night before. Content with each other's company, our mind slowly wakes up to seize the day—with only the sweet sounds of ABBA hung in the air between us.

When we were done eating, I was about to stand up and grab both of our empty plates to put them in the dishwasher. But Colton stopped me before I could, engulfing my hand in his instead. 'Dance with me.'

'What?' I said, amused by his request.

'Come on.' He got out of his stool and got me out of mine, pulling me into him as we softly swayed to the music. My hands around his neck and his hands on my waist.

It wasn't until the chorus that I realized what song it was.

It was 'Andante, Andante'. The song that I had dedicated to him on one of our dates at his aunt and uncle's bar, just a little over a month ago. The date that I had surprised him by going onstage by myself to sing on my own. While I was extremely nervous, I thought Colton would appreciate the gesture. The awe-struck look on his face—forever captured in a photo, thanks to his aunt—made the whole thing worth it.

I could tell Colton was remembering the same thing from the fond look on his face.

'Are you remembering my sweet serenade to you again?' I said to him, my voice teasing.

He grinned back at me. 'Can you blame me? It's not every day your girlfriend dedicates *and* sings a song to you at a bar.'

I just giggled at him, Colton joining me with a small laugh of his own.

As we continued to sway to the song, the playful look on his face started to sombre, replaced by a serious one instead.

I furrowed my eyebrows at him. 'What?' I said, suddenly nervous.

He shook his head, trying to avoid eye contact with me. 'Nothing.'

I put my hand on his cheek and lifted his head to me. 'What is it?'

Colton was quiet for a moment. Then, taking a deep inhale of breath, he gently grabbed my hands that were around his neck. Dropping it at my side as he took a few steps away from me.

I merely stood there, confused at what was happening.

And then he started signing. Slowly. Taking his time between each word.

There were only three.

Three words we've been floating around on but have yet to say to each other.

Just as he signed the last word, I was already launching myself into his arms. I wrapped my legs around him, as I placed my head in the space between his neck and shoulders. He stumbled slightly at the sudden impact, but with his arms around my waist, he held me tight.

I love you.

He signed '*I love you*' to me.

I pulled back slightly, just enough so I could see his face.

He told me again, this time out loud. 'I love you, Clara.'

I pressed my lips against his and whispered, 'I love you too, Colton,' meaning each word wholeheartedly, with every inch of me.

Falling in love can be scary.

Especially since you don't know what lies ahead.

But if you look at it a bit closer, you realize that falling in love is a series of steps—a series of choices that you have to make.

The choice to open your heart to someone, the choice of who to let into it, and ultimately, it's the choice to keep falling in love with the same person every single day. Through all the good days and the bad days.

So yes, falling in love can be scary. But with each moment that I get to spend with Colton, I learn that falling in love can also be easy when you choose the right person to do it with.

And with Colton's arms wrapped around me, standing here in my college apartment's living room, I couldn't be happier with the choice I'd made. My heart filled with so much happiness that this boy never fails to bring me each day.

Even if he is a cliché love interest and the curse might be real, I'm choosing to embrace it.

Yesterday, today, and forever.

And you can't forget, in every fairytale story that starts with a curse, it always ends with the curse getting broken.

And who knows? Maybe we'll be the ones to break it.

Well, that's what I'm choosing to believe in.

Acknowledgements

Book-wise, I had always considered my biggest accomplishment was to have my name in the acknowledgements. I never thought that one day, I would be writing the acknowledgements for my own.

First and foremost, my family. To my parents, thank you for supporting my love of reading, even though you might not have fully understood it. You probably had no idea that I was writing a book in silence during the gap semester that I took, but I will forever be grateful that you understood I've reached my limits and allowed me the time off. This book wouldn't have been written without your unknowing support. And shout-out to my siblings, Vivieanna Isak, Eldreian Isak, and Willdeanna Isak. (Incorporating their full names, so they can have bragging rights. You're welcome.)

Next are the best group of bookish friends a girl could ask for.

To Elynn, just as the sunrise and sunset, our friendship was fated in the stars. Hard to believe our love of books could evolve into an everlasting connection. Thank you for being my biggest cheerleader in my moments of doubts.

To Sufina, the one who made me believe that my book was worth more than what I could fathom. For making me believe that I was worth more. From curating subscription boxes to celebrating life milestones together, thank you for always being by my side.

To Sonia, thank you for nudging me and continuously helping me believe that it was okay to dream bigger for my book. This book wouldn't be in its current published form, if it weren't for your constant support in what I could achieve.

To Intan, your excitement for books is a quality in you that I deeply admire and I'm so fortunate that you have generously expanded that love to my book. Thank you for your friendship and the love you have shown to me and this story.

To Lilian, thank you for showing me the ropes whether it be correcting punctuation or navigating the publishing journey. As someone who's still new to this, your advice and guidance helped make the process less overwhelming than it could possibly be.

Moving on to the Wattpad readers, the ones who have read this book in the best form that I could have offered at the time. Thank you for loving the story, the characters, and being the best readers I could have only wished for. You have made the experience so much more than I could have hoped for. Special shout-out to Deethea, Yana, Aakriti, Lassie, and Belle—your excitement for each update along with each of your comments made those Wednesday updates a happier occasion. I will forever cherish them.

To Amelie and Bobbi, for taking them time out of your day to read this story, while it was still updating on Wattpad, and for saying yes to writing blurbs for my book. I admire you both and your works tremendously; I'm forever grateful to have had your support since the beginning.

To my publisher, Penguin SEA. Thank you for allowing me the chance to let this story reach an audience beyond my wildest dreams.

To everyone else I've met through Bookstagram, whether we've only talked virtually or have met physically, thank you for your never-ending support.

To myself. Thank you for writing this story, for believing that writing a complete book is an achievable dream and persisting to write *Clichés and Curses* until the end. Past-Deidre would not have believed that we have made it this far, thank you for making her proud.

And lastly, to everyone reading this, thank you for taking a chance on this book and spending your time with Clara and Colton. These two and their story will forever hold a special place in my heart, and I'm honoured to have gotten the chance to share them with all of you.